THINGS WE INHERIT

A Novel

Draven Aurora

ISBN: 979-8-9881332-1-6 (paperback)
ISBN: 979-8-9881332-0-9 (ebook)
Library of Congress Control Number: 2023910229

Cover design by: Kelly Carter
Printed in the United States of America

Published by: Draven Aurora
Austin, TX
dravenaurora.com

To those who relate to Joy—I'm sorry,
and I'm so glad you're here.

CONTENTS

CONTENT WARNING

This book contains themes of child neglect/abuse, suicide, death, eating disorders, generational trauma, alcohol consumption, and violence. It is not suitable for all ages and can be intense and/or triggering. If you or someone you know is having thoughts of suicide or struggling with any of the above, a list of resources can be found below. A full list of resources can be found here: https://ncadv.org/RESOURCES.

National Child Abuse Hotline/Childhelp

1-800-4-A-CHILD (1-800-422-4453)

www.childhelp.org

National Suicide Prevention Lifeline

Call or text 988

www.suicidepreventionlifeline.org

Crisis Text Line

Text HOME to 741741

www.crisistextline.org

National Resource Center on Domestic Violence

1-800-537-2238

www.nrcdv.org and www.vawnet.org

CHAPTER 1

Joy Hayes was really fucking tired.

She hadn't slept well the night before, but, in all honesty, she hadn't slept well in years. Sitting at her office desk, she ignored the way her cardigan brushed against her arms, the cotton material chafing her skin in a way that made her want to fling it across the room. Her fingers hovered over her keyboard, twitching as she fought the urge to take off her sweater, and she stared blankly at the blinking cursor of the email she had begun to type.

She winced at the throbbing in her head. Reaching her hand out for her pen, she cursed under her breath as she knocked over her pencil cup, sending her pens, pencils, and the odd unfolded paper clip scattering across the wooden surface. Her neck cracked as she rolled her head from side to side.

The smell of her discarded meal, a frozen plant-based lunch, wafted up and through the air. She wasn't a vegetarian, nor a vegan, but had decided after sobbing to a particularly cruel PETA Facebook ad to try and eat less meat. The brutal assault of soggy Brussels sprouts and beans on her nose and the way her stomach rolled in response made her regret ever opening Facebook.

Tick.

The clock sitting on the wall above her ticked loudly. She

pulled a bottle of pain pills from her desk drawer and chased the white capsules with the small sip left in her lukewarm, flat Diet Coke. The phone on her desk rang, and she jumped. Swearing, she picked up the phone.

Tick.

She finished her conversation, a quick question from a manager of a different department that veered off into him bragging about his recent vacation and the car he was thinking of buying, and put her head in her hands. Every tick hammered into her, and she gritted her teeth.

Tick.

A coworker passed by her desk, and she smiled instinctively. The older woman didn't even glance at her, but Joy held the smile until after she passed. The moment she was out of sight, Joy's smile slipped back into a frown. She zoned out, eventually catching her reflection in the darkness of her computer screen as it dimmed into sleep mode. The bags under her eyes made her grimace.

Tick.

An award sat framed on her desk, an outstanding employee certificate given to her a few months into the job. She loved praise, needed it, but it all felt so superficial. The frame itself was similar, perhaps identical, to the one showcasing her accounting degree at home. Both papers were supposed to bring her happiness. Both made her feel trapped in a purgatory of beige walls and cubicles.

Tick. Tick.

She glanced at the clock, noticed it was only three, and wondered if this is all life could offer. If there was nothing more than watching the clock crawl to five, the mindless chatter about vacation plans and wedding venues, the routines, the alarm clocks, the traffic, the bills.

Tick. Tick

Groaning, Joy rubbed her temples and puffed out a breath of air. Her temple pulsed under her touch, the pounding echoing throughout her body.

Tick. Tick. Tick.

"Just shut up," Joy hissed at the clock, grinding her teeth and glaring at the object.

As you wish, a deep voice responded.

Joy's lips parted in surprise. She looked around for the source of the voice, halfway expecting someone to be standing behind her. Something tickled her throat, and she coughed.

Tick. Tick. Tick.

A thin black mist floated out of her open mouth and toward the wall above her desk. It condensed, forming a solid dark plume, and hurled itself at the clock.

Tick. Tick—

The clock shattered as the black tendril smashed into it. It rocked back and forth for a second before slipping off the nail it sat on and colliding with the office carpet. Joy flinched as the fog shot up from the clock and twisted in her direction. She gagged as the cool mist launched up her nostrils and slid down the back of her throat. A phone rang in another office. Joy stared at the broken clock.

CHAPTER 2

The clock lay in pieces beside Joy's desk, finally quiet. Joy's eyes flicked between it and the ceiling, convinced she would find a hidden camera poised—to record her reaction. Her manager, Carmen, startled her by clearing her throat behind her. She stood beside Joy's desk, her eyebrows raised in question.

"You alright, Joy?" she asked.

Joy nodded slowly, eventually dragging her attention away from the clock. She took in the concerned look in Carmen's eyes and winced. Carmen was her favorite person at the company, a curvy woman with long black hair, deep brown skin, and a sunny personality that made it difficult to dislike her, either as a boss or a person.

A single mom to three kids, Carmen worked harder than anyone else in the office, consistently putting in overtime while juggling soccer games and early morning bus pickups. Joy had been excited and proud when Carmen told her she had been promoted to manager.

"Joy?" Carmen repeated.

"Yeah! I'm sorry," Joy replied. There was a lilt to her words: a slight southern accent that thickened when she was emotional or tired. "I think I might have eaten something bad. I'm not feeling great."

She bent down, scooping the broken glass into her hand

and tossing it in the trash beside her desk. Shaking her head, she placed the base of the clock on the wood of her desk. She smiled up at Carmen, waving her hand and turning back to her computer in a poor attempt to look like she was busy. Carmen raised her eyebrows.

"If you're sick, why don't you head home early?" Carmen suggested, rapping her knuckles on Joy's desk before walking back to her office. "Don't need the rest of the office catching it."

"But—"

"I'll see you tomorrow," Carmen tossed over her shoulder.

Joy scanned her open inbox. Deciding nothing couldn't be pushed back a day or two, she pulled on her coat and threw her keys into her pocket. As she rode down the elevator, Joy thought back to the clock falling, the cold sensation in her throat, and the pounding in her head. She walked through the parking lot toward her car, her cheeks stinging and her lungs burning as she breathed in the frigid October air.

The nip of inhaling the winter chill reminded Joy of the cold she had felt in her throat earlier. She reluctantly pulled her hands out from the warmth of her coat pockets and pushed the button to unlock her car. The pounding in her head had subsided, probably thanks to the medicine she had taken earlier, and she laughed as she thought of how ridiculous she had been. It was nothing more than a silly, perfectly timed coincidence.

It was not a coincidence.

The voice startled Joy, and she fumbled her keys. They fell from her fingers, slipping between the bars of the grate under her feet and landing in what Joy prayed was a pile of mud. She whipped around, a scowl on her face, but she was completely alone in the parking lot.

"Uh...Hello?" Joy called out.

Hello.

Joy blinked. The voice sounded as if it was right next to her, speaking into her ear. She pinched herself harshly and hissed at the stinging sensation.

It is not a dream.

She scanned the area, searching for a TV crew or friend recording on a cellphone.

It is not a prank, either.

"Is this all in my head?"

Yes.

Joy sighed, decided to deal with her mental break within the confines of her own home—after a cup of coffee and a snack—and dropped to her knees beside the grate. Her hand squeezed through the slots, her fingertips brushing against the metal of her keys. Pressing her face against the cold bars, she cursed her short, stubby fingers, willing them to lengthen slightly.

"That's a good look for you, bent over like that," a voice called to Joy.

She jerked backward and rolled onto her knees. A man leaned against the office building, a smug smirk on his lips and a lit cigarette in his fingers. He ran his other hand over his balding head, touching more skin than thin brown hair. He winked at Joy from behind his glasses.

Joy glared back at him. "Something I can help you with, Keith?"

Keith took a drag from his cigarette, puffing the smoke out slowly.

"Nope. Just enjoying the view. God sure took His time when He made you, didn't He?"

Joy curled her lip, the need for a shower washing over her as she watched Keith's eyes trail from her legs to her chest. It wasn't the first time he had used this line. He had said the same to an intern a week ago as she helped him make a coffee run. The intern had filed a complaint with HR and resigned shortly after the HR manager blew it off. Joy heard the manager tell the girl, only in her freshman year of college, that she needed to "grow up" and that she should be "flattered Keith had complimented her."

"And He must have been punishing your mom when He

made you," Joy spit back. "Screw off, Keith, I'm busy."

Keith raised his hand in surrender. He put his cigarette out on the side of the building before tossing it at the nearest bush.

"But now you must rid yourselves of all such things as these: anger, rage, malice, slander, and filthy language from your lips." Keith took off his glasses and began cleaning them with his shirt. "You really should think about cursing less; it's not good for the soul."

Joy rolled her eyes. She had nothing against Christians; she even considered herself one. After her aunt and uncle adopted her, she attended a Baptist church, going to a youth group after school on Wednesdays and a service on Sunday mornings. She was pretty sure she still believed in God, and she prayed nightly, but had long since rejected most of the things she had been taught.

Joy smiled kindly at Keith. He narrowed his eyes in suspicion.

"Don't you know that you yourselves are God's temple and that God's Spirit dwells in your midst? If anyone destroys God's temple, God will destroy that person; for God's temple is sacred, and you together are that temple." Joy blinked innocently. "Oh! Or how about 'Don't you realize that you become the slave of whatever you choose to obey? You can be a slave to sin, which leads to death, or you can choose to obey God, which leads to righteous living.' One of my favorite verses, really."

Rolling his shoulders back, Keith sneered and waited for Joy to continue. She was more than happy to.

Glancing to the side, Joy tossed out a final remark. "Smoking kills. You are slowly murdering God's temple, and, at least according to Corinthians, it sounds like God might not be happy with you."

Keith's eye twitched. He made a move to step forward, shook his head, and stalked back into the office building, slamming the door open without bothering to look backward. Joy turned her attention back to the grate, using her phone flashlight to light up the dark space. The keys glinted below, and Joy lowered herself back down, nostrils flaring as she failed to reach them.

Would you like help?

"Yes, voice in my head, I would like help. If you could float my keys up to me or something, that would be swell."

Joy rolled her eyes. Giving up, she rocked back into a squatting position.

Okay.

Joy coughed as the cold sensation returned to her throat. Snapping her mouth shut, she breathed out slowly through her nose, bewildered as a black mist floated from her nostrils. The mist drifted below through the gate and down to her keys. It wrapped around them, obscuring them from Joy's view. Her mouth gaped as flashes of gold floated up along with the dark cloud. She held out a hand, and they fell into her open palm. The mist swirled around her neck for a few seconds before shooting into her open mouth. She stared at the keys. Then stumbled to her feet and sprinted to her car.

Joy, what are you doing?

"Nope. Nope. Nope," mumbled Joy as she flung herself into her vehicle and locked the door. "This isn't real. I'm stressed and overworked, and this is all in my head."

Yes, you are overworked.

"Not helpful." Joy stared at herself in the rearview mirror, halfway expecting something else to be looking back at her and breathing a sigh of relief when she met with only her own reflection.

Joy grabbed her purse from where she had flung it in the backseat. She whipped out her phone and opened her camera app. "Can you prove this isn't just my imagination?"

What would you like us to do?

Joy looked around her car.

"There's a book in my backseat. I want you to pick it up and put it in the front while I record."

As you wish.

Palms sweaty, Joy clutched onto the phone and waited. The cold of the smoke drifted through her nostrils.

"Okay...go." She lifted her phone up, hitting the record button as she fought back a gag.

The mist floated lazily from Joy toward the back seat. She stared intently at her phone screen. The dark mass did not appear on camera, but Joy could see it as she peeked around her device. The book lifted from the back cushion, hovered in the air for a few seconds, then dropped onto her passenger seat. Joy paused her recording and wheezed as the smoke slid back down her throat. Pressing play on the video, Joy watched as the book lifted seemingly of its own accord and floated to the front. She set the phone on the console and stared off into space.

"Huh."

The book still lay in the passenger seat. Joy checked every few seconds for the five minutes she sat in the car, processing.

She slumped in her seat. "The video could be in my head, too, though."

She rubbed at her temple, slouching further and further into the upholstery as she contemplated. Her phone dinged beside her, drawing her attention.

"Ah!" Joy shot up, grabbing the device and pressing the most recent contact in her call log.

"Ethan!" Joy practically shouted as the call connected.

"My Joy!" Ethan replied, easily matching her energy. "Need any help slaying dragons today?"

Joy could hear music from what she assumed was a new video game playing somewhere in the background. Joy and Ethan had met in a class three years ago, having been paired up for a project by their professor, and had spent the entire assignment bickering over everything humanly possible. Joy preferred the Switch; Ethan loved his Xbox. Ethan's favorite franchise was Lord of the Rings, and while Joy tolerated the books, she couldn't stand the movies. They disagreed on starter Pokemon, with Joy always choosing a fire type, and

Ethan favoring water.

The two even looked like they wouldn't get along.

Ethan towered over Joy's 5'8 frame at 6'4. Joy's hair was usually pulled into a bun, her blue eyes hidden behind a pair of glasses. Ethan's brown hair hung freely to his shoulders, his brown eyes squinting due to his refusal to wear contacts.

Joy's wardrobe consisted of black and gray, an assortment of cardigans, trousers, and blouses she wore in almost precise rotation. Ethan could typically be found in a brightly colored game or movie-themed t-shirt and cargo pants or jeans faded from wear.

Joy had always been too afraid of needles to get a tattoo. Ethan had two: one on his shoulder with text reading "Los tiempos van cambiando" and one extending down his forearm that looked like his skin had been ripped off to reveal machinery underneath.

Ethan was a year younger than Joy, an engineering major, while Joy had debated getting a degree in English, with reading and writing being her first love, but ultimately stuck with the safety of her accounting program.

Although they were seeming opposites, Joy soon found herself looking forward to what had once been her least favorite class. When the class ended, the two kept in touch, and Joy now considered Ethan her best friend. Every now and then, she would get a flicker, an intrusive thought, that she might want to be more than his friend, but if he felt the same, Ethan had never shown it, and so she let the flicker die.

"I'm sending you a video. I need you to watch it and tell me what you see." Joy tapped her phone.

"Uh... yeah, okay," Ethan said.

Joy waited a few seconds, holding her breath and trying to release the tension in her shoulders. Ethan laughed over her speaker.

"Well, that's super random. Is film editing your newest thing? It looks good, though. I couldn't tell where it was edited or see any strings or anything."

"So you see it then? You see the book flying on its own?" Joy asked excitedly.

"Yes?" Ethan hesitated. "Was I not supposed to? What's going on?"

"I promise I'll explain later. Thanks, Ethan!"

"Wait, Joy—" Ethan cut out as she hung up the phone and tossed it aside.

Joy's heart pounded in her chest.

"What if Ethan is also in my head?" she whispered.

There was a pause in her mind. Silence stretched until it was too awkward for Joy to stand.

"Still there?"

Yes, we were simply contemplating the stupidity that was your previous question.. Joy rolled her eyes. *Ethan is real, and we are always with you.*

Joy frowned as a shiver rolled down her spine.

"First of all, that's freaky. Please never say that again. Second, what are you?"

We don't know.

Worried she would look crazy talking in the car by herself, she grabbed her headphones from her purse and popped the buds into her ears.

"Do you have a name?"

No.

"Do you want a name?"

The voice remained silent.

"I'm going to give you a name."

Oh, goody.

Joy laughed nervously.

"Of course, the demon in my brain would be sarcastic. Couldn't get someone friendly or helpful."

Silence. The heater in the car finally kicked in, and Joy placed her hands over the vents.

"Joey?"

Are you naming us after your fish that killed itself?

Joy's mouth pinched.

"He did not kill himself. His head got stuck in his rock statue and his gills couldn't open."

So he drowned himself.

"I'm not gonna name you Joey. You don't deserve the honor of being named after him." Joy huffed. "I'm assuming you can see my memories, then?"

Yes.

"So you're me? I'm imagining it after all?"

Joy crossed her arms and looked down at her feet. Although she still didn't completely believe what had happened, a part of her wanted to believe it was real, that she had some power that made her special. The rest of her was terrified by what that would mean for her.

We are a part of you.

Joy sighed.

"Are you trying to confuse me on purpose?"

Silence.

Joy bounced her leg. "Cool. How 'bout Buttercup?"

Buttercup?

"Well. I have a creepy ass voice in my head. I figured a cute name would help lighten my anxiety about it."

We are not creepy.

"Agree to disagree." Joy shifted the car out of park, pulled out of the office parking lot and headed home. She took her earbuds out and tossed them into her cup holder.

You do not have to speak aloud to converse with us.

Joy rolled her eyes. "Yeah, I got that after the whole clock thing. Talking out loud makes me feel slightly less crazy."

You think speaking out loud in an empty car makes you seem less crazy?

This time Joy remained silent.

Joy?

"Yes, Buttercup?"

We can hear the curse words.

CHAPTER 3

Birth

"It's a girl," the doctor cooed, cradling the baby in his arms before passing her to her mother.

Most mothers would be excited to hear the words, relieved the labor was over and eager to meet their child. Instead of the tears of joy new mothers on tv always seemed to shed, sixteen-year-old Joanne cried out of bitterness, sadness, even a bit of fear. She was tired, sore throughout her body, and terrified by the lack of connection she felt toward the baby.

They say some women were born to be mothers. Joanne was not. When Joanne found out she was pregnant at fifteen, she already had a history of behavioral problems, a wannabe rockstar mother with a drug addiction, a father she had never met, and a younger half-sister who was terrified of her.

Joanne gave the baby the name Joy in an attempt to make up for her absence of emotion as she peered at its pale blonde hair and blue eyes. Joanne's eyes were brown, her hair dark and curly. The child looked very little like her, outside of the upturned, button-like nose. She decided on the middle name Aurora, after the lights in the sky. Joy's last name did not come from her biological father, but rather the man Joanne was with at the time of her birth. Joanne had married the man in a ceremony that was not even close to legal, but they separated a few weeks after. Joy never saw him again—as was the pattern with her mother's love interests—but she was left with his name as a permanent reminder of how fleeting affection could be.

Joy's biological father stuck around for a bit, but ultimately left shortly after she turned two. Although it hurt to think about as she got older, she didn't hold it against him. She was too young to understand the man leaving should have played a bigger role, and, as she had been too young to remember her time with him, she ignored his absence in her life.

The two reconnected when Joy was an adult, long after an indifference to abandonment had become ingrained into her personality. But still, she didn't blame him, not entirely. She couldn't find it in herself to condemn a man who fled from the tumultuous mess that was her family.

"It's a girl!" Like an echo, the words were spouted by another doctor as Joanne gave birth to Joy's half-sister, Clara, a little less than two years later.

Joy and Clara had different fathers, different last names, and different expectations thrust upon them by their mother. Clara was born with her mother's brown hair, brown eyes, and more of her affection than Joy had been. But as with Joy, Clara's father and Joanne were already broken up by the time Clara was born. Clara was also given a different last name than her biological father, the last name of their future, slightly more long-term stepfather.

"It's a boy!" A slight twist on the words heard before.

Joanne gave birth to Joy and Clara's half-brother, Sammy, a year and a half after Clara was born. Joy and Sammy shared blue eyes, but Clara and Sammy shared a last name and brown hair. Sammy's father was a military man serving in the U.S. Marine Corps. He moved Joy, her mother, and her siblings up to a base in North Carolina, only an hour or so from Myrtle Beach, South Carolina. Joy didn't remember anything from before North Carolina. That was for the best. She realized as she got older the majority of the things that stuck out to her were unhappy, dark memories living in the depths of her mind. Joy's first memory wasn't one of the dark ones. Her first memory was of seagulls.

CHAPTER 4

"I wasn't made for you!" Joy sang with the radio, tapping her fingers along her steering wheel as she coasted down the highway.

Joy. Please stop.

Joy sang louder. "You weren't made to haunt me!"

You're going to give us a headache.

This had been going on for nearly fifteen minutes now, Joy screeching along to whatever song played on her phone while she ignored the voice speaking in her head. She had been joking when she named it, fully convinced she was having a stroke or some response to a traumatic brain injury that had somehow happened without her noticing.

"When we said goodbye, I thought it would be the last time."

People are going to call animal control. You sound like a dying cat.

"But you can't get enough of me!" Joy threw her head back as she belted the final lyrics.

Are you done?

The opening beats of a new song played over the car, and Joy sucked in a deep breath, preparing to launch into the next 80s pop song.

We are not going away. We are a part of you. We have waited so long for you to discover this power.

Joy hesitated.

"Power?"

The mist came from us.

"So I'm not possessed by the devil?"

Buttercup didn't respond immediately, but its silence felt like the disappointment of a parent realizing their child might not be the sharpest tool in the shed.

No. You are not possessed by anything. We are the same.

"Huh," Joy murmured, lost in thoughts no longer belonging solely to her. "On the off chance I believe this is real and I don't need to see a doctor or a priest, have you always been inside me or what? Why have I never heard you before?"

We have always been one. You have simply pushed us to the side.

"Mm. You're sure you're not a demon? That was, like, the perfect demonic tagline."

We are not a demon. We are you.

Joy glared at her reflection.

"You didn't answer my other question. Why have I never heard you before?"

You have.

"Like hell I have. Pretty sure I'd remember that."

We have always been here, speaking to you, waiting for you.

"This is giving me a headache."

We know.

Joy rubbed at her temples.

"Okay, last question then. Does everyone have a Buttercup?"

No, we exist only within your mind.

"Yeah, I got that part. Does anyone else have another voice in their head?"

We do not know. Possibly.

"I guess that makes sense. You'd only know what I know, right?"

Buttercup didn't respond.

Joy pulled her car into the parking lot of her apartment complex. She grabbed her purse and slipped her phone into her pocket before locking the car door and heading for the stairs. Stepping into her apartment, Joy felt her shoulders slump. She exhaled slowly and let her eyes flutter shut.

Joy didn't live in a great neighborhood, but there were few affordable neighborhoods in Austin. Her rent here was cheap, and she had learned to tune out the sounds of police sirens and the yelling of drunks and angry people. Although she lived on the second floor, her apartment opened up to the outside, almost like a motel would.

The apartment itself was small; it had one bedroom, one bathroom, a decent-sized living room, and a tiny kitchen. The floors were wooden, which Joy loved, and the furniture was mismatched, pieces Joy had collected from family members and Facebook marketplace.

Tossing her keys onto her coffee table, Joy trudged to the kitchen, threw open a cabinet, and pulled out a mixing bowl. She grabbed a box of cereal from deeper in the cabinet and poured herself a healthy serving. Her couch, a mustard-yellow section with a few questionable stains, sagged as she plopped herself down. Flipping on the tv that sat on a dresser across the room, Joy turned on a cooking video on YouTube and contemplated the last hour as she ate.

You are calm.

Joy shrugged. "Would you prefer I panic?"

No.

"I have a lot of questions, but I honestly don't know where to start."

We know.

Joy took a big bite of her cereal.

"Do you sleep?"

Yes. When you do.

"What am I supposed to do with this, I mean *your* ability?"

What do you want to do?

"I don't know. In movies and comic books, people become superheroes and save the world or whatever. Am I supposed to use your powers for good or be some kind of hero?"

Do you want to be a hero?

Joy's lips pressed together in a slight grimace. She had daydreams now and then where she chased down a purse-snatcher or raced into a fire to save a screaming infant or family pet. She wouldn't deny she would enjoy the attention and the praise being a hero would bring her. She craved attention as much as she hated it.

The fame and money would also be nice if she could find a way to make money doing it, but she wasn't sure she could handle the responsibility. And that's if it was only a positive thing. For all she knew, she would be captured by the government and dissected to figure out what gave her the abilities. Or she could be hated, rejected, and labeled as a vigilante, like Batman.

"Not really," she admitted.

Why not?

"I... I'm not sure. It doesn't seem like me, I guess. But is that wrong? I'm not planning on robbing a bank or being a villain or anything, but is it worse if I have these abilities and choose not to do anything with them?"

We do not know. We are you.

"So, technically, I'm talking to myself?"

Yes.

"But you respond without me thinking of a response?"

Do we?

Joy threw her head back and laughed. "I know you're not trying to be, but that's so unhelpful."

Gordon Ramsey yelled at someone on the television, drawing Joy's attention. She pulled her phone from her pocket, Googled Mr. Ramsey's age, sighed in discontent, and then tossed her phone on the coffee table, tucking away that knowledge for later reference.

"So. If you're me because you have my memories and see what I see, but you have your own thoughts and responses, that would make you kinda like AI, right? You have all the programming and knowledge and can make decisions without prompting, but are limited to what I interact with, like how AI is limited to a computer screen?"

We are… We suppose so.

Joy grinned.

"Cool."

Joy set her cereal bowl on her coffee room table and paused her show.

"Alright, Buttercup, should we try you out?"

If you wish.

"Well, that's not very enthusiastic."

Yes, Joy. We would love for you to test your new abilities we have waited twenty-two years for you to discover. Yippee, Buttercup deadpanned.

"Close enough."

Joy hopped up and down, stretching her legs and shaking out her arms.

What are you doing?

"Stretching. I don't know what you do to my body. I figure I oughta be as prepared as possible."

What would you like to begin with?

A soft meowing echoed through the room as Panda, Joy's five-year-old black and white cat, pranced inside. The cat rubbed against Joy's leg, staring up at her with sad eyes before turning and waddling over to her food dish.

"Alright. Let's start by feeding chunky over there. The food is—"

In the pantry. We will get it.

"So do I have to think about where you're going? Do I, like, move you with my hand, or how does this work?"

We do as you say. When we are away, we hear your thoughts and feel your actions. If you gesture toward something, we will follow. It is your power.

"This is so fucking cool! Alright. Buttercup, please feed Panda."

Joy coughed as the cold mist tickled her throat. It drifted out of her mouth, floating lazily toward her pantry. She followed behind the fog, watching as it solidified into a black mass around the door handle. The door tugged open. Buttercup lifted a can of cat food from the shelf and carried it to the kitchen counter. It cracked the tin open and poured it into the cat bowl. Panda meowed happily, then began to eat.

Buttercup placed the can in the trash. It shot back into Joy, and she gagged as it rushed back down her throat.

"Why do you always come out of my mouth?" Joy frowned as she thought of the way she worded the question.

Where else would we come from?

Joy snorted.

That is disgusting.

"I didn't say anything!" Joy exclaimed.

Yes, but you thought it.

"What about my ears?" Joy snorted. "Like one of those old cartoons, except far more ominous."

We are simply a physical manifestation of your power.

"Oh. That's cool." Joy pondered for a second. "So I could just like—"

She bent her knees as she flicked her wrist out, pressing two fingers to the center of her palm.

Nothing happened.

You are not Spiderman.

Dropping her arm to her side, Joy cleared her throat.

"I know. I thought it would look cool."

It did not.

Joy scratched her neck.

"But can you come from my palms instead? Or my fingertips? Does it have to be an orifice?"

We can come from any part of you.

"Why can no one else see you?"

We do not know.

"Where does the power come from?"

You.

"Am I the only one with this power?"

We know only as much as you do.

Panda finished eating, waddling through the kitchen and choosing to lie on the couch. She stretched once, yawned, and closed her eyes. Joy followed her, flipping off the television and fiddling with her phone.

Opening Google on the device, she searched "I have superpowers, what do I do?" A quick scan revealed nothing of use. Instead, Joy found a few parody articles and dozens of lists of the coolest superpowers and what people would do with those powers. Flight topped almost every list. Joy bounced from foot to foot, eyes lighting up and smile growing.

"Buttercup?"

No.

"I didn't even get to say anything!" Joy pouted.

We know what you were thinking.

"Okay. Good point. But I think it's possible."

Would you like to try?

"Yes. Yes, I would."

Spreading her arms out, Joy watched as the black mist quickly surrounded her body. She thought of it as a giant plastic hamster ball, a sphere circling her and allowing her to move.

What she failed to consider, however, was her complete lack of balance. The sphere lifted her from the ground, and she wobbled, her arms flinging out for stability. Trying to walk forward, she slipped, her face colliding with the edge of the black ball. The ball continued to move, Joy rolling with it as it moved forward.

"Nope. Hate this," Joy concluded as the sphere dropped her back on the floor.

The smoke dissipated, absorbing back into Joy.

We warned you it would not work.

"Yes, I know, but it will! What about under my feet? Like an escalator."

Going up vertically was manageable, but Joy slipped as Buttercup shifted to the side. She tumbled over the edge of the smoke, bouncing off the arm of her couch and landing sprawled on her floor.

"Not that way either," she wheezed out, clutching her stomach and staring at the ceiling.

She tried it like a child's swing set, the black mist forming a harness that gave her the worst wedgie of her life.

She tried having Buttercup lift her by the armpits. Joy had crutches for a bit as a child, having sprained her knee in a game of dodgeball. She hated them. The way the plastic cut into her armpits left her sore for days afterward. The throbbing in her arms after Buttercup's attempt was reminiscent of that. Her shirt chafed her underarms, leaving ugly red splotches.

"What about like a conveyor belt? The ones at the airport people use to get from one gate to the next quickly? Only, slightly tilted so I can step from one to the next. So maybe more like a mix of stairs and a ramp. Or just a ramp. Does that make sense?"

No.

Nonetheless, Buttercup drifted through the air. It formed a small black square, and Joy stepped on. Lifting about two feet in the air, Joy swayed a bit as she steadied herself. A second black square appeared, floating beside her hand. She flicked her wrist and watched as the square aligned itself with the first.

She stepped onto the second square. The first faded away.

Flicking her wrist again, she watched another square appear in front of her. She continued this pattern for a few minutes, stepping on squares a few feet from her living room floor. She gestured down, and the square descended, placing her gently on the ground.

She caught her reflection in the mirror, noticing her wide, excited eyes and the beads of sweat popping up along her neck from trying to remain balanced. She smirked.

CHAPTER 5

Joy, Age 4

"Birdies!" Clara, now three years old, shrieked as she ran at a flock of sitting birds.

They scattered, spreading their wings and taking off into the air. The beach was a bit chilly but bright, and the waves lapped the shore. Joy pulled the hood of her coat up and over her ears, nestling down into the fur as the cool ocean breeze stung her cheeks. She rode on the shoulders of her stepdad and chastised her sister for bothering the animals.

Her mother stood with Joy's brother on her hip, a calm smile on her face as she looked over the sea. Joanne was twenty now, too young to drink legally but old enough to live with her husband on a military base, old enough to have three kids, old enough for the regret and desolation of motherhood to set in.

Joy tapped on her stepfather's head and gestured to the ground. He placed her onto the sand, and she giggled as a seagull hopped closer to her. She patted her lap, beckoning the bird closer as one would a dog. Small feet sunk into the sand as she crouched down, pulling a bit of bread from her pocket. Joy squealed as the bird took the food from her palm. She glanced from her mother to her stepfather to her sister. She threw herself at her mother's legs, hugging her tightly and grinning up at the woman. Her mother patted Joy on the head awkwardly before prying herself away from the girl and turning her gaze to the ocean. Joy wandered away, searching the sand for a souvenir to take home.

Clara ran up to Joanne next, brown ponytail bobbing as she sprinted along the sand. Joanne's eyes lit up, and she held back a laugh as Clara tripped. She landed on her hands and knees before popping right back up—a benefit of youth—with a wide grin on her face. Joanne smiled down at the girl, passing Sammy to their stepfather and hoisting her up and into her arms.

Joy tugged a shell from the sand. Stepping up to the water's edge, she squatted and carefully rinsed the muck from the object. It was rough against her hand, hard lines etched into the yellowish-white color. She turned the shell over and hissed as her finger caught against the ragged edge. A small drop of blood fell into the water, lost in the white froth of the waves.

She glanced back to her family, hiding the object and her hurt hand in her coat pocket. Sammy gurgled in her stepfather's arms. Joanne laughed at something Clara said. Joy stood alone, watching the happy scene in front of her. She frowned, then remembered how her mother hated it when she did so.

"I don't understand why she looks like that, so serious and always judging me with her empty eyes. And she's so quiet. I can't tell what she's thinking or feeling, and it freaks me out," she had once heard her mother tell her grandmother.

She had been born reserved, somber even. Clara's grandmother joked Joy had been possessed as a baby, never crying and with an intense stare that unnerved her. At first, her family had found it amusing. They assumed she would grow out of it. She never did. Even as young as four, she could understand she wasn't quite right, that it made her mother sad and others uncomfortable. So she began mimicking the actions of others, laughing when they did, speaking as they did, showing affection when they did.

Walking away from the water, she forced a smile on her mouth. If it didn't quite reach her eyes, her family never noticed.

CHAPTER 6

Joy swung her arm out, striking blindly at her phone as her alarm blared. Her hand knocked into the device, sending it crashing to the ground. She groaned as she heard it collide with the carpet. She yanked her covers off of her and reached under her bed to retrieve it.

Good morning, Joy.

Joy shrieked, flinging her phone toward the wall as she lost her grip. She coughed as black mist shot from her nostril. It encircled the phone, stopping it from hitting her *Doctor Who* poster, and floated it back gently to Joy's open palm.

"Thanks, Buttercup. Totally forgot you were in there," Joy said aloud.

We apologize.

"For what? Existing?" Joy glanced down at her blaring alarm. "Son of a gun, I'm going to be late."

Joy hopped out of her bed.

"Shi—" Joy slipped on a discarded sock on the floor.

She steadied herself, then lunged forward. She grabbed a pair of jeans lying on a pile of clean laundry that had been tossed onto her desk chair. She crawled on hands and knees, searching for a company t-shirt. One of the perks of working for a tech company was the ability to wear whatever she wanted to work. Most of the engineers wore jeans and t-shirts. Although Joy usually tried to dress a bit more professionally than they, it was Friday, and she was exhausted. A work shirt and sneakers would have to do.

When she moved in, the apartment had been in a state of disarray. The walls had been off-white, with stains of various colors and shapes. She had spent her first few nights seeing images in the shapes of the stains, her own disgusting version of cloud watching. She had since painted the walls a clean white, although the room was still messy.

Early morning sunlight slipped through the sheer curtains and onto her gray bedding. Her bed held numerous pillows and two cream-colored stuffed bears. A bookcase overflowing with books, journals, and small trinkets sat in the corner of her room. Her desk was opposite her bookcase and was covered in unfinished homework assignments, various makeup brushes, and a dried tube of mascara that made her eyes water when she used it. A university hoodie was slung over a lavender, tufted armchair. Joy couldn't help but wince at the half-empty bottles of water scattered around the room.

She plucked the sock from the ground and pulled it onto one foot. She fist-pumped the air when Buttercup found the sock's match under her bed and floated it to her. Reaching into her closet, she tugged out the fabric on the top of the pile.

She hesitated as she stared down at the garment. It was a jersey for the Pittsburgh Steelers, and she traced the vinyl of the number on the back. Her step-grandfather had given it to her a few months before his passing. Money had always been tight in her grandparents' house, and she knew he must have saved for months to buy it from the official website. She folded it and stood, placing it on her bookcase beside the *The Princess Bride* DVD she had saved from his unwanted belongings after his funeral.

She threw on a shirt from the chair she had thrown her fresh laundry on and viciously combed her disheveled hair back into a bun with her fingers. Buttercup drifted her keys, as well as a banana and a light jacket, to the counter by her front door as she brushed her teeth. She pulled on her shoes and headed for the front door.

"Good call," she chirped to Buttercup, peeling the banana as she locked her apartment.

She munched on the fruit as she jogged to her car, unlocking it and scooting herself into the driver's side. Yawning, she flicked on her car radio and glanced worriedly at the clock. Ever the pessimist, she ran through all of the possible outcomes from a meeting she had scheduled for later in the morning as she pulled into her usual parking spot. She narrowed her eyes at her reflection in the mirror and chastised herself for her negativity. Squaring her shoulders, she walked into her office and forced a grin. It was going to be a great day.

* * *

The day had sucked, and Joy was in a mood. The type of mood that made her coworkers avert their eyes as they passed her desk. She mumbled under her breath, fingers flying over her keyboard as she tried to fix yet another mistake caused by Keith. He had a habit of taking the data Joy pulled and shifting it into graphics that made very little sense and were usually inaccurate. He would tell her he was older, he knew the design preferences of the members of upper management, and she should trust he would make her look good.

Today she had been chastised after a meeting in which Keith had changed the data set entirely, failing to mention the change to Joy, and left multiple typos. But Keith, with the audacity only a mediocre middle-aged man could have, couldn't be bothered to apologize for the mistake.

Instead, he looked her in the eyes, shook his head sadly, and said, "That's not like you, Joy. Making such basic mistakes. You can do so much better."

Nick, the company's CEO and absolute douchenozzle, had nodded his head in agreement before turning to the next item on the agenda. Not that he would have said much to her, even if the graphic hadn't contained numerous glaring errors. Nick was as bad as Keith, constantly promoting an atmosphere of sexism and pretty much every other form of bigotry under the guise of "joking." Joy had been looking for a new job for a few weeks now, finally sick of how terrible the men at her company were, but hadn't had any luck yet and couldn't afford to be jobless with her crippling medical debt and addiction to fancy coffees.

She sighed as she watched a man wheel in a cart of hard liquor and little cherries, internally debating if she actually needed to pay her bills and whether she had the stamina to become a stripper, should the need arise. A smaller tech company, Joy's office tried to keep up with the trends of the larger companies while constrained by its undersized budget. The corporate happy hour held every other Friday was a product of this. Instead of meeting at a bar or restaurant, Nick had a traveling bartender come in and serve drinks in the office boardroom. The women in the company, Joy included, absolutely dreaded it.

The men in the office often drank too much, making inappropriate comments or "accidentally" getting handsy as the women huddled together, rolled their eyes, and waited for enough time to pass so they could leave. They were expected to attend. If they didn't, would be labeled frigid or bitchy. The only time Joy had ever missed it, for a dental appointment of all things, Keith had sent out a company-wide email emphasizing the importance of "being a team player" and expressing his disappointment that some in the office didn't seem to understand the significance of bonding opportunities.

Joy had printed twenty copies, shredded to be unreadable, and stuffed Keith's desk drawers with the scraps. Keith had laughed, writing it off as a prank between colleagues, but Joy hadn't missed how his beady little eyes had narrowed.

"Screw this," Joy muttered, turning her computer off and heading for the exit.

Grabbing her things, she trod carefully by Keith's office, praying he wouldn't catch her trying to leave. She made it just outside of the elevator before she heard Keith's door open and his voice call out her name. Carmen stepped out of her office as he began walking toward Joy, blocking his path with a question about a report he had submitted. Carmen turned, sent Joy a quick wink, and gestured at the papers in her hand as Keith's cheeks flushed with embarrassment. Joy could tell by the glint in Carmen's eyes that she was questioning Keith about the mistakes in the data.

Joy smiled thankfully at Carmen's back. The elevator dinged in front of her, signaling an arrival, and she stepped back, making room for whoever was inside. Three children piled out of the elevator, various toys and snacks dangling from their hands. The smallest of the children glanced up, her eyes brightening as she saw Joy. The girl dropped her doll, grinning a gap-toothed smile as she threw herself at Joy.

Joy stiffened as the kid wrapped her small arms around Joy's legs. "Hi, Paula."

"Hi, Ms. Joy." Paula hugged the woman tighter as Joy awkwardly patted her head.

The only boy of the three children sprinted by Joy, his brown curls bouncing as he ran to his mother. Carmen dismissed Keith with a shake of her head, ignoring his glare as he slunk away to his office. She plucked the boy from the ground and placed him on her hip.

"Still not a kid person, huh, Joy?" Carmen teased.

Joy eyed the child in front of her. "I'm working on it."

Paula sneezed, then wiped her nose along Joy's cardigan. Joy grimaced, extracting the child from her legs and guiding her back to her missing doll. Carmen was a single mom to three: Paula, who had celebrated her third birthday last weekend; Marcus, who was four; and Chelsea, who was seven.

Chelsea had recently started dressing herself, something that terrified Carmen and never failed to amuse Joy. Today she skipped into the office in gray Nike sweatpants, a bright pink princess tutu, and a white button-down shirt. Chelsea waved and twirled toward Joy.

"I like your outfit, Chelsea," Joy complimented the girl.

"Thank you. Momma said I can start picking out my own clothes, and I wanted sweatpants cause I can run in them and a tutu because it's cute, and I like the pink and my button shirt because it's warm and matches my sneakers." Chelsea rattled on, a wide grin stretching her chubby cheeks as she explained.

It also amused Joy how all three children looked so similar to their mother, four sets of big brown eyes framed by wild dark curls. Chelsea was the most like her mom, with a big personality to match her vibrant wardrobe choices. Chelsea was a beautiful, happy kid. She had regained the shine in her eyes, the excitement in her small body previously lost to a cruel father and a few weeks of homelessness.

"Makes sense." Joy patted the girl on her head as well, her universal sign for both affection and discomfort. "Are y'all here to pick up your mom?"

Chelsea nodded enthusiastically.

"Yup. Alheri is dropping us off cause she's got a work thing to do. Momma said they do a whole hour of happy here with snacks! That doesn't seem very fair, though, because my snack time at school is only twenty minutes."

As Chelsea spoke, Joy noticed Alheri stepping out of the elevator. Alheri was a tall woman, a little over six feet, with dark brown skin and springy coiled hair that barely brushed her shoulders. She grinned as she saw Joy, throwing an arm around her shoulders and pulling her into a quick hug.

"Hi, Joy. Sorry I have to go, but I'll see you at next week's game night?"

Alheri and Carmen hosted a game night every few weeks, a small gathering of various friends playing whatever board game they could find at the local comic book store. Joy's mouth watered, thinking of the Malva pudding Alheri had made for the last game night. It was genuinely one of the best things Joy had ever tasted, warm apricot jam baked with spongy bread and topped with a vanilla cream sauce.

Joy shook her head sadly, images of baked goods dissipating.

"No, I'm heading back to West Texas for my mom's wedding."

"And that's... a good thing?" Alheri cocked her head to the side. "You like the guy she's marrying, right?"

She did. When Joy's biological aunt turned adoptive mother announced she and Jonas, her future step-dad, were getting married, Joy wasn't surprised. She had very little in common with the man, a conservative farmer with two young sons, but she couldn't deny she liked him for Trini. He was sweet to her, called her Sunshine, and never pressured her to be anyone but herself. Trini had been through some shit and deserved to be happy, which Jonas seemed to make her. Still, she dreaded going home. So many bad memories were woven into her small town, flashes of the person she used to be, a young girl she'd rather leave behind.

Joy sighed. "Yeah, he's great. It's West Texas that sucks."

"Bad Joy!" Chelsea scolded, her eyebrows creasing as she frowned. "Mama says that's a bad word."

Carmen laughed as Joy struggled to think of how to respond. "You're right. That's a naughty word."

Chelsea nodded curtly. Something caught her eye in the distance, and she scurried away.

Alheri smiled at Carmen, stepping forward to press a chaste kiss on her cheek. Someone cleared their throat from behind the three women. Joy turned to see Keith scowling at Alheri and Carmen, his nose wrinkled in disgust.

Alheri stepped away.

She slipped her hands in the pockets of her jeans, her grin stretching too far to be natural. Joy glared back at Keith, her jaw clenching. She knew Alheri and Carmen didn't need her defending them; they had faced plenty of obstacles on their own, but she hated Keith with a fiery passion. She would be damned if she let him make her friends uncomfortable.

"Don't you have a report to fix, Keith?" Joy shook her head sadly. "Such a shame, I know you can do so much better than that."

Keith narrowed his eyes, opening his mouth to speak. Joy smiled back, one eyebrow raising as she dared him to say what he was thinking. The vein in his neck throbbed, and he spun on his heel, stalking back into his office.

"God. He sucks." Joy stared at his office.

Carmen hung her head and let out a shaky laugh.

"Could be worse." She rolled her shoulders back before lifting her head, searching the office for the kids.

Joy's chest squeezed, a flutter of guilt floating through her stomach. Could she have done something more, told Keith something to make him back off permanently? Carmen didn't deserve his disrespect. As Joy studied her friend's reaction, she thought back to the nights Carmen and the kids had crammed into her small apartment, too scared to go home and having nowhere else to go. Carmen's parents passed away when she was in her early twenties. Carmen got pregnant with Chelsea a few years later, deciding to get married for the sake of the baby and for the health insurance her boyfriend's job would provide.

They were happy for a few years, but something flipped in the boyfriend shortly after Marcus was born. He started staying out later, drinking more. He was a mean drunk, a violent one who used both his hands and words as weapons. One night he got rough with Carmen, and she fled, taking the kids with her and staying with Joy for a few days while she filed a restraining order and looked for a new apartment.

It was a bad time in Carmen's life, but she met Alheri a few years later and they had, as Carmen described it with starry eyes after drinking a hint too much wine, an "instant connection." Joy thought it sounded cringy, but she was happy for her friend. The two began dating and had been for almost a year now. Not everyone had been so happy for the couple. Keith had once filed a complaint to HR against Carmen, citing

PDA in the workplace after Alheri had come to pick her up and pecked her on the lips.

Marcus squirmed in Carmen's arms as her hold unconsciously tightened around him. She set him on the ground, and he waddled off after his sisters. With the mood made uncomfortable by Keith, Alheri gave Carmen and Joy a quick goodbye and headed out. Joy patted her pockets, checking for her wallet and her keys, before turning to leave too. Carmen's phone dinged in her pocket as Joy scanned the office to say goodbye to the kids. Carmen cursed under her breath, fingers flying over her screen as she typed a reply.

"Everything alright?" Joy asked.

"One of the Perger Corp. guys just emailed me. They said the document Keith sent them was from the wrong year. I'd ask Keith to fix it, but he's obviously incapable. Ugh, they need it before close today."

Joy glanced at her phone,. There were only thirty minutes left in the workday.

"Do you need help with it? I can stick around."

Carmen smiled sheepishly.

"I can get the document done pretty quickly, but I have the kids..."

Joy pursed her lips.

We will regret this.

"I'll watch the—"

Carmen swept Joy into her arms, hugging her tightly before she could even finish her sentence.

"Thank you!" She released Joy, jogging toward her office. "Don't kill my kids or let them kill each other!"

CHAPTER 7

Joy, Age 5

Sammy wouldn't stop crying.

He had been for hours, even as Joy rocked him in her arms, her tiny limbs aching from trying to hold him the way their mother did. Sammy was two now, already too large for Joy to pick up. Clara's cheeks were flushed red from crying. She tugged on Joy's shirt to get her attention.

"I'm hungry," she said, looking up at Joy through wet lashes.

Joy nodded. It had been a few hours since their mother had left them alone, and Joy was also really hungry, but she wasn't allowed in the fridge without asking and didn't want to get in trouble.

"I know. Mom will be back soon," Joy reassured the younger girl.

Joy was far too young to remember if this was the first time their mother had left them locked in the room, but she also couldn't remember, and would never discover, the reason. According to one of the rumors she had been told over the years, her mother had simply abandoned the children completely, running away from her responsibilities and fleeing to a different state. In another, her mother had left the three, driven down to Texas, and checked herself into a mental hospital.

There was some truth to this story, as at some point in her life, her mother had checked herself into a hospital in Texas. The most likely rumor, the one she heard the most often, was that her mother had locked them in the room so she could go freely to their neighbor's house.

When a kid is born, relatives talk about the things they inherited from their parents, small noses, curly hair, their mother's eyes. With Joy and Clara, there was more discussion about the repercussions of the things they inherited. Mental illness was rampant on her mother's side: bipolar disorder and chemical imbalances that led to bursts of anger. The women in her family were also incredible liars and manipulators, with poker faces rivaling those of professional gamblers.

Joy never found out what happened the day her mother abandoned her, or even if it was a common occurrence, but she did know it was the last time.

It was quickly decided she and Clara would be shipped down to live in Texas with their maternal grandparents while Sammy stayed in North Carolina with his father. She didn't remember the plane ride to Texas, or saying goodbye to her soon-to-be ex-stepfather or brother.

She did remember her grandparents waiting to pick the two girls up from the airport. The first thing she noticed about her grandmother, Sarah, was her hair. It was dyed an unnatural shade of red, a color reminding Joy of *Clifford the Big Red Dog*, one of the books she had left in North Carolina. Sarah's eyes were green, cold and distant, as if she were a million miles away from the conversation. She wore fuzzy Ugg boots, ripped jeans, and a long-sleeved band t-shirt. She had a nose ring, and when she pushed her sleeves up her thin arms, a hint of a tattoo peeked through. Sarah pulled Joy into a hug, and Joy wrinkled her nose at the confusing smell, an odd mix of jasmine tea, cheap perfume, and cigarettes.

Her step-grandfather, Tom, stood behind, smiling kindly at the girls. He was tall and lanky, with long, thin brown hair pulled back into a ponytail. He also smelled slightly like cigarettes, a habit he was never quite able to give up, but also of green apple shampoo and Old Spice deodorant. He wore jeans as well, gaping holes in his knees from years of wear, and a Star Wars t-shirt. He was five years younger than Sarah, in his late thirties when the girls arrived in Texas. The drive to their new home was mostly quiet, an occasional question asked by their grandfather the only break to the classic rock station playing over the radio.

As Joy wandered around the house, she couldn't help but notice it seemed to be divided between her grandmother and grandfather. The living room obviously belonged to her grandmother. Guitars leaned against one wall of the room. Those with scribbles on them were hung up and out of reach of the children. There was a large couch facing a small television, shelving crammed with books on both sides. Articles with pictures of Sarah were framed, hung throughout the room and sitting on empty shelves. Sarah had once been in a band, had big dreams of living the rock-star life, dreams she clung to with her collections of amplifiers and stories she claimed were her good days. She had once even performed as the opener for the Los Lonely Boys, a tale she brought up every chance she could.

The art room, no bigger than a closet, belonged to her grandfather. He was an artist, an incredibly talented one, a trait that rubbed off on Clara but was lost on Joy. The walls were plastered in sketches and comic book panels, all drawn by her grandfather. An old computer he used to mix audio dramas sat in the corner of the room, and various paintbrushes, pencils, and sketching paper lay scattered about the multiple tables he crammed into the small space. Pieces of brightly colored vinyl littered the floor, clung to the fabric of his shirts, stuck to the occasional shoe.

After completing service in the United States Navy, Tom came home to Texas and got a degree in graphic design. He found a job in a nearby city and helped design and prep vinyl stickers on the side. It didn't pay well, but he loved it. He had been divorced once before meeting Sarah and had a child a few years younger than Joanne. He and Sarah had decided on a small wedding, marrying beside a local creek with only their close friends and family.

Joanne must have been heavily pregnant; Joy was born only a month later. It was odd, albeit not surprising, that there were very few pictures of Joanne in attendance. They surely existed; it would be difficult to avoid getting the daughter of the bride in a few pictures, but they were never the ones Sarah showed others or posted on Facebook when showing off throwback images of her youth. Sarah was huge on image, and a pregnant sixteen-year-old would have ruined that.

The room belonging to Joy and Clara was a lot bigger than their room in North Carolina. Their grandparents had done a good job of fixing a room up, buying them toys in frantic haste and building a bunk bed for the large room. Joy quickly claimed the top bunk as her own, tossing her suitcase to the side, clambering up the steps, and marveling at how tall she felt as she looked down.

She waited to unpack until later that night and frowned at the empty shelves that remained even after all her belongings had been carefully placed. Her small chin wobbled as she placed her now empty Barbie suitcase beside her door. She wanted to be ready for when her mom came back for her and Clara, for when she could see Sammy, for when they would be a family again.

CHAPTER 8

The kids had yet to kill each other in the half-hour since Carmen had disappeared behind her door. Joy stood waiting outside of the woman's bathroom, waiting for Paula, who had insisted she was a big girl who could go to the restroom on her own. Joy rubbed at the red, phallic-shaped ink on her arm. Marcus wanted to play artist and begged Joy to let him give her a "tattoo." He had insisted it was a truck, but with only two wheels and an oddly round cab, Joy had been essentially branded with a washable penis.

"All done!" Paula cheered, waddling out of the bathroom.

Joy stooped down, plucking away the toilet paper stuck to the girl's sparkly pink sneaker.

"Did you wash your hands?" Joy narrowed her eyes at the toddler, who nodded.

"Did you really?

The little girl paused. She stared up at Joy with big brown eyes. She shook her head no.

"Go wash your hands."

Paula pouted but trudged back into the bathroom. She returned a few moments later, rubbing her wet hands on her pants.

"Did you wash with soap?"

Paula nodded. Joy raised her eyebrows. The girl nodded harder.

"Look, smell!" Paula thrust her hands in Joy's face.

Her hands did smell like soap. Joy nodded. She began to lead Paula back to the main office, where she had left Marcus and Chelsea. Paula reached up, tugging on Joy's work pants with her damp hands. Joy bent slightly, scooping the girl into her arms and lifting her in the air. Joy nodded along as Paula rattled in her ear about the latest movie she had seen, what she wanted for her birthday, the gum she had stepped on this morning, and the lady who was pooping in the bathroom, in that order.

Joy sighed in relief as she saw Marcus sitting in her chair, exactly where she had left him. He clutched her phone in his chubby hands, eyes fixated on the animated show playing. He had a Fruit Loop stuck in his dark curly hair. Had it always been there? Had he managed to find Fruit Loops in her office? Kids never failed to surprise her.

Her relief at the boy staying still was short-lived. The seat beside him, where Joy had left Chelsea, was empty. She placed Paula down in the seat and scanned the office.

"Where'd your sister go?" Joy asked Marcus, squatting beside the boy.

He didn't look up from the screen. "She was thirsty."

"And where would she go to get a drink?"

He shrugged his shoulders, then giggled at the cartoon shark swimming on the screen. A quick glance at the title of the video revealed he was watching a ten-hour compilation of *Baby Shark.* Joy shuddered then turned to look for Chelsea.

She jogged through the building, glancing in each office as she passed. A flash of color caught her eye through the break room window, a bright pink among the neutral tables and chairs.

Chelsea held a Coke, probably grabbed from the communal fridge. She rocked on her heels, smiling as she chatted with Keith.

"Do you think it's weird that your mommy lives with another woman?" Keith asked.

She shook her head no, grinning to reveal one of her front teeth missing.

"Nope!" she exclaimed. "Alheri is really nice. Plus, she makes this weird food that I can eat with my hands that I thought was gonna be really gross, but was actually pretty good."

Keith patted the girl on her head. It made Joy feel uncomfortable, how familiarly he was acting with the girl. Keith never did anything without a motive, was never kind without cause. He leaned into Chelsea, whispering something into the girl's ear. Tears quickly filled her eyes, and she sprinted off. Joy ran after the girl, waving at Carmen through the glass of her office to join her. Joy found Chelsea in the bathroom, locked in the furthest stall, small hiccups escaping her as she tried to calm herself down.

"Chelsea?" Joy whispered, tapping lightly on the door. "Are you okay?"

The door creaked open, and Chelsea threw herself at Joy's legs. She rubbed the girl's back in what she hoped was a soothing way and waited for her to catch her breath.

"He said. He said that Mommy and Alheri. That they—they—they were sinners and that they were going to go to Hell. I heard 'bout Hell. It's where the bad people go, and there's fire and I don't—I don't want Mommy and Alheri to go to Hell cause then I'll be alone and they—" The girl choked on a sob, tears overwhelming her words.

Carmen appeared in the entranceway. She scanned the room, saw the crying girl, and rushed over. Joy passed the girl to her mother wordlessly, jaw throbbing as anger flashed through her.

"I'll be back."

Joy stormed through the office back to the break room. Keith wasn't there.

Neither was he in his office, but his keys and wallet remained on his desk. She yanked open his bottom drawer. The pack of cigarettes he usually stored there was missing. A quick trip downstairs revealed nothing, as he wasn't in his usual smoking spot.

Knowing he was still in the building, she stalked from room to room, floor to floor, her anger growing as she failed to find him. She pounded on the men's restroom door, kicking it open at the silence that responded. It was also empty. She paused in the middle of the office, eyes narrowing at the door to the stairs. No one in her office used the stairs, as sad as that was, making it a perfect spot for an asshole to smoke without having to go outside.

She threw the door open, and sure enough, there was Keith, leaning against the wall, a lit cigarette in hand. He didn't bother to move when she walked in and shut the door behind her, instead raising his eyebrows and taking another drag.

"What the hell is wrong with you?" Joy demanded.

Her fingers itched at her side. They yearned to reach out, to strike at Keith, shove him so he lost his balance and fell down the stairs.

Then do so.

Joy shook Buttercup's words and her own dark thoughts from her head. Keith stared at Joy before smirking.

"But now you must rid yourselves of all such things as these: anger, rage, malice, slander, and filthy language from your lips. You really should think about cussing less; it's not good for the soul."

Joy's eye twitched.

"You know what's not good for the fucking soul? Telling a seven-year-old that her mother is going to Hell, you absolute asshat," she spit back.

Keith shrugged.

"I only spoke the truth. She should be aware of the consequences of her mother's sins. What that girl needs is a father, a true man, not a woman dressing like one, to discipline her. Instead, that poor, innocent child is stuck with those nasty fa—"

Joy's hand whipped out before she could even think about it, a satisfying crack accompanying the interruption of his words. Keith stood stunned for a second, then his eyes darkened.

"Maybe the child isn't the only one in need of discipline." He walked toward Joy, towering over her as she pressed herself against the door. "I do not permit a woman to teach or to assume authority over a man; she must be quiet. You've been running your mouth an awful lot, Joy. You'd be a lot happier if you stayed home, found a husband, played the nice little housewife. As all women should."

He leaned into her, breathing the canned tuna he had eaten for lunch into her face. She realized she was standing in an abandoned stairwell, with an angry man, while her coworkers were drinking on the other side of the building. The hair stood on the back of her neck, and she shied away from Keith, her hand reaching behind her back for the doorknob.

Let us take care of him.

"You want that, don't you? You want me. Let me put the fear of God in you."

Joy gagged, then stomped on his foot, threat be damned. When he bent over in pain, she shoved him, knocking him backward. He slid down the wall and onto his ass. The cigarette rolled down the stairs, leaving a trail of ash behind. She yanked the door open and only got a step out before—

"They'll never believe you if you try to report me. I know you've made a couple complaints. Steve will write them down and shove them in the box, like he always does. And you'll just look like a stuck-up bitch."

How ironic, the man who quoted a Bible verse and chastised her for cursing calling her a bitch mere seconds later. It had only taken one rejection for him to give up his piety. He had a point, though; nothing would happen if she reported him. She thought of leaving, her hand still on the door handle, but Chelsea's tear-streaked face flashed in her mind. She jerked her head, gaze flitting from the door to Keith's hunched-over form.

God, I wish there was something I could do to put this asshole in his place, Joy thought.

As you wish.

Joy gagged as the mist invaded her senses. It pushed against her skull, and her head pounded. Tears leaked down her cheeks, but Joy found herself unable to control her body. She felt a smile spread across her lips, her tongue darting out to lick at the tears. She was sure she looked psychotic as she gently shut the door behind her.

The sensation was odd, being able to feel what she was doing but having no way to stop it. It was like a movie, a first-person perspective of her actions. She watched herself yank Keith off the ground.

"Oh, Keith. You shitty, racist, homophobic, sexist, small-dicked bastard," Joy heard her voice say. "I hope you remember the only reason you're even at this company is that you have your lips glued to the CEO's asshole. And the only reason he allows it is because it gives him someone to shit on. Someone to make him feel better about himself. You've done nothing on your own, and your life means nothing in the grand scheme of things. Do you think maybe God's plan for you was to be a pathetic waste of space? Just another mediocre man the world will forget seconds after his death? Because I can't picture you amounting to much else."

Enraged, Keith lunged at Joy. She lifted a single hand, black mist pouring from her body and surrounding him. It lifted him from the ground, dangling him over the edge of the stairs. He kicked his legs and opened his mouth to scream. The fog shot down, choking him into silence.

"No, that's not necessary. There's no need for you to speak, Keith. I think you've done enough of that."

Keith began to cry, fat droplets streaking down his face, and Buttercup retreated from his throat. It wanted to hear the man's sobs. Buttercup was usually just a voice, just words in her head. With it in control, however, Joy could feel its intentions. She knew it wanted Keith terrified. She was also terrified. Joy was the type of person who stared down fear, who confronted it head-on. This was different. This was powerlessness, the inability to act or even flee.

"Witchcraft," Keith managed to choke out. A wet spot spread across his khaki pants as he spoke. "You're—you're the devil."

"Perhaps." Joy shrugged. "Or maybe I was sent by your God to punish you for your wicked deeds. Either way, I want you to remember this moment. You so much as look at Carmen, or her children, or any of the women in this office..."

Joy twisted her hand to the side, slamming the man into the wall, then bringing him back to float above the stairs.

"I will rip your heart out of your scrawny chest and eat it for dinner."

She dropped him on the edge of the stairs, close enough for him to fear falling but far enough away that he wouldn't actually fall. She spun on her heel and headed for the door.

"I'll be watching you. Keith. I can see you, everywhere you go, everything you do and say. Even one passive-aggressive comment muttered under your breath, and I'll—" She turned around, mimed herself biting into a burger, and smirked when he paled.

She walked to the restroom and entered. No one seemed to be inside. The pressure in her head receded, and the mist floated down her throat, allowing her to regain control of her body. She gasped, crouching on the floor as her head throbbed.

There. He will never bother you or any of the others again.

And there she stood, alone with the voice in her head that had the power to take over her body and act on her darkest desires. The thought of being alone with Buttercup, the faceless actualization of her anger, scared her, and she darted out of the bathroom. She ignored Carmen shouting after her, avoiding the elevator and sprinting down the now-empty stairs. A few drops of blood and a cigarette butt were the only proof that what happened wasn't all in her imagination.

She knew as she ran that her actions weren't rational. She didn't want to be alone but was running from an office full of people.

An office full of people she liked, or at the very least, didn't dislike enough to let get hurt.

We would never hurt anyone.

She couldn't trust Buttercup, couldn't trust herself.

That did not deserve it.

Chills ran down Joy's spine at Buttercup's words.

She had treated Buttercup like a pet, chatting with it, laughing at its oddity, even as she had no idea what it was. And then she was surprised when it turned out to be something more, something dangerous. It was foolish, how easily she had accepted it as part of her. Maybe it was a part of her. Maybe her family had been right to think that something was off about her as a child.

She burst through the doors of the building and jogged down the road toward the parking garage. It was bright outside, the sun still high in the sky. Texas had a habit of ignoring the time of year. Although it was midway through October, it was still hot. Sweat trickled down Joy's neck and soaked through her blouse, a result of sprinting down multiple flights of steps and the heat.

She fished her keys out of her pocket.

She paused.

She didn't know where she would go, even if she were to drive away. Home meant being alone.

A passerby walked around her, bumping her lightly and causing her to drop the keys. The situation felt eerily familiar. She bent down to grab her keys. A hand wrapped around her bicep.

CHAPTER 9

Joy, Age 7

The DS in Joy's hand chimed, and she and Clara giggled from their place under the bed.

"Do you think we should try 'mean aunt' and see if they will fight?" Clara asked, reaching for the gaming console.

"I bet they would." Joy laughed.

"You fucking bitch!" Their grandmother shouted in the next room, followed by the sound of glass breaking.

Joy clenched her jaw, pulling Clara closer and turning up the music of the game. The pair were playing Scribblenauts, a game in which you could write out a noun to make it appear and use it to finish puzzles. The version the girls were playing allowed them to add adjectives to the nouns, thus changing how they acted in the game. They put in 'mean aunt' and 'mean grandmother' as a joke, but found the two began to fight in the game, eerily reflective of the scene outside of their bedroom.

Their great-aunt, Sarah's sister, had come for a visit. It started out peacefully, but soon escalated into a shouting match, as most family reunions did. The girls had been outside when it began, waiting for Tom to return from work. Clara colored on the concrete using a large bucket of chalk they had found at Dollar Tree while Joy read a book on the swing in the front yard.

The screaming startled the girls, Clara jerking a bright pink line across her flower drawing and Joy dropping her book. They exchanged a look before sprinting inside the house. The cold air of the air conditioning bit at Joy's skin, slightly burned from sitting in the sun for too long. Throwing herself through the front door, Joy faltered as her aunt shoved Sarah.

Sarah crumpled as she rammed against the guitar hanging on the wall. Her nostrils flared as she looked up at her younger sister, a good hundred pounds heavier and half a foot taller than she. It wasn't a fight she would win, and yet she let out a guttural shout as she dove for her knees.

"Joy?" Clara asked, trying to peek over her shoulder.

Lindy grabbed Sarah by the hair, and Sarah jabbed her fist into Lindy's side. Joy remained still, praying they wouldn't see them. Clara tugged at her shirt, and Joy whipped around, grabbing the younger girl's hand and pulling her through the house. They cut through the kitchen, Joy holding her breath as her grandmother chased her aunt down the hallway. The idea of calling the police flashed through Joy's mind.

Joy shook her head, knowing the consequences of the police coming would be far worse than if their aunt or grandmother turned on them. Instead, she yanked Clara down the hall and into their bedroom, locking the door behind her. Tossing Clara the DS from the top of their bookshelf, Joy pulled the comforter from the bed down, covering the small gap between the frame and the floor.

"Like a fort," Joy had explained, grabbing a stash of candy she had hidden after Halloween and throwing it under the bed.

Clara nodded, gaze following the candy before wiggling under the metal frame. After double-checking that the door was locked, Joy crawled in with her. And that's where they stayed, playing a video game as they hid from the fighting, giggling as they chewed on slightly stale candy corn. Numb from the excess of violence they had witnessed in their short decade on Earth, the two soon became sleepy, drifting off into a nap even as the shouting and thudding of thrown objects continued.

CHAPTER 10

Joy jerked back, the hand immediately retreating as she stood.

"Joy? Are you okay? What's wrong?" The speaker shook Joy lightly, and she blinked.

Ethan stood in front of her, his eyes wide with worry. She panted, her breath coming out in short bursts of air. She shook her head, wincing as the dull throbbing intensified. She looked up at Ethan, staring at him blankly. His eyebrows furrowed.

"Joy?" he asked.

Finally able to focus on Ethan instead of the panic clawing its way up her throat, Joy felt the tension leave her shoulders. Ethan scratched at his neck, then stuck his hands into the pockets of his jeans. She lurched forward, throwing her arms around his waist and resting her head on his t-shirt-clad chest. She felt him stiffen, only to relax a second later. He didn't hesitate to pull her closer, placing his chin on her head and waiting for her to speak. The straps of Ethan's backpack rubbed at Joy's neck, but she didn't move. A few moments passed. Sensing Joy wasn't going to break the silence, Ethan pulled back slightly.

"Are you feeling sick? I can drive you home if you—"

"No!" Joy interrupted, shaking her head vehemently. "No, I'm not that kind..."

Going home meant being alone with Buttercup. She wasn't sure she was ready to think about what had just happened, much less confront it. Changing her mind about avoiding others, she tugged him closer. There was something about him that had always made her feel safe. Maybe it was his height or his strong frame that was a result of time spent in the gym. Maybe it was his sunny disposition, his optimistic attitude. Either way, she clung to him tightly and relished Buttercup's silence.

"Um, okay?" Ethan faltered. "Do you want to come over to mine then?"

Joy bit the inside of her cheek. Ethan lived in a cute apartment in the nicer part of town. It was small but entirely too quiet for the chaos that was her mind right now. She needed a distraction, somewhere loud and bright.

"What about Pinballz?" Joy asked, staring at Ethan as sweat started dripping down her face.

Ethan's eyebrows shot up.

"The arcade?" he asked.

"Yeah, it's been a while since I kicked your ass at air hockey. It'll be my treat." Joy winced at the desperation in her voice, but Ethan only grinned.

"I mean, who could turn that down? Do you want to swing home first? Because, no offense, but your sweat is slowly seeping into my shirt, and it's grossing me out." Ethan laughed.

Her panic reawakened, Joytrembled violently. "No. No, um. We can go to, uh, your apartment first. It's...it's closer to Pinballz, and I can get ch-changed there. If that's okay?"

Ethan's smile slipped from his face. Usually, she would be teasing him back, laughing or smacking him over his comment. He could tell something was wrong, could see the signs of an oncoming panic attack. He grabbed her hand, guiding her through the parking garage and toward his car, conveniently parked next to her own. He opened the passenger side door, and she slid in.

"Need anything from your car?" he asked as she buckled herself in.

She nodded. "My bag. It's in the trunk. But I can—"

He gently took her keys from her hand, shut her door, and walked to her trunk. Grabbing the bag, he locked her car and rounded to the back to throw the bag and his own backpack in his trunk. Joy swept her sticky hair off her face and back into a ponytail. She adjusted the air conditioning in the car and placed her forehead against the grate.

Joy?

Joy stiffened. She bounced her leg as she waited anxiously for Ethan to join her.

Joy, you can't deny it's what you wanted.

Joy flung open her door.

"Need any help?" she called out to Ethan.

"Nope," he replied, slamming the trunk shut and jogging to the driver's side.

Ethan nodded as he connected her phone to the car's Bluetooth. Joy bit back a smile. She had once mentioned to him that music helped her relax when she was anxious. It was a passing comment, something she hadn't thought much of at the time, but he'd given her control of the music in every vehicle they'd been in since. The two chatted on the drive, Ethan catching Joy up on his day on campus and Joy asking him about his plan for the next semester.

"You can borrow some of my clothes," Ethan offered as he pulled into his apartment complex. "Those heels can't be comfortable."

Joy laughed as she opened the car door. "Mm. Might have to pass on that one. The last time I borrowed clothes from you, you made me wear a Hawaiian shirt with a t-shirt underneath that announced me as a 'MILF Hunter.' Plus, I have a change of clothes in my bag."

"I was actually thinking more Dungeons and Dragons onesie," Ethan joked, grabbing their bags from the trunk and swinging them over his shoulder. "And in my defense, the shirt was a gag gift from Christmas and the only one that wouldn't have reached your knees."

Joy snorted. She followed Ethan up the concrete stairs and

into his apartment. His home represented Ethan well, a perfect mash of his personality and hobbies. Subtle Star Wars, Lord of the Rings, and video game decor lay scattered around the living room, complete with a Boba Fett Lego head and a Skyrim pillow reading 'hey you, you're finally awake.'

His furniture was sleek and black, a leather couch flanked by two matching armchairs and a dark fuzzy rug. His coffee table was white, with black metallic legs. A few textbooks and notebooks lay scattered on the table, as well as an unhealthy number of Monsters, a few fast food wrappers, and a pile of letters from Ethan's father.

"Can I have some water?" Joy asked, and Ethan wandered off to the connecting kitchen to grab her a glass.

Although she would never admit it, she was incredibly jealous of her friend. Ethan grew up middle class, and except for his parents' divorce, he had a fairly happy childhood. His mother took him on international trips during school vacations, and his father never missed one of his basketball or football games. In fact, his father had given Ethan a framed picture of Ethan playing football in high school. In the picture, Ethan was running alone, ball in hand, the end zone in sight. The frame had a sticky note on it that read, "You got this, son."

On top of his near-perfect attendance at any event that even somewhat involved Ethan, Ethan's father offered to pay for his college, from tuition to rent to living expenses. He also hand-wrote and mailed him a letter every Sunday, never failing to include a few of the comics from the local paper. Ethan pretended it wasn't a big deal, even laughed a bit at the cheesy notes his father sent, but had never thrown a single one away, always storing them in a box in his bedroom closet. A momma's boy through and through, Ethan talked to his mother frequently over the phone, and she sent him a gift basket for every major holiday. She stopped in Austin every chance she could to have lunch or breakfast with him.

Ethan had never been worried about money, never doubted his parents' love for him. He had siblings he talked to regularly, a successful career ahead completely free of the student debt those around him faced, a nice apartment, a decent car, a nice, normal backstory for his life. Hell, he had never even broken a bone.

He doesn't deserve his privileged life.

Joy shook her head as Buttercup's thought floated through her mind. She cringed, realizing she had been thinking the same. It was unnerving to hear her darkest thoughts in a different voice. She felt guilty, ashamed even. Ethan and his family had shown her nothing but kindness and acceptance. She smiled sheepishly as he reentered the room and passed her a cup of water.

"What did you do?" He narrowed his eyes at Joy, scanning the room quickly.

Joy raised her hands in mock surrender, a genuine smile replacing her forced one.

"Nothing! I didn't do anything. Are you sure you should be going to Pinballz tonight, though? It looks like someone should be studying." She nodded toward the textbooks on the table. "Why, I remember when I was still in college. I never went out, I was so busy studying."

Ethan rolled his eyes. "You 'never went out' because you hate people, and that's a load of BS because we went out practically every weekend after we met."

He nudged her toward the bathroom as she grabbed her change of clothes.

"You go first. Lord knows I can't handle your stench for a moment more."

She knew it was a joke, but she couldn't help but wince at the truth of the statement. She marched into the room, shutting and locking the door behind her. The room was silent outside of the hum of the bathroom fan. Joy swallowed harshly as she stared at her reflection.

Please don't shut us out. We are a part of you.

Her face paled as Buttercup spoke. She trembled, shivering as droplets of the cold rain raced down her spine. She took a step forward, examining her face. She leaned closer to the mirror. She watched her pupils seep through her iris and into the whites of her eyes, black strokes dashing from the center until only darkness remained. Joy bit back a scream and slammed her eyes shut.

Ethan tapped on the door. "I'm just gonna change; I don't think I need a shower. I'll be in the living room if you need anything. Take your time, though, there's no rush. And... Joy? If something's bothering you, you know you can talk to me, right?"

Joy flinched and glanced back at the mirror. She sighed in relief at the flash of blue she saw in her eyes and the normal appearance of her pupils. She quickly stripped out of her sweaty clothes, tossing them into Ethan's sink and yanking on dry ones. Deciding against showering, she swiped on some of Ethan's deodorant.

Please.

Joy's chest tightened at the sadness in Buttercup's typically monotone voice. At least, she thought she heard sadness. Did she hear sadness? Or did she imagine it? She hesitated, her hand on the door handle. She thought back to the cold, the helplessness as she lost control of her body. Pressing her lips together, she opened the door.

"Do you have something I could put my wet clothes in?" Joy asked from the doorway.

Ethan hummed, tugging an old grocery bag out from under his sink. Joy transferred the clothes from the sink to the bag and stepped into the living room.

"Ready to go?" Ethan asked.

Joy nodded, then followed Ethan out of his apartment and back to the car.

The ride was usually only fifteen minutes long, made slightly longer by six o'clock traffic, but the two spent the time singing along, horribly, to the odd mix of classic rock, Disney songs, and today's hits that encompassed Joy's downloaded songs. The sun began to set, shining directly in their eyes.

Ethan reached over and lowered the car visor for Joy. She glanced up and caught her reflection in the small mirror.

She flipped the visor back up.

"You good?"

Joy chuckled awkwardly. "Yeah, just don't like not being able to see the road."

"Alright, weirdo," Ethan laughed as he pulled into the arcade.

* * *

"And that's game!" Joy shouted, hopping up and down as the puck slid into Ethan's goal.

Ethan groaned, putting down his paddle and scanning the room.

"Fine. I'll go reload the cards. Want anything to drink?" he asked.

Joy stepped to the side as a pair of shouting children ran by her, stuffed teddy bears and overflowing cups of soda in their hands. The drink sloshed over the side, spilling onto the already sticky linoleum floor. Joy was an introvert through and through, so the crowded arcade caused some stress but allowed her to escape the day's earlier and more upsetting events. The smell of the place—stale beer, buttered popcorn, and sweat—hadn't helped her headache. She figured caffeine would help.

"Diet Coke would be nice. Wanna use my card? I did offer to pay for the opportunity to whoop your ass."

Ethan waved her off.

"I got this one. Don't miss me too much." Ethan gave Joy a cheeky wink before strolling toward the front of the arcade.

Joy grinned as she watched him walk away, his 6'4 distinct among the four-foot-tall children. She pulled out her phone as she waited, shooting a quick text to her younger sister and scrolling through her Instagram.

You cannot ignore us forever.

Joy fumbled her phone, the device bouncing from one hand to the other before she put it into her pocket. She looked up slowly. Her reflection stared back at her from the glass of the Star-Wars-themed pinball machine. Although her image was warped by the flashing of blue and yellow lights, she could still make out the black fog drifting around her, framing her face in a demonic shadow.

We were doing as you wanted, acting on your thoughts. If you ignore us, you will be alone again.

The word *alone* bounced around Joy's mind. Her stomach flipped, both out of fear for herself and pity for Buttercup. She bit her lip, sighing before pacing forward and ducking into the photo booth in the corner.

"Okay. Go ahead," Joy whispered.

We are the same, Joy. We would never do anything you didn't ask for.

Joy blinked as the camera in the booth flashed.

"Look. I get that you thought you were doing something to help, but it made me super uncomfortable. I didn't like...I didn't like not having control over myself."

We will only do as you want.

The booth flashed again. Joy's head pounded in time with the flashes of light, and she shut her eyes tightly. A number was called over the speaker, probably for a food item. Children continued to squeal around her, accompanied by the occasional chastising of a parent and the overlapping symphony of multiple arcade games' music.

Sighing, she opened her eyes.

"Fine. If you promise never to control my body again, I will forgive you."

She shook her head softly, conflicted about the words even as they left her mouth. Does something that exists within her even need forgiveness? Would she even be able to fight it off, should it take control again?

Thank you for your benevolence. You are right; we could take over.

Joy's hair raised off the nape of her neck. The camera flashed again. Her breath caught in her throat as she waited for Buttercup to continue.

But we won't. Joy, we are the same. No one will ever truly know you. There is no need to hide yourself. Your flaws, your memories, the sadness and uncontrollable anger. We understand. We share them.

Joy let out a puff of air. On the one hand, she never had to be alone again. On the other hand, she found Buttercup terrifying. It was fine, everything was fine. But.

"Who are you talking to?" Ethan asked, yanking open the curtain to the photo booth and glancing around.

"Your mom," Joy retorted, shoving Ethan out of the way and stepping back into the arcade.

He rolled his eyes and handed her one of the cups in his hands. "Wow, so clever."

Joy took a sip of the water, scanning the arcade for their next game. She began walking away but stopped when Ethan called out to her.

"You forgot your pictures. It's a little weird you wanted to take them on your own, but I'll try not to be offended."

Joy snatched the strip from his hand and shoved it into the pocket with her phone. "Didn't want you breaking the camera —"

"With my charming good looks?" Ethan finished, smirking.

A game chirped behind Joy, and she turned, grinning wickedly as she contemplated.

"Let's do that one. Whoever gets the smallest one has to buy dinner."

Ethan narrowed his eyes in mock suspicion.

"Are you sure about that, Joyous? You're terrible at claw machines. Like probably the worst I've ever seen."

Joy shrugged, grabbing Ethan's hand and pulling him toward the opposite side of the arcade.

"What can I say? I feel like I got luck on my side today," she tossed over her shoulder.

"I'm feeling extra generous, so I'll go first." Ethan stepped up and swiped his card along the machine. "I'll even let you go until you either go broke or win some consolation prize."

The machine dinged, cheery music playing as Ethan concentrated. His tongue poked slightly out from between his lips. He adjusted the claw, bouncing back and forth from the front of the machine to the side before smashing the big red button in the middle. The hook swung down, grabbing a medium-sized stuffed toy and lifting into the air. It teetered slightly, then shot to the side, dropping the prize in the metal slot.

Ethan fist-pumped, then bent down to grab the object. He knelt down on one knee, holding the stuffed R2D2 out in both hands.

"For you, fair maiden, a token of my affection."

Joy laughed, accepting the Star Wars character with a dramatic curtsey.

"A shame, good knight, for I shall take great pleasure in beating you, even as you kneel before me so kindly."

She stepped up to the game. If she had to live with the voice in her head, she might as well use its powers to her advantage.

"Buttercup, I'm going to need your help on this one," she whispered.

"Hmm?" Ethan asked.

Joy smirked. "Don't worry, just whipping out some ancient war chants to guarantee my victory."

Ethan ruffled her hair.

"You don't stand a chance, J. I'm already picturing the piles of free tacos I'm going to make you buy me. And maybe some queso. And perhaps a drink or two—"

Ethan turned, the music from a different game catching his attention. Joy quickly swiped her card, eyes narrowing in focus as she watched the claw swing into motion.

This time, Joy kept her words to Buttercup inside of her

thoughts. "You got it?"

Yes.

The dark mist trickled from her mouth, her lips parting as it seeped through the cracks of the machine and surrounded the largest stuffed animal in the giant glass box: a bright pink narwhal that was bigger than most of the children in the arcade, complete with an ice cream cone horn and colorful sprinkle patterns along its back. The fog nudged the toy toward the hook as it descended, wrapping around the item and hook, and lifting alongside the game. The toy dropped into the basket. Joy bit back a grin as Ethan turned to her, eyes wide and lips pursed.

"You've never once won a claw game around me, and you happen to win the biggest prize possible when food is on the line?" Ethan paused, looking from the machine to the boasting Joy. "I feel like I've been swindled, and by my best friend, of all people. This betrayal cuts me to my core."

Ethan wiped away a fake tear, dramatically throwing his head back.

"C'mon, drama king, dinner's on you tonight, and I'm starving." Joy skipped forward, giant toy and the R2D2 both clutched against her chest.

Ethan laughed even louder, jogging to catch up with Joy. He threw an arm around her, pulling her closer and leaning down.

"You know, you're awfully cute," he whispered, causing her cheeks to glow red.

He leaned in closer, his lips brushing against her ear.

"For a traitor," he murmured, then jabbed into her ribs with his opposite hand.

Joy gasped, laughing as she pulled away from him. She twisted, holding the toys with one hand while trying to poke Ethan with the other. He smirked, grabbing the attacking hand and tugging her toward the exit.

He pushed the door, his body smacking against it as it didn't budge. Joy hid a grin as Ethan shook his head. She stepped around him, pulling the door open and stepping aside to let him pass.

CHAPTER 11

Joy, Age 8

"Why don't we go watch a movie?" Tom asked.

Clara's eyes lit up, her small frame practically trembling with excitement. Joy stood beside her, the three huddled together in the living room. At first, Joy didn't look at Tom, her attention stolen by the tiny reindeer barely clinging to their Christmas tree. She expected it to fall, but it remained.

"Like at the theater? With candy and popcorn and sodas?"

Joy frowned, tugging at the pajama top that was a pinch too tight on her.

"But it's Christmas?" she asked, finally turning to look at him.

Tom nodded his head, wincing as he spoke over the shouting from down the hallway. "That's what makes it extra special! We can go watch a Christmas movie in the theater and eat so much popcorn that your tummy will pop!"

Clara giggled as he lifted her in the air. He set her down, nudging her toward the girls' shared room so she could change. She skipped away, mumbling about which candy she would choose.

"What about Mom?" Joy whispered. She glanced toward the back of the house.

Tom looked down at her, eyes softening. He squatted, his adam's apple bobbing as he swallowed harshly, before nodding his head.

"Joy, she—"

"Can I bring the Wii?" Clara sprinted back into the room, device in her hand.

Tom scratched his head. "No, the Wii has to stay here."

Clara pouted, holding the game close to her chest.

"But I heard Grandma say that Mom and that guy stole something from her. What if they take the Wii too? Trini and Connor just got it for us, and we haven't even gotten to play it yet."

Tom sighed.

"You can leave it in my art room. Put it in the box under the desk and leave some comic books on top of it."

Clara dashed off, leaving Tom and Joy. The man Clara had mentioned was yet another of the boyfriends Joanne had brought around to their house. They weren't always bad. In fact, Joy had liked quite a few of them, especially the ones that brought her toys. She didn't like some of the others, like the one who had pushed her for asking what his tattoos meant or the one who, according to what Sarah told Tom, had been arrested for vandalizing the cemetery the day after showing up at Clara's birthday party.

She really didn't like the one who had asked her to sit on his lap. His smile had been scary when she said no, his hand trailing up her leg in a way that made her jump up from the couch and run to find Tom.

Joy thought back to his earlier words, to the idea that her mom was stealing things.

"Is Mom a bad person?"

Tom tried to smile, started to shake his head no, but stopped.

Joy's stomach hurt as she watched him debate what to say. Usually, when grownups were quiet with her, it was because something bad had happened, because they didn't know how to tell her.

Joanne had a habit of popping in and out of Joy and Clara's lives. Sometimes she stayed a few days. Sometimes only a few hours. Joy clung to those moments with her mother because that's what she thought she was supposed to do. She barely knew the woman, but she knew she wanted her mother to love her. Moms loved their kids; everyone knew that. And sometimes, there was a flicker of Joanne attempting to be a mother.

Last month was one of those attempts. Joy had learned to shift with her mother's moods, to show happiness when she did, to hide when she was upset. So when her mom had shown up, camera in hand, in a flurry of motion and energy, she had rolled with it. Her mom wanted to have a photo shoot, changing Joy and Clara's outfits, posing them in different places around the house. Joanne had left the next morning without saying goodbye, off to find the next thing that would capture her attention.

Sarah hadn't taken many pictures of Joy and Clara as they grew up. There was a drawer in their kitchen with envelope after envelope of printed photos, mostly of Sarah's life events, her in the band, her and Tom's wedding, but also a few of Joanne and Trini as children. A few weeks after the photo shoot, a packet of the pictures came in the mail. They had since been stuffed in the drawer.

Joy and Clara weren't supposed to touch the pictures. Sarah had told them that they would ruin them, but sometimes, real late at night, Joy liked to sneak into the kitchen and pull them out. The bulk of her childhood pictures had been taken in one afternoon, but with the different outfits, it almost looked like something more, like a happy family, the type of family who took pictures for all their special occasions. On those nights, Joy pretended they were. She was good at pretending.

Joanne had come back for Christmas, but just like with Lindy, something had happened away from Joy's small ears and observant eyes that led to a fight between her mom and

Sarah. Their gifts and dinner had long since been abandoned, the food growing cold, and the excitement Joy felt from opening her gifts replaced with a restless nervousness Tom had quickly picked up on.

Tom cleared his throat, and Joy looked back at him.

"Sometimes good people do bad things. Your mom, she's sick, and sometimes that means she does things that are naughty."

Joy's eyebrows furrowed.

"Mom's sick? Shouldn't she go see a doctor, then? If I get sick, I won't be able to play the Wii tomorrow with Clara, and she'll be upset."

"Not that kind of sick. Sometimes people are sick in the head."

Joy nodded, then turned to gather her thoughts. Her eyes lit up, a small gasp of understanding slipping through her lips, and she glanced back at Tom.

"Is that why she had a needle in her bra? To make her feel better?"

"Did..." Tom paused. He took a deep breath. Joy noticed his hands, clenched into fists, were shaking. "Did your mom have a needle in her shirt?"

"Yeah, Grandma saw it earlier. That makes sense, though. She didn't yell at Mom or anything, which I thought she would, but she said something really quietly, and the two went back to Grandma's room."

A muscle in Tom's jaw jumped. He hugged Joy tightly before pulling away.

He pushed her gently toward the door. "Go get changed. Maybe after the movie, we'll grab some pizza. Does that sound good?"

Joy nodded, smiling reluctantly. After Joy and Clara changed, the three left, shutting the door gently behind them. The reindeer continued to cling to the tree.

CHAPTER 12

"Kindly explain to me how I still ended up paying?" Joy sighed, taking a large bite of her taco.

The blanket she sat on, a spare one Ethan kept in the back of his car, was warm, but grass pricked at her legs from underneath. They had grabbed tacos from a food truck and were currently sitting by Lady Bird Lake, a large body of water in the center of Austin. Joy could see downtown from her spot by the water, the tall glass buildings glittering in the pink glow of the setting sun.

"Because I'm a broke college student, and you can hold it over my head when I graduate?" Ethan smiled cheekily.

Joy polished off her taco and eyed the extra one in front of Ethan. He pushed it toward her.

"How are classes?" Joy asked.

"Exhausting."

Joy stretched her legs out, leaning back on her hands and taking a sip of her drink.

"How much longer do you have?"

"Just next semester, and I'll be done, thank God."

Joy glanced at Ethan, her stomach constricting at the thought of him leaving Austin. A lot of people would assume, given Ethan's size and friendly demeanor, that he was all brawn and no brains, but this couldn't be further from the truth. Ethan had graduated valedictorian of his high school class, like Joy, and had even made it to the state science championship in physics.

That isn't to say he had spent all his time studying, like the nerd he was deep down. No, Ethan was born with good looks, intelligence, natural athleticism, and an easy-going charisma —the perfect mix He played varsity football and basketball, was a member of the student council, and starred in the school play, all while having a healthy social life. Joy hated him a bit for it.

"What are you going to do after you graduate?" she asked, taking a gulp of her drink.

Ethan shrugged. "Flee the country, move to Switzerland, become a sheep farmer."

"A sheep farmer with a degree in electrical engineering?" Joy raised her eyebrows. "Sure you're not just going for the beer and milkmaids?"

He threw his head back and laughed, brown eyes crinkling at the edges and hair brushing against his shoulders.

"I'm not sure yet. Probably find a job around here and work for a few years. I'd like to go back and get a Master's someday, but that's pretty expensive."

Joy nodded, her shoulders relaxing from where they had bunched up near her neck. Although she was friendly with many people, she could count on one hand the number of real friends she had, mainly due to her extreme aversion to going out. She would be upset if any of her close friends moved away, but something about Ethan leaving made her chest hurt.

We're in love with him.

Nope. Joy disagreed with Buttercup completely and wouldn't allow herself to get lost in that train of thought.

"Have you thought about going back?" Ethan asked.

Joy hesitated, then forced a laugh. The sun had dipped below the horizon, casting a shadow over her face. It made her smile look odd, stretched too far across her lips, the shadows hiding her dimples and making her eyes look like pools of dark water.

"For what? People don't exactly get a Master's in accounting."

"I mean for writing. You could get an MFA, finally write that book. I've read your drafts. You're talented, Joy. A bit rough around the edges, but talented."

Joy pressed her lips together, her teeth nibbling at a dry strip. She shivered as a cool breeze brushed against her skin, no longer protected by the warmth of the now-retired sun. Streetlights flickered to life around the two.

"It's just a hobby. Plus, I like my job—"

Ethan snorted his disbelief as he gathered the trash from their makeshift picnic. "You hate your job."

"Okay, maybe I don't love it, but I like the people," Joy defended.

Ethan rolled his eyes.

"Yeah, Keith is so much fun to be around."

Something shifted in Joy. She felt her face flush but couldn't tell if it was from embarrassment or anger. Those around her and Ethan began to pack things; footballs tossed into cars, joggers pulled on their jackets, and children placed into strollers and walked out to various vehicles.

"I have Carmen and a decent salary." Joy's smile twitched, but she did not allow it to fall.

Ethan studied Joy's expression, his thick eyebrows furrowing at her forced grin.

"But are you happy?"

Joy picked at the corners of her nails, wincing as a strip of skin peeled down her thumb.

"I can't risk not having the health insurance they provide," she muttered.

Ethan sat up, grabbing Joy's hand in his own.

"I know it's scary, but sometimes you have to be willing to take a risk. You can rely on those around you more, freelance on the side as you get your degree. You'd be so much happier. It's scary, but wouldn't it be worth it to do something you actually enjoy for a living?"

Joy yanked her hand away and narrowed her eyes, her smile finally slipping.

"Who exactly would I rely on? Trini, who's busy getting married and building her dream house? Connor, who didn't pay a dime toward my education the first time? Clara, who doesn't even text me back most of the time? And you can't just completely ignore health insurance. What if the cancer came back? My shots alone were $25,000 a month, and there's no way in hell I could afford something like that. I don't need to hear this from you of all people."

"What's that supposed to mean?"

"You've never had to worry about money. You had a happy childhood with two parents who adored you. The worst thing that's ever happened to you was your parents divorcing, and even that was done in the least traumatic way possible. Your dad literally built a house a mile from your school so he could see you more. You have no idea what it's like to grow up the way I did, having to work constantly for the smallest chance at a halfway mediocre life, and yet you make it sound like I'm choosing not to be happy. I'm doing my fucking best."

Joy's chest heaved. She swallowed thickly. She refused to look up, fists shaking as she processed her outburst. Ethan shifted beside her.

"I'm sorry," Ethan said.

Joy stilled. She turned to look at him, scared to see anger or hatred in his eyes. Instead, he smiled sadly at her.

"What?" she choked out.

"I'm sorry," Ethan repeated, pulling her into a half-hug. "What I said was insensitive. You're right, I don't know what it's like. Joy, I want you to be happy, but I understand where you're coming from. Just know, if you ever choose to pursue writing or slime making or professional basket weaving, or anything else that catches your attention, I will be behind you. I'm sorry your family kinda sucks sometimes, but I'll always be in your corner."

Tears welled in Joy's eyes. Until that moment, she didn't

know how badly she needed to hear those words from someone.

"I'm sorry. I shouldn't have reacted that way. I know you've worked hard for where you are too."

"It's cool. I know what you meant and I get how what I said would have hurt. I also know your anger is something you've been working on, and I see so much improvement. I'm proud of you, Joy. It takes a stronger person to apologize and work through your faults than it does to pretend you have none. You're killing it, kid."

Joy laughed, tucking herself under Ethan's chin as she wiped the tears from her cheeks.

"I'm still older than you," she murmured.

She felt Ethan's chest vibrate as he chuckled.

The cold air bit at Joy's cheeks, burning her lungs as she inhaled Ethan's cologne and the smell of the water. Those who had been packing up had long since left, leaving only the occasional jogger and couple strolling along the streetlights.

"Help!" A desperate voice called from down by the water.

Ethan and Joy's heads shot up. Joy squinted into the darkness, barely making out the outline of a woman with a stroller.

"My kid fell in the water. Please, I can't swim," the woman shouted.

Ethan leapt up, dragging Joy with him.

Along with a few others who had heard the woman's cry, the two friends raced to the edge of the river. The women trembled, leaning over the edge of the concrete beside the river on hands and knees. Joy immediately fished her phone from her pocket, dialing 911 and giving a twenty-second explanation while describing their location. The operator assured Joy that an officer would be there shortly.

She jogged back to the alcove, scanning the small crowd for Ethan. Without the sun, only the harsh glow of cellphone flashlights illuminated the dark water. A child, one who must have only been a year or two old, cried from within the stroller, and Joy's forehead wrinkled in confusion. The mom clutched a cellphone in her hand, staring intently into the water. Seeing Joy's confusion, a young woman stepped up to explain.

"Her toddler was walking along the edge, holding her hand. The baby started crying ,and she let go to check on it. The kid slipped. Your friend and another guy are in the water searching."

As she finished explaining, Ethan's head popped up. He rubbed the water from his eyes and slapped the surface. He shook his head grimly as another man swam up beside him.

"It's too dark. I can't see anything."

The man echoed his sentiments.

Ethan dove again, his bright yellow socks flashing above the water as he continued searching. It had been a minute, probably closer to two, since the woman had first cried out. Even if she had yelled as soon as the child had slipped, that meant the kid was more than likely already unconscious. If that were the case, they only had a few minutes to find and resuscitate the child before brain damage, or worse, set in.

You know all of this through Criminal Minds. *You could be completely wrong; the child could be already gone.*

Joy grimaced, realizing Buttercup was right.

"Buttercup, how far can you spread your mist? Could you thin it out along the bottom?" Joy thought.

We are unsure of the point. The child would not have much time left.

Joy paced to the edge of the water. "Yes, I get that. Hence, why I'm asking. If you could find the kid, we could lift it out of the water and get started on CPR."

Yes, we could, but we would need to be in the water.

Joy began taking off her shoes, stripping off her jacket and tossing it, along with her phone, to the side.

"Are you going in?" The woman who had spoken to Joy earlier asked, eyes wide in surprise.

"I was a lifeguard. The least I can do is help search." Joy turned back to the woman. "I called the police. Keep an eye out for any emergency vehicles and help guide them here."

This was only a half-lie. Joy had worked as a lifeguard at a church camp a few years and almost twenty pounds ago. She perched on the edge of the concrete. Buttercup drifted out of her mouth as she scanned the water. Joy's heart only had time to beat twice before it returned.

The child is to the right of the alcove. Get in, and we'll lead.

"Can you grab the child and bring it to the surface?"

We are not yet strong enough.

Joy nodded, and the black mist floated from her hands, solidifying into a dark cloud and shooting downward.

She shook out her hands, took in a deep breath, and dove. She choked back a gasp as she hit the cold water. Swimming blindly for a few seconds, Joy flailed her arms out and searched for Buttercup.

A burst of cold wrapped around her hands, guiding them to what felt like a frozen rope. She followed the rope, kicking her legs and pulling herself hand over hand until it abruptly stopped. She pressed her hands forward, jerking as they sunk into a muddy wall.

She felt along the smooth slime, moss and mud coating her hands and feet until her arms bumped into something warm. She yanked at the warm limb, pulling a small body into herself. A cold tentacle wrapped itself around her torso, and she gasped, immediately choking as water filled her lungs. The lasso pulled taught around her waist, dragging her and the child upward. She cradled its head into her neck as they broke the surface. The rope retreated, leaving Joy gasping for air as she kicked her legs to stay above the water.

"She has him!" A voice called in the distance.

Seconds later, warm hands wrapped themselves around her, lifting her and the child out of the water and onto a patch of grass. She lay on her back, breathing deeply and staring at the sky. Her vision swam, the glare from the streetlights swirling into abstract streaks of light.

"He's not breathing," a voice choked out.

A panicked murmur shot through the crowd.

Joy's veins froze, and she forced her eyes open.

Go to the child. We can save him.

Joy pulled herself to her feet, too tired to do anything but obey. She stumbled through the crowd, dropping to her knees beside the child. She tilted his head back, vaguely remembering the first aid training she had received years prior. She felt the boy's chest rise as she blew air into his mouth. Cold air tickled her throat as Buttercup shot from her mouth and into the boy.

The mist worked its way down to the boy's heart, squeezing in rhythm to "Stayin' Alive" by the Bee Gees, as Joy had seen in an episode of *The Office*. Less than a minute passed before the boy began to cough.

"Thank God," Joy sighed, turning him onto his side as he threw up water.

She slumped, breathing a sigh of relief that turned into a gag as Buttercup returned.

I thought we were gonna do the whole angry cartoon ears thing, she thought.

Buttercup laughed, and Joy shivered. Its laugh was cold, and jarring, as if something was trying to imitate a laugh. The child's mother sobbed, clutching the boy's hand and repeatedly thanking Joy. Ethan pushed his way to the front of the cheering crowd, scooping Joy up and spinning her in the air. Cameras recorded the scene, onlookers patting Joy on the back and telling her how well she had done.

You did amazing, Joy. You are amazing, almost heroic.

Joy grinned. The strip of pictures from the arcade had slipped from her pocket when she dove and now floated along the surface. It would wash up on the shore in a few days, her terrified expression distorted by the waters of the lake.

CHAPTER 13

Joy, Age 10

"That skirt makes you look like a slut," Sarah scoffed.

Joy's outstretched hand dropped to her side. In it was a list of the awards she had won during her academic competition. She had competed against five other schools, winning or coming in second in a number of events. She accepted any competition that didn't overlap with others, desperate for Sarah's approval.

Sarah loved nothing more than appearances, than the ability to brag to others. When those around her had grown tired of listening to her talk about her short-lived band glory days, she started talking about Joy and Clara. Joy had grown to be fairly plain in her features, hair a straw-colored blonde, body just shy of being too skinny. Her physical appearance would give Sarah no bragging rights. There were plenty of children, even within their neighborhood, prettier than her.

Joy didn't develop socially the way the other kids did. She was quiet at first, a bit awkward even. Sarah would never be able to tell her friends how popular Joy was at school. Joy lacked the charisma her mother and grandmother used so easily to get their way.

The one thing Joy had going for her was that she was smart.

Her teachers often praised her for her intelligence. Joy was top of her class, thrived in academic competitions. At first, school came easily to her. She grasped concepts much faster than her classmates, aced tests without having to study. Sarah latched onto it, bragging about Joy to anyone who would listen.

Joy found her worth in those brief moments. The most warmth she had ever felt from her grandmother was when Sarah had first been told that Joy was reading at a level far beyond those her age.

She was animated the evening after her competition, excited about her success as she boasted to Tom on the drive home. Tom had been proud, offering to make Joy a special dinner.

She had rushed straight to Sarah's room, a room separate from Tom's for reasons she wouldn't learn until she was a bit older, to tell the woman how the day went. She fully expected Sarah to be as happy as she was, to praise her, show her the warmth that only came with success. Instead, Sarah had spit words at her, her glare an indicator of worse things to come.

"I'm sorry," Joy said automatically, dropping her attention to the carpet.

She wasn't quite sure what the word "slut" meant, but she could tell from her grandmother's tone of voice that she had done something wrong. Joy lowered her head as Sarah raised her voice and yet, she remained in the room. The anger Sarah so easily spewed was better than being alone with her thoughts, and a small part of Joy still held onto the hope that this could be turned around, that she could still earn Sarah's affection with the list still clutched in her shaking hand, that it could all be a misunderstanding.

Sarah narrowed her eyes. "You went behind my back to wear that, didn't you?"

Warning lights flashed through Joy's mind. The venom in Sarah's words was not unusual, but it was rare that it was aimed at Joy. She sidled toward the door, refusing to make eye contact with her grandmother.

"What?" She hesitated to ask, afraid that she would say the wrong thing and make it so much worse.

"I've never seen that skirt before. You were wearing pants this morning. You had to have changed at the school. Why? For the attention? So you could make me look bad by dressing like a little whore? I bet all the boys loved seeing those skinny little legs of yours all on display." Sarah stood, pacing forward so she was in the girl's face.

"I didn't. I don't know—" Joy bumped into the mirror on the outside of the door.

"Doing things behind my back is a form of lying, Joy. And you know we have to punish liars." Sarah opened her closet door, grabbing her belt.

"I didn't lie! I told you Mick was gonna let me use a skirt to wear at UIL. I did poetry today and all the girls in the speaking events had to wear a dress or a skirt. I didn't have one, and I told Mick, who told her mom, who gave Mick a couple of skirts to let me try on." Joy rushed the words out, tears forming in her eyes.

She couldn't stop herself from staring at the belt in her grandmother's hands. Sarah was a fan of corporal punishment. Not of the gentle swats given by hand to a misbehaving toddler, no, Joy was too old for that to have any impact. Instead, Sarah had two belts, one brown and leather, the other black and studded, that she used on Joy and Clara, drowning out their screams and the sound of leather on flesh with reassurances such as "this hurts me more than it hurts you." The red welts on Joy's butt said otherwise.

And maybe the swats had started as small reminders to behave; maybe they could have originally been normal. In Texas, principals often gave swats to misbehaving children, often with a wooden paddle and often, especially for the high school students, hard enough to sting for a few minutes. But there was something different about the look in Sarah's eyes when she reached for a belt, something sadistic in the way her arm would extend over her shoulder, pulling the belt back as far as it could reach before swinging it down with a brutality previously unknown to Joy.

Just the week before, Joy had gotten in trouble for saying a cuss word at school. She knew she was going to get into trouble, probably even deserved it after dropping an f-bomb at a boy who was teasing a friend over her weight. She had dragged her feet on the walk home, coming back five minutes later than she usually did. Clara had gone over to a friend's house, and Tom was working late, leaving only Joy and Sarah. After seeing the discipline slip Joy had in her backpack, Sarah had screamed at her for embarrassing her and making her seem like a bad guardian. When Sarah slipped into her closet, Joy knew what was coming.

She lay perpendicular to the bed, hands spread over her head. Sarah ripped Joy's jeans down and began to swing. Tears welled in Joy's eyes, but she refused to make a sound. Sarah swung harder, waiting for Joy's response. Joy whimpered as the edge of the belt broke skin. She couldn't help but try and wiggle away, the pain too much for her to handle, her knees buckling as she tried to roll away from the bed. Sarah didn't stop. She swung blindly, striking across Joy's back. Joy screamed and dropped to the floor. Sarah puffed out a breath, rolled her eyes, and told Joy to go to her room and think about what she had done. Tom brought a bag of frozen peas to her room that night, apologizing and telling her that Sarah would never do that again. It had only been a week. And the belt was back in her hand.

"And you just happened to wear a skirt that was that inappropriate?" Sarah said. "You know that skirt was too short. It makes me look bad, as your parent, if you wear something like that. Do you want me to look bad?"

Joy shook her head.

"Mrs. D said it was long enough. They made me do the fingertip test."

Joy put her hands against her sides, demonstrating how the skirt was a few inches longer than her fingertips. Sarah glared at her, eyes wide with barely concealed rage. Joy glanced around the room, looking everywhere but at her grandmother, her eyes catching on an open bottle of pills and a glass of wine on the bedside table. Sarah followed her gaze, jaw clenching. Tom tapped lightly on the bedroom door. Joy didn't dare to respond, standing as still as possible. The door handle turned, and Tom peeked his head into the room.

He glanced at the bedside table, then at the belt in Sarah's hand.

"Joy," Tom softly called for her attention, "I think Grandm might be feeling a little sick. Why don't you head to bed?"

Joy nodded, crumpling the paper in her hand and dashing out of the room and into her own. She locked the door behind her, throwing herself on the bed and burrowing underneath the covers.

Her stomach rumbled from her lack of dinner. Outside of the safety of her blankets, she heard muffled arguing. She wrapped the blankets tighter around her ears, turning on her side and willing herself to go to sleep.

Joy had been rejected or left behind by so many that it had eventually become second nature. She numbed herself to the loss of affection, accepted it as a part of her. She no longer placed the blame on others, but instead thought that it was because of her, because there was something fundamentally wrong with her personality or her appearance or her worth that made her unlovable.

Please don't leave me.

Joy had found her validation in achievement. What Clara lacked in praise, she got in affection. Joy was the oldest, the smart one, the one who would grow up to be the pride of her family. And she was treated as such. But Clara was the fun one, the kind one, the artistic and emotional one. They praised Joy, putting her up on a pedestal, using her as an example for Clara to live up to, something Clara resented.

Please be proud of me.

But when placed so high above others, one not only risks

the fall but also has to learn how to live with the distance. There was no warmth for Joy in her household. They didn't greet her from school with an embrace as they did Clara, only questions on today's successes. But if Sarah was no longer interested in her academics, what was left for her?

Please love me.

CHAPTER 14

"A real life hero," Ethan teased, tossing a newspaper onto his coffee table.

Joy pursed her lips, putting on an expression of nonchalance. She glanced at the paper, her face staring back at her. The picture was of her grinning down at the child, her hair plastered to her forehead and water dripping down the side of her cheeks.

She declined a few requests for interviews, saying anyone in her position would have done the same with that fake humility people often display. In actuality, she was proud as hell. She simply hadn't wanted to be on camera. The picture in the paper wasn't bad, as the terrible phone camera obscured most of her features, and the crowd hid most of her body. An interview would be different, bright lights and high-quality images showcasing her acne scars and potential double chin. She would much rather enjoy her five minutes of fame in blurred anonymity.

She shifted, pulling her feet up and under her and tugging a white, fluffy blanket closer to her.

"What are you thinking for dinner?" she attempted to change the subject.

"It's Wednesday, wings are half-off at Seolju?" Ethan suggested.

"Eh. Wings sound good, but their stuff is always so much better in person, and that would require me to put on real pants and shoes."

She gestured down at her sweats, wiggling her toes in her fuzzy socks.

"Fair enough." Ethan plopped down on the couch beside her, handing over his phone.

"Chinese?" Joy asked as she scrolled through his delivery app.

"Too greasy."

Joy nodded.

"Greek? Cava has a coupon."

Ethan shrugged. "Sounds good to me."

"The usual?" Joy turned the phone toward Ethan, pointing at a previous order.

"Yup."

Joy ordered the food, then passed the phone back to Ethan. She stretched, her shirt riding up a bit and exposing a strip of pale skin. Ethan stared at the strip. Joy pulled her shirt down and raised an eyebrow in question.

"Sorry, I just..." Ethan started. He frowned, turning to face the front. "The scars, they look a lot better."

Joy's hands smoothed the fabric of her shirt across her stomach. She left them there for only a second, tracing along the cotton wrinkles before crossing her arms over her stomach.

"Yeah, they're pretty faded now, other than the one on my belly button."

"And you... you're feeling okay?" Ethan asked, fiddling with his phone case.

Joy knew this question like the back of her hand. So often, she had been asked how she was feeling, if there was any news about her health. Ethan refused to look up at Joy, but the frown she saw broke her heart. It was never his intention to make her feel bad, but the look of sadness, of nervous unease, that crossed his face whenever her illness was mentioned never ceased to light a spark of guilt in her stomach.

"Yup. I'm feeling great," she replied.

When she was diagnosed with cancer at twenty, Joy learned the hard way that sometimes a lie was kinder than the truth. In all honesty, Joy had spent the last few weeks alternating between constant states of nausea and a fatigue she had never known before, even when she was undergoing cancer treatment.

She knew she would need to return to her doctor at some point, but it would have to wait. The bill on her dining room table, a reminder of the hundreds of dollars she still owed to the oncology center, was constantly lurking in the back of her mind. Between rent, her car payment, and the credit card debt she had accumulated in college, paying off her medical balance wasn't feasible. Maybe in a few years when she got a promotion, or even moved to a different job, things would be different, and she would feel financially stable enough to do the things on the bucket list she had typed out on her phone.

The list seemed to mock her, reminding her of the small things that were out of reach. Things like "regular haircuts not given by Clara," "dermatology appointment for the moles on my back," and "work clothes not bought at Goodwill." There was nothing wrong with Goodwill; Joy loved Goodwill. But it would be nice to be able to get new clothes from a nicer brand, the spots on her skin looked at, and a haircut given by a professional instead of her younger sister with scissors bought at Dollar General.

Still, Joy didn't want to seem ungrateful. She had a roof over her head, food in her fridge, and a drive to work harder, earn more, make a name for herself in whatever field she ended up in. She knew if she told Ethan, he would try to help, even go as far as to offer her his father's money or the money he had saved during his summer internship. He would pity her. The thought made her stomach churn.

"Good." Ethan paused. "That's good."

An awkward silence settled over the living room, a product

of the unresolved anxiety and uncertainty that seemed to follow a cancer diagnosis through treatment and into remission.

Joy coughed. Ethan coughed.

Joy frowned. Ethan frowned.

Joy's eyebrows raised, and she turned to face him. Ethan followed suit, turning to her, raising his eyebrows, and sticking out his tongue. Joy laughed, shoving him away and reaching for her laptop.

After a few episodes of some tv show that played in the background as Joy and Ethan swiped through their phones, occasionally laughing and showing the other a video they had found, the food arrived. The delivery driver dropped his bags at the front door, knocking once before leaving for his next order.

The two munched happily, pausing only so Joy could take a picture of the food and send it to her youngest sister Caden. Joy grinned as Caden responded with multiple middle finger emojis and a picture of the frozen pizza their mother had made for dinner. She showed the response to Ethan, who snorted.

Joy and Caden hadn't grown close until Joy left for college. The seven-year age gap, the tensions of Joy and Clara being adopted by their Aunt Trini and Uncle Connor, and Joy's busy schedule hadn't left much room for sisterly bonding. Caden was Trini's oldest biological daughter, a lanky now-sixteen-year-old with fringed blonde hair, thick black eyeliner frequently lining her blue eyes, and an effortlessly cool persona. Caden was everything Joy wasn't in high school: confident, proud of her interests in anime and art, and unapologetically herself. In her tiny school in West Texas, she easily stood out, a liberal, black-clothes-wearing teenager with a bit of an anger problem among the oil field yuppies and the conservative farmers' kids. Joy thought Caden was cool as hell.

"I should probably head home; I have work tomorrow," Joy declared after a few hours of talking, eating, and alternating between YouTube videos and the earlier background tv show that Joy had decided she enjoyed enough to actually pay attention to.

"You could stay? The guest room is open," Ethan offered.

Joy yawned, stretched, and stood.

"Normally, I'd take you up on that offer, but I desperately need a shower, and I don't think I have any clothes left here."

Ethan stood, tossing Joy's keys to her and reaching for his own.

"I'll walk you to your car."

Joy laughed. She threw her phone into her pocket and grabbed the leftovers from the table, frowning as her finger dipped into the small plastic cup of a jalapeno-feta whip.

"I think I can make it there on my own," she said, quickly licking her finger as Ethan turned his back.

"I know you could, but I'd feel better seeing you off. Who knows what kind of assholes are out there, especially in your neighborhood. Didn't someone get attacked by a guy with a machete last week? And remember when you had to take an exam in a SWAT lockdown?"

Joy grimaced. Both were unfortunately true.

"Yeah, but how is walking me to my car here going to protect me from my neighborhood?"

Ethan shrugged but still insisted on walking her to her car.

"Text me when you get home," Ethan demanded.

Joy rolled her eyes and agreed, waving as she pulled out of the parking lot. Ethan stood watching until she was long out of sight.

The drive home was quiet and uneventful. When Joy got home, she showered, threw her leftovers into her fridge, and crawled into bed. She scrolled her social media for a few minutes, pausing as she came across a video on Facebook of her emerging from the water with the child. Her body looked unnatural as it broke the surface, as if an outside force was dragging her upward. At the time, she had been too drunk on adrenaline and praise to think about the way the invisible rope had yanked her through the water. She sat up. Clicking her phone's power button, she stared at her reflection in the black screen.

"Did you lie to me?" Joy said aloud.

When?

"I know you know what I'm talking about. You can literally read my mind. You lied when you said you couldn't pick up the child on your own, didn't you?"

Buttercup remained silent.

"Answer me!" she demanded in a shrill screech, ignoring the banging on her bedroom wall and her neighbor's shout of complaint.

Yes.

"Why?"

Why did we not lift the child, or why did we tell you we could not?

"Both!" she snarled. Her hand gripped her phone tightly, fingers shaking and turning white.

Joy, we only want what's best for us.

"That doesn't answer my question."

We wanted to save the child. You had always dreamed of being a hero.

Joy paused, the tension leaving her shoulders. She pulled her blankets around her neck and dropped her phone onto her mattress.

"What are you talking about?" she asked.

We know what you want. We were there every time you fantasized about saving the day: running into burning buildings, stopping a shooter. You cannot lie to yourself, Joy. We've seen it all. Felt it all. We know all of your desires and doubts.

"So I can't lie to you, but you can lie to me? How's that fair?"

You lie to yourself as well. How is that any different?

Sirens sounded from somewhere down the road. This wasn't unusual in her part of town, and Joy didn't even flinch. The sirens in her head, however, rang with Buttercup's words. She didn't know what it would say next, if she even wanted to know what it meant. The air around her felt stale, smothering her, making it hard for her to breathe.

Despite her discomfort, she breathed out a near silent, "What?"

Sarah loves me; she just doesn't know how to express it.

Joy's stomach burned.

Mom is coming back for me.

She grabbed her covers, pulling them over her head.

I'm happier alone.

Tears pricked her eyes.

Tom's death was my fault.

The tears dripped down her cheeks.

I don't ever think about hurting myself anymore.

She pressed her hands to her ears.

I'm feeling great.

"Stop."

I don't need any help.

"Please."

I'm fine. It's going to be okay.

"Please stop."

All lies you have told yourself.

"I know, just stop! I get it!"

She huddled under her blankets, wiping the moisture from her burning eyes with the back of her hand. She was filled with anger at Buttercup, hatred toward herself and her insecurities.

Perhaps you should call a therapist.

"You're a dick."

We are the same.

* * *

BANG.

Joy's eyes fluttered open. She lay on her side, facing away from her window. She sat up slowly, groggily, glancing around her dark room. The fan hummed overhead. She reached for her nightstand, hands fumbling for her phone. Squinting at the bright screen of the device, she frowned as she saw it was a little after three in the morning.

She didn't remember falling asleep, but her stinging eyes reminded her of the argument with Buttercup. Uncertainty crawled over her skin, goosebumps rising along her arms in response to an unknown danger. Nothing seemed to be out of place. The only light in the room came from her bathroom down the hall, a single sliver of yellow among the dark shadows cast by her furniture.

BANG. BANG. BANG.

The noise startled Joy, and her phone slipped from her hand. Grabbing the device, she rose from her bed and trod lightly through her bedroom, stopping at the front door. There was a bat by her bed, but she didn't think to grab it, convinced that the warnings flashing through her mind were dramatic, an exaggerated response due to her love of horror movies.

The chill of the living room slid through her, and she pulled her cardigan closer around her body. She flinched as the pounding continued. Shouting floated through the air, a deep voice slurring incoherent words together.

We can handle it if you would like.

"We don't even know who it is. Plus, I don't trust you at all. So far, you've taken over my body and lied to me. It's probably just some drunk asshole," Joy murmured under her breath.

She stepped forward. Lifting onto her toes, she pressed her cheek against the door and raised her eye to the peephole. A man stood in front of her door, his frame dimly lit by the streetlight. He was on the shorter side, standing at about 5'8, with dark hair and eyes. He fiddled with the hood of his gray jacket, pulling its strings so that only a small circle of his face showed. He grinned, his eyes wild and lips peeling back to reveal yellowing teeth.

Joy, there is no need to pause. He means to harm us. Let us take care of him.

Joy's head jerked from side to side, the motion robotic. She stared through the peephole, muscles locked into place and breathing shallow. The man stumbled, his head rolling to the right. He regained his balance, his neck snapping forward and gaze fixing on the peephole. He wiggled his fingers with one hand. Silver flashed in his other. She squeaked, a small gasp falling from her lips. The man cocked his head to the side, his smile widening. He took a step back.

Joy, you need to move.

The man took another step back.

Joy.

He took another step.

JOY. MOVE.

He stopped.

Joy gulped. She stared out, unable to move and unwilling to let the man out of her sight. Her hand locked around her cellphone. The man stood with his back against the metal banister. He rolled his shoulders. He bent his knees. He sprinted toward the door.

THUD.

Joy jerked backward, landing on the ground as the door shook. The wooden floorboards sagged beneath her weight. She hissed as she tried to catch herself, her wrist bending at an odd angle and sending a sharp pain up her arm. She flipped over, crawling on hands and knees toward her bathroom.

THUD. THUD. THUD.

The walls seemed to shake with every impact. Joy's eyes flicked to the kitchen as she stopped in front of the bathroom door. She leapt up, her socks slipping as she sprinted toward the block of knives on her counter. She grabbed the largest one and darted back to the bathroom, shutting and locking the door behind her. With trembling fingers, she dialed 911, pressing the phone to her ear and crouching in her small shower.

"911, what's your emergency?" A female voice responded.

"Ye-yeah, um. My name is Joy Hayes. Someone's trying to get into my apartment," Joy whispered, shaking her head to clear her thoughts and rattling off her address.

"Are you somewhere safe?"

Joy blinked. "Um. I don't... Yes, I think so for now. I've locked myself in my bathroom."

The heating unit in the next room kicked into life, its clanking and humming overtaking the pounding on her front door.

"Good. Can you describe the man you saw? What was he doing?" the operator questioned.

"He was...kinda short. Dark hair. Had a hoodie pulled over his head. Um. He was knocking on the door, and then he smiled at me and stepped back and threw himself at it."

Joy glanced at the door, debating pressing her ear against it to listen for the man.

"You said he smiled at you. Could he see you?"

Someone shouted from the other side of the wall, not the smiling man, but a neighbor having to listen to the attack on Joy's front door and the incomprehensible babbling.

"Uh...no. I don't.. I don't think so. He looked up at the peephole and smiled," Joy said reluctantly.

The operator cleared her throat.

"Mm," she hummed, her tone expressing her skepticism. "And did the man seem intoxicated?"

Joy frowned.

"Maybe? He did sway a bit," Joy allowed.

Her shower curtain was molding at the edges. Had it always been moldy? Why didn't she notice this before? Each stain, each imperfection, now glared back at Joy. It wasn't the time for that to hold any significance; it shouldn't have been her focus. Her vision swam, the room growing blurry. The operator sighed.

"Okay, Ms. Hayes. I understand how that would be frightening, but it sounds as though the man may be confused."

"But he didn't seem—"

"There's a unit on their way. An officer will reach out soon. Keep the door locked."

"Oh...okay." Joy stared at the phone in her hand.

The line clicked dead.

I could take care of it.

And for a second, Joy considered it. As she crouched inside the shower stall in her cheap apartment, in her terrible neighborhood, a man attempting to break into her shitty place, she contemplated letting the thing inside her loose, regardless of the consequences. Then she thought of how she felt when Buttercup took over her, how much it terrified her that she had no clue what it was capable of.

And so she forced herself to say, "The police are on their way. We'll wait for them."

The heater finally clicked off, leaving an unsettling silence. Her phone lit up in her hand, and she recognized the local area code. Her legs began to shake as she crouched. She sat, one hand resting on the knife balancing on her thigh while the other held her phone. The water from her earlier shower seeped into her sweatpants. She pressed her forehead against the tile and answered the phone.

"Hello?" she mumbled.

"Hi, Ms. Hayes. This is Sam with the Austin police department. Are you okay?" a male voice replied.

"At the moment, yes. The banging on my door stopped," Joy said.

"We get this call a lot. It's usually just someone too intoxicated to find their way home or to figure out they are at the wrong apartment. A unit will patrol the area, but he should go away on his own."

"I—" Joy thought back to the man, how he seemed to stumble, the drunken sway to his movements. Perhaps they were right. She bit her lip. "Okay. But will someone come check?"

"Yes, ma'am. A unit is on the way, but feel free to call back if something else should happen."

Joy thanked the man and hung up. She contemplated waiting for the police, but the silence of the apartment, the fear of not knowing where the man was, was overwhelming.

"Will you..." she whispered.

We will see if he is gone.

"Thank you."

Buttercup drifted from Joy, floating under the door and out of the bathroom. It returned a few seconds later.

The man is gone.

Joy sighed in relief. She picked herself off the ground, scowling at the water that dripped from her sweats as she stood. She waited for a little over an hour and a half, sitting on her couch in the living room in the dark, the knife on the table and her phone in her hand. She contemplated calling Ethan but knew he wouldn't be awake for a few more hours and didn't want to bother him. The police never came.

You should try and get some sleep.

Joy climbed back into bed, hesitant, but willing to try and sleep. She curled into her blankets, flinching at any small noise she heard. Her ceiling fan spun overhead, and Joy stared at it, blinking sleepily in time with its movement. She turned on her side, facing toward her window. Her eyes fluttered closed and her breath steadied.

Tap.

Joy jolted at the small sound coming from her bedroom window.

Tap.

A shadow walked in front of the window, only barely visible through the cracks of her blinds.

Screeeeeeeeeech.

Joy covered her ears, wincing at the sound of metal on glass.

Panda hissed from somewhere under the bed. Joy had completely forgotten about the cat in her panic. Her apartment felt different now, darker, a strange energy buzzing throughout. Joy lay silent in her bed, refusing to move, holding her breath as she listened.

BANG.

Angry fists beat against the wooden frame of her front door, filling the apartment with echoes of bad intentions. Joy forced herself to stand up, pulling the covers away from her body and grabbing for the phone beside her. She crouched beside the window, below her shutters, and waited.

She squinted into the darkness but couldn't see anything. The man grew silent, the banging fading, and she shifted the blinds to peek out.

He stood in front of her window, leaning on the metal railing. His head jerked toward the window, dark eyes narrowing as his gaze flicked down to where she crouched. A brown bottle dangled from his hand, and he swayed on his feet. He lifted the bottle up to his shoulder, cocking it back with a grin on his face. Joy furrowed her eyebrows. He chucked the bottle, and Joy gasped.

Joy, let us handle him.

Joy remained beneath the window, squatting with her hands covering her head. She rocked back and forth and stared at the ground.

Tap.

Joy looked up, her eyes meeting the man's as he crouched in front of her window.

Tap.

A blade, slightly longer than a foot, glittered in the man's hand.

Screeeeeeeech.

He ran it along the glass, then pointed it at Joy.

"I see you," the man whispered. His grin widened.

Joy panted out a panicked breath.

The man jumped up, saluted, then sprinted by Joy's window and down her concrete stairs.

He stopped, glancing around the gravel in the dog park below her apartment. He jerked, his attention caught by a large rock in the center of the gravel. He lifted it. Tossed it in the air once. Then twice.

"What is he..."

Joy, we should move.

He turned and squinted at Joy's window. He wound his arm up, rock in hand, and lobbed at the window above Joy. The glass cracked, but did not shatter. Joy screamed, dashing from her room and into her bathroom.

"FUCK!" she shouted, realizing her phone had slipped from her grasp.

Glass shattered from somewhere in the apartment, and Joy locked the door.

The man whistled in the next room.

"LEAVE ME ALONE!" she screamed.

Joy.

"Get him out of my apartment," Joy begged.

With pleasure.

Buttercup shot out, its mist curling under the door.

"What the—" The man's gravelly voice faltered.

Joy heard dragging, feet being pulled along the smooth surface of the ground, followed by a cry of pain.

Thump.

Thump.

Thump.

Three dull thuds sounded from outside of the apartment. A few more moments passed before Buttercup returned.

He will not bother you any longer.

"What do you mean?" Joy asked, though she knew.

Buttercup remained silent. Joy unlocked the door, creeping out of the bathroom and toward her bedroom. The man's knife lay in the middle of the floor. She kicked it to the side. The shards of glass that remained around her window frame were tinged pink, a strip of dark fabric dangling from the edge. She grabbed a pair of Crocs, a gag gift from Ethan that Joy secretly wore around the apartment, from where she tossed them in the corner of the room.

Stepping carefully across the scattered fragments of glass, Joy stared at the gaping hole where her window had once been. She stuck her head through, searching for the man. Her attention caught at the bottom of the stairwell, where a body lay still in the slowly rising sun.

CHAPTER 15

Joy, Age 11

"I want you to draw yourself."

Clara giggled, grabbing the pencil and paper from her grandmother's outstretched hand. Something hard settled in Joy's stomach. There was a look in Sarah's eyes, a smile that stretched too far on her thin lips. Sarah didn't do things like this with the girls, fun little activities just for the hell of it. There was always something more, an ulterior motive tucked away to be pulled out at her convenience. Joy sat on the bed for a half-hour or so, watching as Clara sketched herself as a princess. She gave herself long hair, big brown eyes, and a large, poofy dress. When she finished, Clara popped up from the desk and raced through the hallway to their grandmother's room. Joy followed behind slowly, a wave of anxiety washing over her.

She stopped outside the doorway when she heard Sarah laugh bitterly. "Is that really how you think you look?"

Clara tilted her head to the side and frowned.

Sarah smirked. "Do you want me to show you how everyone else sees you?"

Clara hesitated, then nodded. Sarah snatched the paper from the young girl's hand. Grabbing a marker from the nightstand, Sarah slashed a bright red x marked over the drawing. Clara's face fell, droplets dotting her eyelashes as she fought the urge to cry. She knew, even as young as ten, that crying would only make her grandmother's temper flare up worse. Joy watched from the doorway as Sarah flipped to the back side of the paper and drew. Her motions were jerky, manic, as she ended her sketch with a large circular motion. She shoved the drawing into Clara's chest. It was silent for a moment, Clara's sniffling the only discernible noise.

"Look at it."

Clara shook her head no.

"Look. At. It," she hissed.

Clara peeled the paper away from her, chest heaving as she looked down. Her chin wobbled, and she glared back up at her grandmother, who gasped in mock surprise.

"How dare you look at me like that. This is for your own good. That's what you really look like. That's how everyone sees you, Clara. And they'll always see you that way if you don't put in any effort."

Clara dropped the picture, running out of the room as a sob escaped her.

Sarah frowned. "You understand why I had to do it, right, Joy? It's not healthy, looking like she does, and I'm afraid she's going to get bullied for it."

She wrapped her bony hands around Joy's, shaking them. Joy clenched her fist and looked to the ground. She nodded once as her grandmother paced out of the room, lighter in hand as she patted her housecoat for her pack of cigarettes.

Joy wanted to call Tom but didn't know what he would say, or if there was anything he could even do. It seemed that Sarah had all the power in the household—to ruin a mood at a whim, to create silence with a single word.

She and Tom had long since stopped sleeping in the same room. They were getting divorced, according to Sarah, which confused Joy. Tom still called Sarah 'babe,' still answered to her every command barely disguised as a request, still told her that he loved her daily. When Joy's friend's parents had divorced, they had two houses, but Sarah showed no sign of moving out. She got a job, but it only lasted a few weeks before she was back in the house full-time. She wouldn't cook or clean during her short stint as a housewife—that was usually left to Joy—but she was there, hidden away in the farthest room, occasionally coming out to smoke or to ask Tom to go and get her something to eat.

It wasn't until years later that Joy learned the truth about their divorce. Sarah had gone on vacation a few times, flying to Boston to spend time with Tom's best friend. Tom had thought it would be good for her to get out of the house, that a change of environment would help distance her from her most recent drug relapse. It seemed like it had. She came back happy, looking younger than she had in years. Tom attributed it to a restful vacation and exploring a new city. Sarah attributed it to sleeping with his best friend. It wasn't the last time this would happen. No, Sarah took many trips up north, leaving for days, sometimes weeks, and coming back to live in Tom's house, enjoy Joy's cooking, and verbally assault Clara.

Joy learned to love the days she didn't see her grandmother, the times Sarah spent in a different state. When Sarah returned, Joy would have to listen for the sound of her grandmother's door opening, wince at the distinct sound of Sarah's slippers shuffling down the hallways. Joy would make herself quiet, pulling Clara to their room when Sarah moved. She would avoid making eye contact for too long in case Sarah was in a bad mood. Joy was sure her sister saw her as a villain, tugging Clara away from her toy and the television at the smallest creaks, chastising her for being too loud. Joy felt powerless, unable to protect her sister, unable to leave.

CHAPTER 16

"I don't understand why you didn't call me the first time that asshole tried to get in," Ethan fumed, picking up a piece of glass Joy had missed and tossing it into the garbage bag.

"I didn't want to bother you. I assumed it was just some confused drunk dude. The police officer that called even said it was probably nothing." Joy sighed.

The man had been knocked unconscious after "falling" down her steps but was otherwise fine. The police cuffed him as soon as the paramedics gave the all-clear. They explained that the man had multiple warrants out for his arrest, two for aggravated assault and one for sexual assault. A part of Joy thought she should still be afraid, especially of Buttercup. Buttercup insisted the man had tripped after it pulled him out the window, that his fall had been nothing more than the stumbling of a drunk madman.

Joy didn't believe it.

She had felt Buttercup surge at the man as he balanced on the first step, the feeling similar to when Buttercup had held Keith above the stairs in her office. It wasn't quite the same, as this time she had control of her body, had been sitting in the bathroom as it happened, automatically going through the motions while her attention was elsewhere. She had still been able to feel herself trembling and her heart racing, but her mind had been focused on getting rid of the man in her apartment, the feel of his cotton jacket and scrape of his back as he was dragged back through her window, the sound of his body bouncing down the concrete, the stillness of his frame as he thumped to a stop.

She knew Buttercup had lied but couldn't find it in herself to care, especially when she thought of the man's grin and the flash of his knife.

It was a little after nine when the police left, taking Joy's statement and information while her neighbors peeked at the scene from their windows. In the silence of her apartment, Joy had stared at her phone for a few moments, unsure who to call or what to do first. She couldn't call the apartment complex yet as they didn't open until ten, but she was able to call and talk to a local repair company about getting her window fixed. She choked when the man on the phone told her it was going to be $350 and prayed her renter's insurance would cover even a small bit of the cost.

She called Carmen next, giving her a brief rundown of what had happened and telling her she wouldn't be able to come to work that day. Carmen had been very understanding, practically demanding she take a few days off to recover and asking if there was anything she could do to help. She then texted her family a brief update, only giving them the most basic details and reassuring them that she was fine and that there was no reason for them to make the five-hour drive to Austin.

She called Ethan last, much to his chagrin. He arrived to find her picking up the final pieces of glass from her bedroom, a bed sheet and duct tape in her hand.

"Can you hold this while I tape it?" Joy asked Ethan, passing him the sheet and ripping off a piece of the tape with her teeth.

Ethan stepped forward. "Why are you putting a sheet up?"

"There's a giant hole in my window." Joy rolled her eyes and began to tape down the bottom right corner of the fabric as Ethan held it against the wall.

She held back a shiver, goosebumps raising on her exposed

arms as a gust of cold autumn air slipped through the cotton. It wasn't that cold, probably around sixty degrees. But Joy stood in front of the window without a jacket and had been since the man fell down the stairs. The cold kept her awake and alert, allowing her to stay focused on the different steps she needed to take. She could handle the cold as long as it helped her stay motivated.

"Yes, I saw that." They shifted to the bottom left corner. Joy fumbled the roll of tape, and Ethan stooped down to pick it up for her before continuing. "I mean, aren't the guys coming in a few hours to fix it? Why bother with the sheet?"

"I don't want bugs coming into my apartment."

Joy's phone rang from somewhere in the next room, but she ignored it, instead stretching on her tiptoes to reach the first of the top corners.

"It's November; there are no bugs," Ethan said bemusedly.

Joy shrugged. "Birds then."

"Flew south for the winter already."

Joy slapped a large piece of tape on the corner and winced at the stinging that shot through her arm. She flipped her palm and frowned at the strip of pink, a thin cut stretching from one side to the other, a hint of glass that glittered in the sun from within the red crevice.

"Then I'm trying to keep the cold out."

"It's like fifty, and the sheet is doing very little to help with that."

"If it's like fifty," Joy deepened her voice in a poor impression of Ethan, "then it's warm enough for bugs and birds."

Ethan hummed.

"What?"

"Nothing." Ethan turned from Joy as she finished taping the sheet.

"What?" Joy demanded.

"Nothing!"

"Okay…" Joy set the duct tape on her bedside table.

Suddenly thirsty, she spun around and strode forward to her kitchen.

"It's just that..." Ethan started behind her.

She looked at him over her shoulder, one eyebrow raised.

"Were you scared?" Ethan asked, rocking on his heels.

Joy blinked. "Was I... scared?"

"I mean, some guy tried to break into your apartment, and you're acting like nothing happened! Joy, you had the place cleaned up, police called, and repair guy on the way before you even called me. You're avoiding it."

Joy groaned. She rolled her shoulders, grabbed a mug from a shelf, and filled it with tap water. Ethan walked to her bathroom. Joy listened to him rummage through her cabinets, thinking bitterly about how scared she had been. She chugged her drink and slammed the glass on the counter as Ethan came back into the room.

"I'm not avoiding it. I'm taking control of it," Joy explained. "It's empowering to be able to do something." Would he understand?

Ethan placed a small box with red markings on her dining room table. He opened the box, revealing brown Band-Aids, gauze, and a few antiseptic wipes. Plucking out a Band-Aid and a wipe, he reached for Joy's hand.

"You're not letting yourself have time to process. You can't just let this kind of thing bottle up," he chastised, swiping the alcohol-covered cloth along the cut on her palm.

Joy jerked her hand back, jaw tightening. He had no clue what she had been through! How dare he try and tell her how to react? She had felt so damn powerless last night, having practically been at the mercy of the man with the knife. Having to accept Buttercup 's help when she didn't want to. She was also frustrated as hell. When the apartment complex had finally opened, they had essentially blamed her for not calling the complex's security officer (never mind that she hadn't even known they had an officer), the police hadn't bothered to come until after the man had fallen down the stairs and needed an ambulance, and the insurance people had been unsure whether or not an attempted break-in was included in her coverage, potentially leaving her with a $350 bill for her window that would take the majority of her meager savings to cover.

"Jesus, Ethan! Leave me alone. Last night sucked, okay? Is that what you want to hear? I've never been that scared in my life. I locked myself in my bathroom, ass wet from sitting in my damn shower, and waited. Waited for some asshole to get into my apartment. Waited for him to get to me. I was powerless. I had nothing I could do, and I hated it. Is that what you wanted? To hear that I'm human too? That I get scared too?"

Joy's chest heaved, and her hands closed into shaky fists. Joy looked up to see Ethan staring at her. She flinched and let her gaze drop to the floor. He reached for her hand once more, wrapping it in gauze before letting it drop to her side.

This was it. She had been too loud, too angry. Her voice had been scornful. He was going to leave her. She was going to lose one of the only people who truly seemed to like her and enjoy her company. She should've known this would happen, should've distanced herself as soon as she started caring about him. She cringed inside, waited for him to yell at her, for his footsteps to walk out of her door.

Instead, he sighed, sitting on her couch and patting the seat beside him. Joy's shoulders slumped, her throat choking on a rising sob. She flung herself forward, launching herself at Ethan. He wrapped his arms around her, rubbing her back as she cried into his shoulder, and murmured soft words into her hair.

* * *

A few hours later and Joy was still curled up on the couch, Ethan flitting about the apartment making coffee, bringing her blankets, and flipping between YouTube videos on her television. The window repairman had finally come by a little less than an hour ago. He had snorted at the sheet taped on the frame and informed Joy that the replacement would be closer to $500 than the initially quoted $350. Her insurance company had also called back with the bad news that they wouldn't be covering the repair, leaving her broke but with a brand new window for an apartment she didn't feel safe in. The repairman had taken her card so flippantly, as if he was completely unaware that he was wiping out the tiny molehill of savings she had managed to stash away since graduating last year.

As if hearing her thoughts, Ethan cleared his throat.

"Come stay with me," he offered.

Joy glanced up from her phone where she had been texting updates to her family and Carmen. Her eyes stung, her head hurt from crying, and she was so tired from the night before that she wasn't sure she had heard him correctly.

"What?"

Ethan nodded toward her front door.

"Come stay at my apartment. You can use the guest room."

"Why?"

Joy locked her phone and placed it on her coffee table.

"I figured you'd want to get away for a couple of nights. And I'd feel a lot better if I knew you weren't alone."

Joy swallowed. She wasn't convinced she could sleep tonight, but she didn't want to be a burden to Ethan, especially after the embarrassing crying episode earlier. She could still practically see the wet spot on his blue Henley shirt, a disgusting patch of tears, snot, and runny mascara she had been too tired to take off properly the night before.

"No, that's okay. I wouldn't want to make you uncomfortable or interrupt any um...visitors you may have."

Joy had to force herself to spit out the word "visitors." The thought of Ethan with someone else made her want to puke, even though she knew she had no say in that department.

Even if she did still have feelings for him, which she definitely did not, there was no way he would reciprocate them. She couldn't understand why he was single. He was attractive, broad shoulders and towering height paired with silky brown hair and warm brown eyes, and he was intelligent and kind. Meanwhile, she was an angry woman a few pounds too heavy and a minor inconvenience away from a mental breakdown.

He chuckled, his mouth flashing a set of straight white teeth before falling into an easy smile.

"I wouldn't be uncomfortable. You're already at my apartment at least twice a week. At least this way, I won't have to waste gas picking you up," he teased.

Joy bit her lip.

"You're sure?"

Her hand twitched, fingers flexing toward the overnight bag sitting in her hallway closet.

Ethan nodded. "I'm sure."

Joy picked at the skin around her fingernails. Silence fell as Joy debated and Ethan waited for her response.

"Okay."

CHAPTER 17

Joy, Age 11

"I don't think it's a good idea for you to visit her," Sarah explained, pulling the phone away from her ear.

"Why not?" Joy asked, picking at the skin between her nails. "Clara and I made a card for her. I bought her a Sprite, too; they always make me feel better when I don't feel good."

Sarah sighed. She rubbed at her nose ring, smoothed her red hair back into a thin ponytail.

"It's not the same, and you know that. She's not sick; your mother hurt herself. And she did it right after talking to you on the phone. She told me you said something that upset her. We want her to be able to rest."

Joy shook her head.

"I didn't...I didn't say anything. I don't remember saying anything. I was just telling her about my day, and she said she didn't feel good and had to go, so I said okay, and she hung up."

Sarah patted her hand.

"I'm sure you didn't mean to, but I think you being there might set her off again. We don't want her hurting herself worse, do we?"

Joy's shoulders slumped. A few hours earlier, her mother had tried to kill herself. Sarah had wasted no time telling her, sparing her the gory details but making sure Joy understood what had happened and hinting that Joy was to blame. Joy didn't know how to react when Sarah told her. She was sad, sure, but mostly ashamed, her mind racing through every interaction she had with her mother recently to try and figure out what she had done wrong. Joy handed the card and the drink over to Sarah.

"No, ma'am, but I promise I won't do or say anything. I just want to see her."

A small lie. A part of her did want to see Joanne, to verify that her mother was alright with her own eyes, but a bigger part of her was scared that Joanne hated her now. Joy wanted to see her because she was sure she would be able to tell if her mother's attempt to end her life had also been an attempt to leave Joy behind. She thought she was being selfish, wanting to see whether her mother still loved her while she was still recovering in the hospital, but she couldn't push down the desire far enough to agree to stay home while Sarah and Clara visited her.

"Fine. But you have to be quiet. Hug her quickly and then let Clara talk to her."

Joy nodded. She forced herself to smile as Clara walked into the room. The three loaded up in her grandmother's red Monte Carlo, Joy claiming shotgun as the oldest. They drove roughly a half-hour to the hospital, parked the car, and rode the elevator up a few floors. Clara had grabbed the Sprite and card from the car, and was swinging the bottle around in her hand. It clipped Joy's hip, and Joy whipped around to glare at her younger sister. Clara stuck her tongue out as the elevator dinged.

Her grandmother approached the nurses' stand, a smile on her face. "We're looking for Joanne."

The nurse raised her eyebrows.

"What's the last name?"

Sarah hesitated. Joanne had been married several times and had a habit of switching between a few of the last names she had used over the years. She was currently single, as far as anyone knew, and Sarah had no idea which last name she was using. Her phone chimed somewhere deep in her purse, and she whipped it out.

"Sorry, she just texted me. Mind pointing me to room 405?"

Clara smiled as she threw open the door to Joanne's room. She hadn't been told the real reason why Joanne was there, instead thinking her mom had been in an accident of some sort.

"Hi, Mom!" Clara exclaimed, throwing herself onto the crisp white sheets of Joanne's bed.

Sarah rolled her eyes, chuckling and pulling her away. "Be careful of her IVs, Clara. Remember, your mom is still recovering."

Joanne smiled. She had gained weight since the last time Joy had seen her, and, outside of her slightly pale complexion and the tubes running from her hand, she looked healthier.

"She's fine, Mom. It's good to see y'all. It was getting a bit too boring around here."

"Mom, look!" Clara handed her the card and Sprite. "We made this for you so you'll feel better sooner."

Joanne gingerly took the objects from her, patting her on the head and gushing about how thoughtful the gifts were. Her eyes narrowed over Clara's head, focusing on the girl still standing in the doorway.

"Hi, Joy," she called out.

Joy stepped cautiously into the room, smiling tentatively at her mom, but keeping her mouth shut. She searched her mom's eyes for the hatred she had convinced herself she would find. Instead, she saw nothing but cool indifference. Joy had a habit of watching her friends talk to their parents. She would listen to the conversations, study how their moms and dads looked at them. There was an eagerness to the way her friends' parents spoke about their children, excitement and pride in even the mere mention of their names. She had come to the conclusion that Tom was the only person in her life to look at her that way, to speak of her proudly at his office, at the grocery store, boasting about Joy and Clara to pretty much anyone who would listen. And that was enough. That should be enough. Joy wished she felt like that was enough.

Her mom had never looked at her that way, nor spoken of her in such a manner. To Joanne, Joy was her oldest child. Joy was the mature one, the one with the sad blue eyes that Joanne joked made her look thirty years old. The one who had inherited her intelligence. The one she resented the most. The one who should've never been born. The one she wished she had gotten rid of. The one who took her dreams away from her. At least, those are the words Joanne had said to Sarah one of the rare nights she had stopped by to see Joy and Clara, and sat up talking after the kids were asleep. She didn't know that Joy had climbed out of bed to ask her mother if she wanted Joy to make her a special breakfast in bed in the morning. Joy had wanted Joanne's affection, but learned that night that she was a burden, the one who had ruined her mother's life.

"Hi, Mom." Joy finally found her voice, her eyes darting around the white walls.

She gave Joanne a quick, light hug, then sat in a chair in the corner of the room. Clara and their mother talked for a while, Sarah occasionally piping in with a comment or small laugh. Joy tried joining the conversation a few times, but the room fell silent every time she spoke. She shrunk into herself, pulling her knees into her chest with a forced smile as the others giggled and chatted until visitation hours were over. Envy burned through her as she watched Joanne give Clara a piece of candy she had stashed in her bedside table, her head tossing back in laughter as Clara pretended the red rope was a mustache. They looked so much alike, from their frizzy brown hair and light brown eyes to the shape of their noses.

Her mother's love had always felt like a competition between her and Clara. The two girls were often pitted against each other, as if one could be better than the other, as if one could be good enough, smart enough, pretty enough for their mother to claim as her own, for her to want to keep.

The comparison wasn't always harsh words and insults hidden in praise for the other sister. At times, it was literal competition, occasionally physical. When Joy was eight, Joanne moved back to Texas, renting a small house in the neighboring city. Joy and Clara would stay overnight with her for a few days at a time, the two girls often planning for weeks for their "sleepovers." One morning Joy and Clara had woken up around eight and flipped on the television to distract themselves from their growling stomachs, knowing their mother wouldn't be awake for a few hours but also knowing that Joanne hated it when they got breakfast without permission. The noise from the television had been too loud, waking their mother up. She had a hangover from drinking, makeup smudged around her eyes, and her breath smelled like a bar.

She told the girls to pack their bags, that she couldn't handle it, that they were going home two days earlier than expected. Clara and Joy had bawled, begged their mother to let them stay. These sleepovers were rare, and they were unsure when they would see their mother again. Joy had watched a smile grow on her mother's lips, cruel and mocking, a reflection of her grandmother's sadistic grin. She told the girls they could stay, but only if they could stay in a wall sit for over ten minutes.

They tried. Tears running down their small faces, blonde and brown hair plastered to their neck, little legs shaking violently, backs pressed perfectly against their wall and knees bent into a perpendicular squat.

But it wasn't enough. Nothing ever was with Joanne. She had sent the two girls back to their grandparents with a smirk and the promise to see them again soon. She moved out of Texas three days later.

Joanne didn't stay in the hospital long either; she was discharged the next day. She hadn't bothered to tell anyone she was leaving, Sarah arriving for a visit to an empty room and a note saying she was off to her next adventure. Sarah had screamed at Joy when she got home, telling her that Joanne was unhappy with Joy for being so quiet.

Joy wasn't surprised to find out her mom had left again. She was used to people leaving. And she was beginning to think that maybe she deserved it.

CHAPTER 18

"You're sure you're gonna be okay on your own? I don't have to go to class. Today's topic is engineering communications, and honestly, who wants to sit around and learn about how to give a presentation to a whole bunch of engineers? Like, 95 percent of them would rather die than have to sit through anything that might require them to be social. I don't mind skipping, especially if you don't want to be on your own yet."

"I'm only going across the street," Joy deadpanned.

The pair had spent a few hours talking to her apartment's leasing office about potentially switching apartments (which they ultimately said they couldn't allow) and waiting for the police to call and give her final updates about the man. Ethan told her he was staying until he came, ignoring her as she insisted she would be fine. After what was probably the thirteenth time, he sprang up and walked out her front door without saying a word. She waited, confused, and texted him to ask where he had gone.

He returned a few minutes later, a bag of snacks from the convenience store down the road in one hand and his switch in the other. He marched silently to Joy's television, plugged the game in, thrust a bag of chips and a controller at Joy, and then plopped down beside her. They spent the next three hours playing Smash Brothers.

Joy was now sitting on the mattress in Ethan's guest

bedroom, Panda curled up into a fuzzy black ball beside her. Joy's suitcase was placed gently beside the bed, along with a backpack containing her laptop and other valuables she hadn't felt comfortable leaving at her apartment.

It had taken her only a few minutes to pack after the window had been repaired, but almost half an hour for her to coax her cat into a carrier. She was originally going to leave the cat at her apartment and stop by to check on her, but Ethan insisted she would be a welcome guest at his apartment, even going so far as to lug her automatic kitty litter box into the backseat of his car.

Ethan had a class starting in an hour, and Joy wanted to use that time to go to the cafe across the street from his apartment and get some work done. Ethan, still in an overprotective fit, wanted to skip class. Joy was debating shoving him out the door. She figured if she dove for his knees, she might have a fighting chance.

"It wouldn't work," Ethan smirked.

Joy's eyebrows furrowed.

"What wouldn't work?"

"Going for the knees."

He laughed at the shocked expression on her face.

"I've got a good eight inches and eighty pounds on you. I'd go limp, squish you like a bug."

Joy stood, grabbed her backpack, and stared him down.

"It's like twenty feet away, and I need to get some emails sent. I can't do that with you here distracting me, and you need to go to class."

Ethan flashed her a cheeky grin.

"I'm sorry my devilishly good looks are distracting you so."

Joy bit back a laugh as Ethan tossed his hair dramatically over his shoulder. He snagged her backpack from her hands, slinging it over his other shoulder, and slipped his hand in hers. He tugged her forward and out the front door.

"Bye, Panda," he shouted over his shoulder as the door slammed behind him.

The black cat continued sleeping.

***

"I'll be back at four." Ethan stood from the wooden table Joy had claimed.

As Joy had stepped into the shop, the smell of coffee and cinnamon rolls wafted through the air. Oak tables and wicker chairs with the occasional occupant were scattered throughout the room. A few people were looking upward, and Joy did the same. There was no distinguishable ceiling, but many small lights shone against an indigo background. Joy traced the shape of the big dipper within the lights.

"Yes, you've said that three times now."

"And you have my number? You can call me if anything happens, I don't care if I'm driving or in class or saving the life of the President."

"Yes, I have your number." Joy rolled her eyes then raised an eyebrow. "Saving the life of the President? Like the U.S. President? Why would he be in Austin?"

Ethan ignored her.

"And you have that pepper spray I gave you?"

Joy patted a small pocket of her backpack.

"Yup. Though I'm not sure why you have it to begin with."

"Pepper spray is a fairly efficient way to ward off undesirables."

Joy smirked. "I agree, but does the llama canister help with the efficiency?"

Ethan averted his eyes. He took a large bite of the Danish he was holding and turned from Joy.

"It was all they had at the store," he mumbled.

Joy laughed. "Go! I'll be here when you're done. Have a good class."

Ethan nodded, shoved the rest of his danish in his mouth,

then turned and walked a few steps. He paused. Dropping his backpack to the ground, he spun on his heel and stalked over to Joy. She froze, hand still reaching for her coffee, and watched him approach her.

"What—"

Ethan grabbed Joy's hand, pulling her out of her seat. He wrapped his arms around her and squeezed tightly. Joy tensed as his head dropped to her neck, his warm breath tickling her collarbone.

"I'm really glad you're okay. I don't know what I would have done if you hadn't been."

Joy relaxed. She put an awkward arm around him and patted him roughly on the back. She felt his shoulders shake and pulled back, terrified he had started crying. Not necessarily because she thought he might be hurt, but because she wouldn't know how to react if he was crying. Did she pat him too hard? Should she have said something?

"Uh. Don't worry. I'm...uh. Not dead yet?" she blurted out, hands waving in panic.

Ethan glanced up, and Joy flinched when she saw tears rolling down his cheeks. She sighed and narrowed her eyes when she saw the wide grin on his face.

"You pat me..." He gasped between laughs. "Like I was a dog. That was such an awkward hug."

Joy shoved him away and plopped back into her seat. She huffed, hitting the power button for her laptop and averting her eyes. He shouted a quick goodbye as he passed through the door, and she settled into her seat to get some work done.

* * *

The coffee warmed her hands as she drank. Every sip was the perfect balance of sweet caramel and acidic bitterness, with hints of hazelnut and cinnamon. The drink was fragrant, notes of the warming spices drifting through the air. Joy sighed in contentment.

"Joy?" A voice asked from the side. "Joy Hayes?"

Joy winced. She debated taking her coffee and making a run for it, but decided against it. Instead, she turned, a tight smile tugging on her lips. A woman stood in front of her table, one she vaguely recognized from junior high as someone she had been on the volleyball team with. The woman was slightly shorter than she remembered, long black hair where she had once had a bob, the large Michael Kors bag in her hand the same tan as her sweater. Joy panicked as her mind blanked on her name.

"Hey!" she said instead, pulling the woman into an awkward hug. "It's been a long time, how are you?"

For a few minutes, the two made small talk. Well, the other woman made small talk. Joy smiled at her awkwardly, half-listening to the woman talk about the wedding Joy hadn't even heard about. The woman apologized profusely for not inviting Joy, telling her it was a small destination wedding at some exclusive resort and she just "assumed you would be busy with other things like your little job." Joy still couldn't remember the woman's name.

They had gone to school together back when Joy had lived with her grandparents, before she had moved a few hours away to live with and be adopted by Trini and Connor. Most of her school life from back then was a blur, a scrambled mess of a desperate attempt to get Sarah's approval, make herself seem as normal as possible to her classmates, and pick up the pieces of her life. The woman in front of her reminded her of those days. She had a faint memory of the woman as a child, one of the more popular girls in her class, a spoiled kid with loving parents who loved to brag in the way only those who enjoy putting others down did.

Although Sarah had been the first to show Joy what it meant to be poor, this woman, and her friend group, had never failed to remind Joy. They flaunted their summer trips while Joy maintained the house throughout the summer. They strutted about in new clothes while Joy wore their hand-me-downs. They showed off their hand-picked supplies, discussing how they occasionally traveled to different cities just to get their pencil cases in a particular color or shape. Joy tucked her supplies, the ugly colors not chosen by other poor kids from a local church's charity drive, as deeply into her second-hand backpack as possible.

It seemed time hadn't changed this woman. She sat in front of Joy and bragged about her husband's wealth and the "new business" she had recently joined.

"You know, my company is looking to recruit more Boss women like you." The woman, whose name Joy still had not remembered, flashed a white smile. "It's a great opportunity to make some cash on the side, and the products are actually SO good. In fact, my hubby was saying the other day how much he enjoyed—"

She continued speaking, launching into a full speech about her "small business." Joy's head pounded.

Buttercup, Joy thought. Please, for the love of God, make her leave.

We could kill her. Make it look like she slipped and broke her neck.

Jesus, I want her to leave me alone, not die. Joy smiled, nodding her head as the woman tossed her hair and gestured to her phone.

Fine. Killing her would be a much simpler solution; however, your reluctance to be associated with her death is understandable. We will do it your way.

Buttercup shot toward the woman, and Joy smirked. The woman coughed lightly into her hand as the black mist circled around her legs, excused herself politely, and then resumed talking.

"And have I mentioned that the tea is so good for weight loss?" Her eye lingered on Joy's thighs, and Joy clenched her jaw.

"Is that right?" Joy balled her hand into a fist under the table and the woman frowned.

Joy's classmate shifted in her seat and crossed her legs together. Although Joy couldn't see it, she knew, could practically feel, Buttercup was pressing on the woman's bladder.

"Yeah!" Her enthusiasm seemed to have waned, her voice tight as she looked to the bathroom.

This is disgusting.

Joy squeezed her hand together, her fingernails digging into her palm, and took a sip of her coffee using the other hand. Buttercup squeezed the other woman's bladder in response. The woman began to stand.

A gentle smile fell on Joy's lips, and she leaned forward in interest. "Why don't you tell me more about that? I'm always looking for new weight-loss products. And I have a couple of friends with too much time on their hands who are looking for a way to earn a bit of cash on the side."

The woman's eyes lit up. She settled herself back into the seat, attention wavering between Joy and the restroom entrance a few feet away.

"I'd love to tell you more!" she said in a strained voice.

Her hands clutched at the sides of the table, her thighs clamping together desperately.

Joy squeezed harder.

"Hold that thought. I'm so sorry, but I have to run to the ladies room." And run she did. "Stay right there! I will be right back," she tossed over her shoulder as she disappeared through the bathroom door.

Joy hopped up the second the woman was out of sight, grabbing her coffee and phone and darting toward the door. Her phone chimed in her hand, and she glanced down to see that Ethan had just arrived.

"Hey!" Ethan greeted, bumping into her on the sidewalk outside the coffee shop.

His hands were full of Target bags, so Joy wrapped her

hand around his upper arm and tugged him in the opposite direction.

"I'm pretty tired. Is it okay if we just head home?"

"Sure?" Ethan chose not to question Joy, instead letting her pull him along.

The two walked in silence to his apartment across the street, Joy occasionally glancing behind to make sure they weren't being followed by her MLM-loving ex-classmate and Ethan swinging the bags in his hands in large arcs. The plastic smacked into a woman waiting at the cross light, and Ethan apologized as Joy laughed.

Back at his apartment, Ethan tossed the bags onto his couch. Joy breathed in relief as the door shut behind them. It wasn't so much that she was afraid of the woman—her years of yearning for her classmates' approval were long behind her—but the idea of having to interact any further, to make polite conversation and pretend she wasn't bored to death, made her want to gag.

She walked over to the couch, glancing at the bags scattered on the black cushions. "What's in the bags? Also, why didn't you ask me to go with you? I freaking love Target."

Ethan smiled.

"Just a couple things I thought you might need."

Joy grinned back, hands already digging through the contents. Inside were a few lavender-scented bath products, a giant, fluffy yellow towel, a plethora of her favorite snacks, and a super long charging cable. Tears pricked at her eyes as she looked back at Ethan.

"Thank you," she mumbled, wrapping her arms around his waist and burying herself in his chest.

Ethan hugged her back, his chin resting on the top of her head. "Anything for my favorite girl."

CHAPTER 19

Joy, Age 12

"You must be so proud of Joy."

Sarah nodded at one of Joy's friend's mothers from her seat in the bleachers, a dangerous smile playing across her lips. Joy felt her heart stutter, having overheard the words as she walked onto the volleyball court. She wanted, no, needed, someone to acknowledge her effort. Sarah left the game a few minutes later, leaving Joy to bite back her disappointment and continue playing. A part of her was grateful Sarah had shown up at all, as it was the first time in a long time that someone had come to watch her play. She understood it was just a junior high sports team, nothing important in the grand scheme of things, but she could never quite quell the sting of rejection she felt as her friends' parents called their names from the stands.

Joy walked home that night in a surprisingly good mood. She strolled through the kitchen door and hallway and stopped outside her room.

"Clara!" Joy shouted, panic rising.

Her room was in shambles. All of her shelves and her entire closet had been emptied onto her floor. Her bed had been flipped; her desk drawers lay on their sides. She feared someone had broken in. The true culprit was much more terrifying to Joy. She flinched as bony hands wrapped around her upper arms.

"Where's my money, Joy?" Sarah hissed.

Joy jerked backward, whimpering as the older woman's grip only tightened.

"What money?" Joy asked, eyebrows furrowing and breath coming out in short, panicked bursts.

Sarah flung the girl's arm, and Joy stumbled away, her back ramming into her wall.

"My twenty-dollar-bill. I know you have it. It wouldn't have just gone missing. I know you've been stealing from me."

Sarah's breath smelt of Misty menthol green cigarettes, her spittle spraying the room along with her accusations. Joy shook her head. The sun had long since set, casting shadows on Sarah's face, highlighting the depth of her wrinkles and the enraged crease of her brow.

"I didn't take anything," Joy ground out, crossing her shaking arms across her chest in a show of defiance that she knew wasn't very convincing.

Sarah cocked her head to the side. "Are you calling me a liar?

Her tone was even, deadly. Any courage Joy had mustered up deserted her, leaving her cowering alone in the corner of her room.

"You're pathetic," Sarah scoffed. "Stealing from me and thinking you can get away with lying about it. I've been too nice to you, given you too much, and now you're a spoiled little bitch. If I don't get my money back, I'm taking everything back. No more phone. No more playing sports. You will come home every day and clean and do homework and go to bed. I'll take your clothes and your cheap, Dollar Store makeup. You will wear only what I tell you to, go only where I tell you to."

Sarah kicked out, scattering Joy's things around the room. Her CD player crashed into her desk, the lid shattering and falling to the side. Sarah's head cocked to the side, and she grinned. She kicked again, aiming at Joy's makeup bag. Her powder cracked open, the fine dust coating all of Joy's clothing in an orange grime.

Sarah paused as the front door opened, Tom shouting his usual greeting. Joy didn't say anything, but Sarah called for him to join her in Joy's room. It filled Joy with hope, assuming that Tom would calm her grandmother down like he always did.

He stepped into the room, listened while Sarah told him that Joy had stolen from her, and sighed.

She waited for him to ask for her side of the story, to apologize for Sarah's rash actions.

He didn't.

He turned his tired eyes to Joy and quietly asked, "Did you take the money?"

In that moment, Joy learned that family could break her heart far worse than any man could.

She was sick of wanting more from the adults in her life, sick of blaming herself for those who let her down, desperate to escape this house.

Above all, Joy was tired. She had long since taken over the cooking and cleaning, especially during the summer months. She was the one who helped Clara with her homework after school. Tom wouldn't be home until at least six, sometimes later, and they didn't want to bother him when he did get home. She clipped coupons from the paper and scrounged for quarters to buy snacks from the local convenience store.

She was growing up, but she was had to do so on her own while also helping Clara and looking after the house. Sarah had always emphasized the importance of image. She told Joy that Joy was plain looking and that she would have to try harder to catch a boy's attention. She bragged about Joy's intelligence to her friends, but warned her that boys wouldn't like her if she was too smart. Joy wasn't sure she even wanted a boy's attention, but she did want her grandmother to be proud of her, so she began focusing on her appearance.

She spent an entire summer scouring fashion magazines at

the local library, watching YouTube videos to learn to do her hair and makeup, and even stayed with Trini for a few days, babysitting her kids so she could save up money to shop at the local Goodwill. Trini had surprised her and Clara at the end of the summer by offering to take the girls on a shopping trip. Joy cried, for the first time in a long time, because she was so excited to be getting new clothes.

The day of the trip, Joy knew something was wrong. There was a storm brewing in her grandmother's eyes as they loaded into Trini's SUV and drove to the nearest town. When Joy would get excited about a piece of clothing, her grandmother would tell her it was too expensive, that she was being selfish. When Clara asked for a new backpack, as hers was a few years old, her grandmother had yanked it from her hand and put it back on the shelf.

Both girls held back tears, clutching onto Trini a bit longer than usual as they said their goodbyes. Sarah had rolled her eyes when Tom had asked for a fashion show when they got home with their new clothes. She stomped back to her room and refused to answer as he tapped softly on the door and begged her to open up.

The morning before school started, Joy stared in the mirror, focused on the small red bumps that had popped up on her forehead. Sarah told her she wasn't washing her face correctly, that the acne was her fault, and she should learn to cover it up. Starting the next day, she refused to leave her house without at least two layers of foundation. Not that Sarah had taught her, or even offered to teach her, how to do makeup—she hadn't even taught her how to take care of her hair properly or how to use a tampon after her periods.

Sarah had tossed her a book about puberty and told her that YouTube had a lot of tutorials for doing makeup. The makeup was easily two shades darker than it should have been, an orange against her pale neck. But it was enough for her grandmother to leave her skin alone. Joy knew better than to wish for more than just enough.

CHAPTER 20

Joy woke slowly, grimacing and struggling to focus in the darkness. She was in her old bedroom at her grandparents' house, but didn't think to question this in her sleep-addled state. Sitting up, she looked around. There was only a single source of light in the room, a candle placed on a table near the door. She brought her hand up, reaching for the lamp that she knew sat on the desk next to her bed. The switch twisted, a soft clicking filling the otherwise unnatural silence, but the light remained off. She reached out blindly, tapping along the desk, in an attempt to find her phone.

Finding nothing, she stepped off of the bed. Joy cried out as something sharp embedded itself into her foot. She brushed the ground surrounding her foot with her hand and found it covered in shards of what she assumed was shattered glass. Pieces of fabric and something rough and plastic-like were mixed in with the glass. It was familiar, Joy thought, this setting, the bits of material scattered around the room.

Grabbing a piece of the fabric and the rough object, Joy retreated onto her bed, cradling her injured foot in her empty hand. Something glinted in the dim candlelight, a fleck of something other than her pale skin. She pinched the foreign object with her fingers, hissing as drops of blood fell onto the bedspread. Tears formed in her eyes as she, fingertip by fingertip, removed it from her foot. Inch after inch, it tore through her flesh until finally, she held a piece of glass roughly the size of her index finger.

She crawled forward on her bed, careful to keep her injured foot from pressing against the blankets. If she got any more blood on her covers, she wouldn't be able to hide it, and her grandmother would be mad. She was tired, too tired to deal with her anger.

She inched toward the candle, glass shard, plastic object, and fabric strip in hand, and stretched her body to reach the flickering flame. She held the pieces up to the light. There was a fluttering in her stomach, not the butterflies that come with attraction, but the discomfort of feeling like you've forgotten something, that there was a piece you were missing. The fabric was gray and polyester. The material was so familiar to her touch, as if it were something she used daily. The rough object was more papery than it was plastic, a dark green and the shape of half of a pine tree. With trembling fingers, she lifted it to her nose. It smelled woodsy with a slight citrus undertone.

A seatbelt. A car freshener. An image flashed through her mind of a lonely man sitting in his car, an action he would never come back from and a granddaughter who would never see him again.

She lost her balance, flailing for a few seconds before slipping off the bed and falling onto her back. She screamed as at least a dozen pieces of broken glass bit into her back and arms. She forced herself to lie still, unable to move without agitating the shards in her body.

Rolling to her side, she bit her lip harshly to prevent herself from screaming again. She groaned quietly as she hauled herself to her hands and knees. Glass scraped against her palms as she pushed aside the pieces in front of her and crawled through the shadows to the door of her bedroom. Sweat fell down her face, mixing with the blood on her back and arms to create a grimy paste.

"Ethan..." Joy croaked out, her voice groggy and thick with blood from biting her lip. Images of the tall man flashed through her head, confusing her. Why would Ethan be here? Could he hear her? Could he find her in this place he had never visited?

Joy's head spun as she approached the door. She shook violently, her arms nearly buckling under the weight of her body as she dragged herself forward. Glass shifted in her body with every movement, some pieces pulling loose and dropping to the floor while others sunk deeper into her skin. Her arm desperately reached upward, fingertips brushing against the doorknob before falling back to her side. A voice laughed mockingly. Her head snapped forward at the sound, squinting at the outline of a figure standing in the darkness she faced.

"Who's there?" Joy whispered.

Adrenaline racing through her body, Joy leaned back to the candle, grabbing it with one hand and thrusting it toward the figure. Joy kneeled in front of the mirror. Her grandfather's image stared down at her from the mirror hanging on her door. He stood, his tall frame leaning over Joy as if it might touch her at any moment. The wax from the candle dripped onto her hand, but she couldn't feel its heat. Joy's eyes were glued to her grandfather's face. His eyes were pitch black, and a sad smile stretched across his mouth. The reflection's head cocked unnaturally to the side, and his eyebrows drew down, as if confused by her fear.

Joy gripped the candle harshly, waving its flame threateningly at the image. She scooted back, legs dragging along the glass and leaving trails of blood.

"Where were you?" her grandfather asked.

Joy shook her head.

"I'm sorry," she whimpered.

"You could have saved me," the reflection accused, its voice causing the mirror to shake. "Did I not deserve to live?"

Joy's vision grew black, her breath coming out in panicked puffs.

"You knew. You could have stayed. But you chose yourself. Selfish, even in the most desperate of times," he chastised.

The mirror fell from the door, the glass shattering on the floor. Her grandfather crawled out from underneath the mirror's frame. He stood, his head brushing against the ceiling of the room. Joy sobbed. Her whole body trembled as she picked up a piece of the broken glass with her empty hand.

She squeezed her eyes shut.

She heard a footstep.

Then another.

"Why do you seem so sad, Joy?" he croaked out, his voice right beside her ear. She felt his breath brush against her hair, the strand sticking in the sweat of her face. "Isn't this what you wanted? To get away from me?"

"No," she gasped out, refusing to open her eyes. "It was never you. I'm sorry. I would never have left if I had known. I'm sorry. I'm so sorry. It's my fault. I know it's my fault."

A hand patted her on the head, just like he used to do when she was a child. "You're just like her. You can't escape it. You inherited her darkness, her anger."

Joy wanted to scream, to deny it, but she found she couldn't. How could she say she didn't inherit a darkness when she hurt the first person to truly care about her, hurt him to the point of no return?

The hand retreated from her head, and silence fell over the room. She waited a few minutes, but nothing happened. She opened her eyes, her heart thudding in her chest. Black, empty eyes met her weeping blue ones, his face only inches from hers.

"You belong with me, here in the darkness," he whispered before his free hand pinched out the candle's flame.

* * *

Joy woke in a cold sweat. She bolted from the bed, tripping as her feet tangled with the blankets, and landed on her hands and knees. She looked up, eyes meeting her reflection in the mirror. She screamed, scampering backward on all fours until her back hit the dresser. She squeezed her eyelids together tightly, shaking her head as tears dripped down her face. The door creaked open, but Joy only curled herself inward further, arms around her legs and head between her knees.

"Joy?" a familiar voice questioned as footsteps filled the room.

Her eyes were wild as she looked up, unfocused and searching. She looked straight through the figure in front of her, shaking wildly.

"Joy. Hey, it's okay..." The voice said. "It was just a dream, you're okay."

A hand stretched out, gripping her arm. She shrieked, flinging herself to the side. Her ribs rammed into the handles of the dresser, and she groaned. Her hands covered her ears as her trembling form rocked back and forth.

"Joy. It's Ethan. You're okay," the voice affirmed. Joy could feel someone squatting beside her, hands hovering over her body as they hesitated to hold her.

"It was... I couldn't," Joy sobbed, "glass... and dark. The mirror... I..."

Joy relaxed as she looked up and met warm brown eyes. Ethan crouched beside her, his brown hair mussed and eyes half-lidded from sleep. Seeing that she recognized him, Ethan grabbed onto her arms and pulled her up into a warm embrace.

"You're okay... it wasn't real. It wasn't real," he murmured, pressing his lips gently against her head.

Joy burrowed herself into his neck, tears forming not out of fear but embarrassment. "It wasn't real?"

Ethan nodded. "It wasn't real."

Quiet enveloped the room as she breathed deeply. Ethan didn't move, didn't loosen his grip or mention the warm tears soaking through his shirt. He rested his chin on her head, breathing steadily in an attempt to help her continue to do the same. She felt ashamed. She wanted to run and hide in the bathroom or shove him out of the bedroom.

She started to wiggle, trying to free herself, but Ethan's arms only tightened. She sighed, letting her body go limp as he walked them both back to her bed. Goosebumps slid down the back of her neck as she blinked sleepily. She tilted her head back and closed her eyes, enjoying the tranquility of the moment.

"Joy," Ethan warned as he set her back onto her bed, "I'm going to go get you some water and an ibuprofen. You hit the dresser with your ribs pretty hard, and I'm sure you're going to have a hell of a headache from crying. You're okay. I'll be right back."

He held her hand a few moments, squeezed tightly, then dashed out of the room. Her stomach churned as she watched him leave, her anxious thoughts returning along with the fear. Her chest tightened as she remembered the nightmare. She gasped and clutched her hand over her heart.

The nightmares had started the night she found out about her grandfather's death. She thought about telling someone, but she was afraid she would be told she deserved the nightmares—that his death was really her fault.

She was also afraid no one would be able to relate. That even if she brought it up, they wouldn't want to talk about it. It was even worse now, even more difficult to talk about, as she thought everyone had moved on. There was no one she could talk to without feeling like a burden. Not Ethan with his loving parents and happy childhood. Not Trini with her new family and upcoming wedding. Not even Clara, with her desperate desire to escape the past, to become more than their shared trauma.

And so, like everything else she felt, she pushed it down, rocked herself back to sleep on some nights and brewed a cup of coffee to keep her awake on others.

Ethan returned, a mug of water and a few small pills in hand. She chugged the drink and threw back the medicine.

"It's okay," soothed Ethan, rubbing his thumb soothingly across her hand, "give it a minute."

Joy took a couple of deep breaths, her constricted torso loosening and stomach settling. She withdrew her hand from Ethan's grasp, the tips of her ears turning red as she averted her gaze. Ethan cleared his throat, taking a few steps back and gesturing toward the door.

"I'm gonna make us some tea," he said. "If you don't think you can go back to sleep, you can come with me. I'll put some cartoons on the TV in the breakfast nook while we wait."

Joy nodded her head, standing and walking toward the open door. She paused in the doorway, turning to meet Ethan's eyes.

"I don't know what you did earlier, but thank you. I don't think I would have been able to calm down on my own," Joy confessed, her cheeks tinting alongside her ears.

Ethan smiled gently before following her. Joy tried to watch the old cartoon playing but found her thoughts drifting back to the nightmare.

"Do you... uh?" he started as he set the drinks down and sat across from her.

Joy raised her eyebrows. "Do I?"

"Do you want to talk about it? The nightmare, I mean? Was it about the guy who tried to break in?"

The mug stopped in front of her lips.

"Yeah," she nodded. "It was about him."

Ethan nodded back. He sat and watched the cartoon for a few moments as they sipped on their drinks. His eyes lit up.

"I know something that could help!"

***

"I feel stupid," Joy said, standing in front of Ethan's projector in her pajamas.

Ethan stood a few feet away in Darth Vader pajama pants and an old t-shirt. She shifted her weight from one leg to the other and debated running back to her bedroom to grab a pair of socks. Her feet were freezing on the hardwood floor.

She took a deep breath, eyes closed as she listened to Ethan tap on his laptop. He muttered under his breath as he scrolled through the app he had opened. The fan above them was whirling slowly. A piece of her hair fell out from her bun and tickled her nose. Ethan laughed as she wrinkled it. She cracked her neck before opening her eyes.

"Learning self-defense will not only help you physically in a fight, but it'll also increase your confidence, should you ever get into a bad situation." Ethan tapped beside his eye, then beside his nose and throat, and finally his upper thigh. "You'll want to aim at the weakest points, especially the groin and throat. People in action movies go for the chest or the knees, but these spots aren't nearly as effective."

His voice seemed odd, too loud and excited for the still of the night. It was almost three in the morning, a fact Joy grimaced at as she stifled a yawn.

"You sound like a cheesy self-defense instructor. Like one of those ones from the really bad commercials that people react to on YouTube. Where did you even learn that?"

Ethan hunched over the laptop, hiding his face. Joy noted the tips of his ears turning a slight pink.

He flipped the projector on. Joy shielded her eyes at the brightness of the video on the screen.

"YouTube video," he mumbled with a sheepish grin.

Joy shot him a skeptical look.

"It's actually really empowering!" Ethan defended, pressing the button to start the video. "Just give it a chance."

Ethan took a few steps back as cheery intro music burst from the speakers.

"Keep your hands around your face. I'm sure you've noticed that boxers keep their gloves covering their face—this is super important. You want to be able to block the vulnerable spots I mentioned earlier. Luckily, you don't have an...um..." Ethan cleared his throat, his cheeks growing pink. "You know, so your focus should be on your face and throat."

Joy laughed and turned to face him while casting occasional glances at the screen. A man stood in a dojo of some sort, his white robes tied together with a black belt. He bowed at the camera, then gestured forward. Another man, slightly younger, stepped forward, bowed, then turned to the instructor.

"Start with your knees slightly bent, it'll help give you a solid base," the first man said, his legs shoulder length apart and knees bent. "Drive your knee up, extend your leg while leaning slightly back, and kick. You'll want to make contact with either your shin or the ball of your foot."

Joy mimicked the motion, legs bent and leaning, then kicked her foot up at Ethan, who was still staring at the screen. He whipped around in time to see her foot flying at him. He blocked her leg with his arm, laughing as she apologized profusely.

"You don't have to worry about me," Ethan grinned. "I'm not afraid of a little kick."

He released her leg, and she stumbled. He grabbed her by the waist, steadying her for a few seconds before letting go.

"If your opponent is too close to kick or punch, you can use your elbow," the instructor continued.

Ethan bent his arm at his elbow, shifting his weight from his back leg to the front as he swung his arm swiftly. Joy copied the motion.

"Now, if they're behind you," the instructor stood behind the second man, guiding him through the next action, "you can still use your elbow." The instructor placed his hand on the other man's arm, bending it at the elbow and pulling it back toward him. "Just rotate your hips and pivot on one foot."

Ethan jogged backward, positioning himself behind Joy.

Ethan tapped her arm, signaling her to try. She swung her elbow, twirling on one foot. He caught it easily and nodded his approval.

"That was awesome! I could feel the force on that one.

Rotating gives you a bit more momentum."

"What about if they already have a hold of me?" The second man asked, staring directly at the camera instead of the instructor. The question was obviously scripted, but Joy's mind flashed to hiding in her bathroom, to being afraid he would find a way in and grab her.

"That's a great question!" the instructor replied enthusiastically, shooting the camera a thumbs up. Joy snorted. "If it's from the front, I would say go for the eyes or throat. You can use your thumbs, or you could use the palm of your hand and strike at their nose. If nothing else, their eyes will water, and it'll be a good chance to escape. If it's from behind, there's a way to get out of it. Let me walk you through the steps."

Ethan mimicked the actions of the instructor, stepping closer behind Joy. She was deep in thought as she ran through all the techniques they had shown her so far.

"I'm going to put my arms around your waist, is that okay?" Ethan asked.

Joy nodded again, gulping slightly. Ethan wrapped his arms around her, bending his knees and pulling her into him. He pressed his chest to her back, his warm breath tickling her ear.

"You want to create space to get free, so the first step would be to get low. Bend at your hips—" The man instructed as Ethan moved one arm from Joy's stomach and tapped at her hip—"and throw your elbow back like I demonstrated earlier. Leaning forward will shift your weight, making it harder for someone to pick you up and giving you room to create the momentum you need for your swing."

Joy bent at her waist and knees. She twisted her body, throwing her elbow forward. Ethan released, taking a few quick steps back as Joy's arm passed through the empty space.

"If they have your hands wrapped up too, you can do the same thing, but kick or drive your knee up instead."

Joy practiced a few times on her own, twisting her body and changing between attacking with her arm, knee, and leg. She grinned as she sparred with Ethan, her confidence building as she swung through the motions. Ethan's phone dinged somewhere in the apartment, distracting him for a second as Joy's elbow connected with his cheek.

"Oh, shit," Joy murmured. "I'm so sorry."

Ethan chuckled, lifting his hand to rub at the spot. Joy stepped up to him, her fingertips brushing the red area. Ethan stepped back, cheeks pink, and cleared his throat.

"I'm fine. Maybe we should try and get some sleep, though? It's been a long night, and I know you have work tomorrow."

Joy nodded. She knew she wasn't going to be able to go back to sleep, having already resigned herself to another night sustained by caffeine, but felt guilty that she was keeping Ethan up. Ethan studied her, searching her face for something. He had a way of knowing what she was thinking that both comforted and unnerved her.

"How about a movie, then? *Princess Bride*?"

She couldn't help but smile. On top of being able to read her like a book, he always seemed to remember even the smallest things she told him. *The Princess Bride* was her favorite movie and had been since she first watched it with her grandfather as a child. She could practically quote the entire thing. She nodded eagerly.

Ethan grinned. "I'll pull it up then."

The two sat on the couch, the opening scene of the movie playing on the projector. A white fuzzy blanket was pulled over their legs. Joy's head rested on Ethan's shoulder as they watched. After a few minutes, Joy's eyes began to feel heavy. She heard Ethan whisper her name as they shut, but couldn't find the energy to respond, instead falling into a deep sleep.

CHAPTER 21

Joy, Age 12

"Joy Hayes to the principal's office, please. Joy Hayes to the principal's office."

Joy frowned as the announcement echoed through the classroom. A few kids laughed, "oohing" dramatically.

"Take your bag with you. The period is about to end," her teacher said, nodding at the girl.

Joy slung her backpack over her shoulder and walked across campus to the admin building. She was in the spring semester of seventh grade now, shoulders perpetually hunched with all that she had learned.

She learned it was best not to talk back to her grandmother, to quietly do as she asked, no matter how unreasonable the task was.

She learned not to eat the snacks on the bottom shelf of the pantry or the sodas in the fridge. Those were reserved for her grandmother.

She learned how to scrounge for quarters in the couch. If she was able to find two or three, she could walk a few blocks to the grocery store and buy herself and Clara a granola bar or brownie to split.

She learned how to find the best school supplies in the piles outside of random churches. Her family was not religious, but the churches offered free school supplies to the kids who needed it.

She learned many teachers were kind, buying her basketball shoes when she showed interest in the sport and coats and blankets in the winter.

She learned it was embarrassing to be poor, to accept help from others, and that she should be ashamed that most of her clothes were hand-me-downs from a friend. Trini had taken them school shopping the summer before seventh grade began, but she had soon outgrown the pants and shirts that had been bought, growing multiple inches in a few months. She was left with a pair of jeans, a pair of sweatpants, and basketball shorts along with a dozen or so shirts.

She had been so excited when the friend's mother had dropped by the house, a garbage bag filled with clothes in hand. Her grandmother had mocked her for her excitement, labeling it pathetic to accept such things.

"We give you everything we can, and that's still not enough for you. Selfish little brat," Sarah had said, pushing her freshly dyed hair out of her eyes. There always seemed to be enough money in the budget for her monthly salon visits, multiple packs of cigarettes a week, and the payment for the shiny red car in the driveway that was only driven once a month. There was not enough, however, for Joy to get volleyball knee pads, cash for field trips, or something else. These were little luxuries not allowed for a child on a graphic artist's income.

Sarah took the garbage bag into her own room, shutting herself in for about an hour before tossing it onto Joy's bed. Joy noticed that the bag seemed a lot lighter than it had. Joy also noticed Sarah wearing new clothes, nice jeans, slightly too big, held to her bony hips by a belt Joy had never seen before.

Entering the principal's office, she saw not her principal but a woman with a clipboard, her blonde hair slicked back into a tight ponytail, a sympathetic smile on her lips, and a coffee stain on her white blouse. She held out a hand to Joy.

"Hi." Joy forgot the woman's name as years passed but remembered the firm handshake, the way she set the clipboard down as she introduced herself. "I'm from CPS. If it's okay, I'd like to ask you a few questions."

Joy answered the questions truthfully, outlining what her homelife was like, describing in detail all of the things Sarah had put her and her sister through. She talked about her mom, how she randomly popped in and out of her life, usually with the presence of drugs and a boyfriend that scared the two sisters.

She talked about Tom, how she didn't want him to get in trouble because he was doing his best. She told the woman how he worked multiple jobs, late into the evening and on most weekends.

Everything tumbled out of her, all of the trauma and hurt from the last few years. By the time she finished, the school day was almost over and her eyes stung from crying. The CPS worker had been patient, listening and taking notes after every question. She told the girl that they were going to visit her house soon, and suggested she not mention it to their grandmother. Joy thought that maybe it was the end for the sisters, that they would be placed somewhere else, maybe even with Trini and Connor.

Then, she fucked up. Her grandmother had been on the warpath, screaming at the two girls about anything and everything. Nothing seemed to soothe her rage, not offering to clean the house, not apologies, not even a call to their grandfather, who was spending a late night at work and didn't answer the phone. They had no clue what set her off, having returned to old sheet music strewn around their living room, a guitar lying halfway off the couch, a harmonica on the floor.

Sarah was smart and had always been clever about her abuse. She had never raised a hand to the girls, always justifying the physical as spankings for being "bad," belts swung in what was deemed as righteous anger. Today was different. There was a look in her eye, crazed and unbridled, her usual stoic mask shattered by rage.

Joy thought about taking Clara and running, going to the neighbors, and calling 911. But what then? Would Tom also get in trouble? She didn't want that. So the girls stayed quiet, trying to make themselves small and unnoticeable. It didn't help; their avoidance only seemed to fuel the anger. For the first time, Sarah raised a hand at Clara, who had spilled the water she was trying to drink.

"This is why CPS is coming!" Joy shouted in fear, desperate for Sarah's attention to turn away from her sister.

Sarah's hand stilled. Her head turned slowly.

"What?" she asked, voice calm.

Joy shook her head. Sarah walked over to her.

"Joy, did you say CPS was coming?" she asked again, leaning close enough to Joy that she could smell her cheap perfume and the cigarette she had smoked earlier that day.

Joy hesitated. The news seemed to have reduced her anger, a perfect calm replacing it. She nodded slowly.

Sarah patted Joy's head. "Thank you for telling me."

She walked away, retreating to her room. Joy and Clara exchanged confused looks.

Sarah spent the next few days coaching the girls on what to say as they waited for the CPS officer to make her home visit. She had informed their grandfather, who pulled them into tight hugs before apologizing and promising that things would be better from then on.

The visit came and went, the girls answering questions perfectly as the worker walked around the spotless house. After the fit in which Sarah had gone through all of Joy's things, Joy and Trini had been speaking more frequently. It was decided not long after the visit that the girls would move in with Trini and Connor, who had two small children of their own, as they could provide a better life for the two girls.

Joy had cried as she packed her things into boxes. She was excited for a chance to start over, to live a normal life, but she was also sad. She didn't want to leave her grandfather, not here, not with her. They both cried as they said their goodbyes, loading into Connor's truck and watching as the house and their grandfather's sad eyes faded into the distance.

CHAPTER 22

Joy woke to the smell of smoke and a black haze drifting along the white ceiling.

Her neck ached from its awkward position pressed into the arm of the couch, but she ignored it and the dull throbbing in her back and jerked up and onto her feet. She sprinted toward the source, nearly tripping over Panda as the black cat darted away from the kitchen. Ethan stood in the middle of the kitchen, rubbing his neck as he glared at the stove.

"What happened?" Joy asked, startling Ethan.

Joy rubbed the sleep from her eyes while Ethan stepped forward, blocking the oven from her view.

"Uh," he stammered.

Joy glanced from Ethan to the stove, the smell of burnt plastic assaulting her senses. Ethan sighed as Joy wrinkled her nose.

"H-E-B sells premade pancakes in these little tubs. It said they were best heated in the oven, so I popped them in and—"

"And you didn't take them out of the plastic container?"

"It didn't say to!"

Joy frowned, pushing Ethan to the side and opening the oven to reveal black plastic dripping down the metal bars. She reached forward, hissing at the heat.

"Ethan, did you not..." She popped her head up and narrowed her eyes at the oven display. "You have to turn the oven off! Why is it still on!"

"I panicked! I smelled it starting to burn and thought I had left it in there too long, but then I saw the plastic melting and didn't know what to do, so I shut the door and—"

A knock on the door interrupted Ethan. Shoulders slumping, he walked to the front, opened the door, and grabbed the paper bag sitting on his doormat.

"Then I ordered Uber Eats," he mumbled.

Joy stood and flipped the oven off. She looked at the oven. She looked at Ethan. Her shoulders began to shake, a squeak escaping her lips as she turned her back to him.

"Are you.... Are you laughing at me?" Ethan gasped, placing his hands on his hips.

The fire alarm blared from the wall above, and Joy lost her composure as the wailing filled the apartment. She burst out into laughter, tears running down her cheeks. She snorted, then laughed harder at herself for snorting, which made her snort again. Ethan stared at her for a few seconds, cheeks flushing pink, before he moved to turn the fire alarm off. Joy shook her head, practically wheezing, and opened the living room window. The two fanned at the smoke, trying to rid the apartment of the toxic cloud the melted plastic had created.

Ethan glared at her, and she raised her hands in mock surrender. "I didn't say anything!"

He flung her hood up, grabbed her jacket strings, and yanked, knotting them tightly under her chin. Joy flailed about blindly, bumping her knees into the coffee table and clawing at the hoodie. Ethan placed his hand on the small of her back, guiding her to the couch and avoiding her hands as she swatted at him.

"You're in timeout while I plate up the food. Sit there and think about how you've made a mockery of my failure."

"Joke's on you, now I can't smell the stench of your failure," Joy jested, her voice muffled by the cotton.

"What was that?" Ethan called from the other room.

"Nothing..." Joy mumbled.

Resigned to her fate, she flopped sideways onto the couch like a fish, head landing on the throw pillow she knew was on the far edge. Ethan returned a few minutes later, graciously untying the hoodie from around her face and passing her a plate of pancakes. They watched TV while they ate, chatting casually about the day's plans before Joy noticed the time on the clock and leaped up to get ready.

"Joy." Ethan sighed, pinching his nose and shaking his head while watching Joy try and leave the apartment. "How do you even see like that?"

"Like what?" she questioned, juggling her lunch, phone, keys, and a binder of documents she needed for the day. She swung her elbows out wide, shuffling the items in her arms to prevent them from falling as Ethan plucked the glasses off her face.

He disappeared back into the apartment. Coming back, he gently guided the frames back onto her face. She grinned sheepishly at her improved vision, so used to her glasses being dirty that she didn't even think about it anymore.

"Thanks."

Ethan patted her head, smoothing out the frizzy strands escaping her half-assed bun. "Welcome."

Ethan locked the door behind him, scooping the binder and Joy's lunch out of her arms as she fumbled to grab her ringing phone.

She answered without bothering to check who it was first, a habit that had left her in quite a few stand-offs with debt collectors and one really awkward conversation with a man who was trying to sell weed to the person who had previously had her number.

"Hello?" she asked.

"Joy?" Trini's voice asked back.

Trini calling was odd. Trini hated speaking over the phone, something she and Joy shared. A solid text, Snapchat, or even email was a thousand times more likely between the two most socially anxious members of the family. Messages were nice, Joy reckoned, because she had time to think about her response, to craft exactly what she wanted to say, to not look like the complete and utter asshole she was. The last time Trini had called Joy, it had been a group video chat with all of her siblings, which was even weirder than Trini calling only Joy.

Joy had nervously blurted out, "Are you pregnant?" and then rattled on for a solid minute about how babies freaked her out and how kids in horror movies were always the worst because you couldn't just bitch slap them like you could a possessed adult without looking like a jackass or getting arrested.

The call had gone silent as Trini blinked in confusion. Trini definitely wasn't pregnant; she just wanted to share that she and Jonas had gotten engaged, which everyone but Joy, as the only family member not still living in their small town, was expecting.

Trini started by asking Joy how she was, if the insurance was going to cover the window replacement, if she felt safe staying at Ethan's, and if she needed to drive up to Austin to give Joy one of her spare pistols for protection. Her rambling was oddly comforting to Joy, who assured her mother that she was fine, her savings had paid for the window, Ethan was the biggest teddy bear she knew, and no, driving to Austin to give her a weapon was not necessary.

"You with a gun is a terrifying thought," Ethan mumbled as the two walked to his car.

Joy could practically hear the grin in Trini's voice. "Is that Ethan?"

She hummed in affirmation.

"Is Ethan coming?"

Ethan cocked his head to the side. He opened the door to the backseat for Joy, allowing her to dump her stuff and walk around to the passenger side.

"Coming to what?" Ethan asked.

"Trini's wedding," Joy whispered back, pulling the phone away from her cheek for a brief second before returning it.

"Trini, I doubt Ethan would want to—"

"I'd love to?"

Joy looked at him as he slid into the driver's seat and raised her eyebrows.

"You would?"

"Yeah. Oliver has been texting me for weeks about wanting me to come down and look at his computer."

Something tugged at Joy's heart, a mixture of warning, jealousy, and affection. She thought it was adorable the two got along so well, but she couldn't help the envy that filled her when Ethan admitted he spoke to Oliver more than she did. She was also worried about Ethan and Oliver getting close, knowing that, eventually, Ethan would move on with his life when he realized Joy wasn't who he thought she was. In that moment, she didn't know how she'd be able to look Oliver in the eyes and tell him that Ethan wouldn't be coming around anymore. They would both lose him.

"Well, that settles it!" Trini exclaimed, warmth settling into her tone. "Y'all can have the upstairs guest bedroom. See you soon!"

Joy sighed. "You have no clue what you just signed up for."

* * *

A few hours later, Joy found herself at work, desperately trying to keep herself from looking at the new clock ticking on the wall. Nick had demanded the clock be replaced on one of his many walks through the office, declaring the cracked one didn't fit the "vibe" of the office. She popped in a headphone, listening to music while typing and retyping her out-of-office email. She figured "I'll be back eventually, bitches" probably wasn't the most professional response.

She and Ethan would be leaving for West Texas the next morning, with Ethan offering his car for the trip. Joy didn't think she was a bad driver, but the state trooper who pulled her over for speeding the day after getting a permit seemed to think she was, and Ethan wholeheartedly agreed.

Her phone buzzed beside her.

"I'm outside," the text from Ethan read. Joy grinned.

He had been driving her to and from work, insisting it made more economic sense for the two to carpool, even though campus was the opposite direction from her office. Living with him had been nice, comfortable even. Joy knew it was a dangerous move, spending so much time with him, but she was confident in her ability to shut down any growing feelings.

She turned off her computer and hopped up from her seat. Her keys jangled in her hand as she walked to the elevator and pressed the button for the ground floor. The elevator stopped only a single floor below, doors sliding open to reveal a waiting Keith. He looked tired, slouched over the phone in his hands, his eyes shaded by dark circles. He glanced up to see Joy staring expectantly, paled, pressed his lips together, and averted his gaze. Joy smirked.

"Going down?" Joy asked.

Keith nodded curtly, stepping into the elevator and fixing his attention on the closed door in front of him. He stood with shoulders tense and breath coming out in quick pants.

Joy leaned back, watching Keith try and avoid her eyes. Was she being cruel by relishing his discomfort?

No.

No, what? Joy thought back.

She tapped her fingers along the wall. Keith flinched with each sound.

It is not cruel. He has not been physically harmed. Yet.

Tap. Tap. Tap. A single stream of sweat dripped down Keith's neck, disappearing down his white shirt. One of his hands dipped into the pocket of his trousers, hand clenching around an unknown object.

Is cruelty defined as physical harm, then? If anything, I'd say inflicting fear can be just as cruel, Joy thought, and yet she did not stop herself from staring at the frightened man.

Although he may be afraid, he has inflicted far more suffering on others. Perhaps he will utilize his fear as a motivator for self-reflection.

Joy hummed in response. The sound startled Keith, and he jerked his hand out of his pocket, the object still clasped within his fingers. It slipped from his grip, metal clanking along the tile floor and skidding to a stop beside Joy's foot.

Joy looked at it, then looked up at Keith through the reflection of the elevator doors, one eyebrow raised. Keith shifted sideways, turning to look at the object: a rosary with golden beads and a silver cross. His body twitched like he was going to reach for it, but ultimately he shook his head and flipped to face the front of the elevator.

The elevator dinged, the doors sliding open on the bottom level. Joy bent down, intent on scooping up the rosary and handing it back to Keith. He held his breath in anticipation and took his phone out of his pocket. Joy didn't miss him hitting the record button on the device's camera. She hissed as she made contact with the cold metal of the cross, yanking her hand back as if it had burnt her and taking a small step back. Keith grinned in triumph, grabbing the object from the floor and holding it up to Joy, who allowed her eyes to widen in fear.

"I knew it!" he cried shrilly, his pitch high enough to make dogs bark while his mostly bald head flushed red. "You're possessed by the devil! These beads have been blessed by a priest and dipped in Holy water. I'll make you regret the day you crossed me, a man of God, you demonic slut."

Joy didn't bother pointing out the hypocrisy in Keith calling her a slut in the same breath he called himself a man of God. Instead, she burst into laughter, snorting as Keith recoiled in fear. She shot her hand out, fingers wrapping around Keith's hand and the cross.

"A man of God, huh?" Joy leaned in close, still holding the object, her warm breath caressing Keith's ear as he trembled beneath her touch. "Maybe I should put the wrath of God in you instead."

Keith shuddered, yanked his hand away, and sprinted in the opposite direction. Joy watched the five hairs he had combed over the top of his head flop to the rhythm of his footfalls as he turned the corner and out of sight. She smirked, pocketing the cross and scanning the parking garage for Ethan's car.

She lit up as she finally spotted it, her leer softening into a warm smile, and bounced over to his vehicle. He sat hunched over in the driver's seat, watching a YouTube video on the phone on his lap. Joy tapped on the glass, and he jumped, his phone slipping into the crevice between his seat and the center console. He groaned as he rolled down his window.

"You scared me. Ugh, it's going to be a pain to grab—"

"I WILL TRY AND SEDUCE THE DRAGON!" A voice shouted from the car's speaker system.

Joy burst out into laughter as Ethan cleared his throat. The apples of his cheeks blossomed red, and he bent to the side, hands desperately reaching for his phone.

"Okay. Roll the D20 to see if you succeed," a different voice directed.

Ethan hopped out of the car, kneeling beside the vehicle as his hand flailed around underneath the seat.

"A NATURAL 20! THE SEDUCTION IS SUCCESSFUL! Ballen leads the dragon further into the dungeon—"

Joy choked on her spit as she gasped out a scream of a laugh. Ethan reached upward, punching the power button for his stereo system. He popped up, phone in hand, and sighed.

"Any chance I can convince you to forget this?"

"Why would I ever want to forget a successful dragon seduction?" Joy giggled, walking around the car and getting into the passenger side.

Ethan only shook his head. The two chatted about their day, Ethan complaining about a group project he was assigned, and Joy detailing how her coworker fell asleep in the company break room after staying up all night playing a new video game.

"Did someone wake him up?" Ethan asked, flipping on the

blinker and turning into the movie theater's parking lot.

"Not on purpose." Joy snorted. "Carmen threw skittles at his open mouth until one finally made it in. He didn't even question it, just asked her for another piece."

* * *

"Popcorn?" Ethan asked, making a beeline for the concession stand.

"On your student budget?" Joy teased. "You sure know how to show a girl a good time."

Ethan winked, grabbing her hand and pulling Joy to the back of the line. Joy had noticed this was quickly becoming a habit of his, grabbing her hand and tugging her along with his every whim. She had long since decided she didn't mind it. In fact, if she was being honest with herself, it made something in her feel warm, content even. Not that she would ever admit that out loud. Or to herself.

"I live to please." Ethan tipped an imaginary hat, and Joy rolled her eyes. "Although, if I'm being honest, I only have $15, so popcorn and split a drink?"

Joy nodded. Ethan glanced longingly at the candy behind the glass counter.

"You know, I wouldn't mind paying. I'm a big working girl and whatnot," Joy offered.

He slung his arm over her shoulder.

"Absolutely not. I invited you on this best friend date and so I will be paying for it."

Joy's stomach twisted at the words. There was nothing wrong with what he said, nothing malicious in his tone. But every reminder of their friendship was a nudge away from being something more, a push away from the feelings she harbored. Had once harbored. She frowned, then pushed that emotion down.

Ethan stepped up to the counter, ordering a large popcorn and a large Diet Coke for the two to share.

"You don't even like Diet Coke?" Joy questioned quietly, leaning into him as the cashier scooped up the popcorn.

Ethan looked down at her, one eyebrow raised. "Yeah, but you like it. And I don't dislike it. It's just not my favorite."

Guilt shot through Joy, twisting and turning through her body, darkening her mood. Maybe she should have been happy that he remembered her favorites. No. She *should* be happy that he treated her this way. That was the normal response, the proper one. Anyone else would be excited that the person they cared for paid them so much attention. But as Ethan grabbed the drink, Joy couldn't help but feel scared.

Someday he will realize that he deserves better.

She stumbled behind Ethan as he happily chatted about the movie, oblivious to the turmoil she felt. Buttercup was right. One day Ethan would wake up and understand that he deserved so much more than her anger, than the demons she kept hidden from her everyday persona. If she wanted to keep Ethan, she had to be better.

And that could begin with…

Her eyes trailed to the boxes of candy hidden behind the glass display case.

Joy unzipped her purse and winced at the cold of Buttercup drifting from her fingertips. The candy, carried by Buttercup, floated around the counter, dropping unseen into her purse.

Ethan passed Joy the soda as they settled into their seat, and she put it into the coaster between their seats.

"I have no idea what this movie is about," Joy whispered.

Ethan nudged her shoulder. "It's almost like I texted you the trailer a few days ago."

Joy narrowed her eyes, grabbed her purse, and tugged out the candy tucked inside.

"Well, I was going to give you this, but…" Joy waved the snack.

Ethan's eyes lit up.

"But..?" he questioned, reaching across Joy for the candy.

She snapped it back and held it over her head.

"You've been very sassy."

"Sassy, huh?"

"Yeah. Sassy."

Ethan leaned closer, and Joy's breath caught in her chest at the sudden proximity. Not that she would ever let that show, save for the slight widening of her eyes. Instead, she stretched her arm out further and raised an eyebrow in defiance. Ethan scooted forward. His eyes dropped to her lips, one hand inching its way around her arm and up her spine, stopping only when it brushed the hairs on the back of her neck.

A child squealed behind the two, but neither flinched, both unyielding in their staredown.

WHAP.

The child rammed the back of Joy's seat as he ran by, the candy slipping from her fingers on impact. Ethan scooped it up and leaned back in his seat while Joy turned and glared at the sprinting child and his obvious lack of parental guidance. She flicked the wrist furthest from Ethan, Buttercup soaring from her in a mass of dark, petty vengeance. The mist smacked into the child's bag of popcorn, sending kernels flying through the theater.

Joy sank into her seat as the buttery snack landed amongst the seats and winced at the thought of some unfortunate employee having to pick it up. She flicked her wrist again, Buttercup following her order and gathering the popcorn into one large pile.

A quick glance over her shoulder confirmed the kid was staring at his fallen treat, his mouth flopping open and close like a prepping-for-a-meltdown fish. A shriek filled the air, followed by two parents sprinting from the entrance, cheeks red in embarrassment. Joy turned around and stared at her hands as Buttercup returned.

Ethan snorted and muttered something about "instant

karma." He turned to Joy, a small smile on his face that quickly slipped into a frown of concern.

"You okay?" he asked, nudging her shoulder with his own.

She wasn't upset about knocking the popcorn out of the kid's hands or making him cry. She couldn't care less about that. It was the action itself, the lack of control she felt as Buttercup acted on an intrusive thought. No. That wasn't quite right either.

It was the secret thrill that shot up her spine at the power she held, at not holding in her feelings, at allowing herself to lose control for a moment.

She forced a smile and pushed down her unease.

* * *

"I think you would be the vigilante type," Ethan declared as Joy exited the theater bathroom.

She frowned at him, brushing her wet hands against her jeans and cursing the electric dryers for never blowing hard enough to rid her of the damp feeling. The movie, ironically, had been about the daughter of a murdered mob boss who discovered she had superpowers and used them to track down the men who killed her family. A little cliche, in Joy's opinion.

"The vigilante type?" she asked.

"Yeah. If you had superpowers," he explained with a shrug. She flinched, but he continued. "In movies and comics, people go one of three ways: hero, vigilante, villain. I think the vigilante is the most realistic of the three. No decent person is suddenly going to go full villain, killing innocent people, stealing stuff, you get the idea. And there are very few people who would go full hero, not using their powers to their advantage. So what you're left with is the vigilantes, the ones who seek out people in revenge and make them suffer, but also just kinda do what they want."

Joy chewed on his words.

"But what if someone got superpowers and chose to do

nothing with them? Like did small things, but didn't go full Batman on people?"

"I'd say it's kinda a waste, especially if they got cool powers."

Ethan tossed their half-eaten popcorn in the trash, and the two walked into the brisk autumn night. Joy pulled her cardigan closer around her, fighting back a shiver as a gust of wind blew through her clothes.

"Okay, so say you get telekinesis. What would you do first?"

Ethan didn't even hesitate.

"I'd steal clown statues and put them in the houses of people I hate. I'd put a big one in their shower, small ones in their fridges and closets, and tuck another big one into their bed. Then set up a camera and catch their reactions. A hundred percent."

Joy nodded twice, half in approval of his diabolical scheme and half in contemplation.

"Where would you get the statues from?"

"Amusement parks. Collectors. Clown-themed restaurants." Joy's eyebrows shot up. "They exist. Trust me."

"You mean like McDonald's?"

"Among others. But I would put ole Ronald right by the toilet in the middle of the night. They get up to use the bathroom and McPee themselves."

Joy sighed at the bad pun, but she knew Ethan caught the way her lips fought back a smile.

"I can't imagine you hating anyone enough to do this. You're the kind of guy who pretty much likes everyone."

Ethan paused a few steps from his car. "I'd make enemies."

"You'd make enemies," Joy repeated. "Just random people or...?"

"I'll figure that out when the time comes."

Joy threw her head back in laughter, her sides squeezing as she gasped for air. "You're ridiculous."

"Then what would you use telekinesis for?"

She shrugged.

Save drowning kids, fight off assholes trying to break into my apartment, get you to notice me, she thought, feeling herself wilt in the artificial light of the slightly blinking movie theater sign.

"Probably stupid things," she said with a forced laugh. "Win arcade games. Steal candy from babies. The basics."

Ethan eyed her, watching her expression closely before bumping her shoulder.

"Lame."

Joy huffed and stalked forward, Ethan chuckling as he jogged to catch up.

"I'm sorry I don't feel the need to seek clown vengeance," she threw over her shoulder.

He quickly caught up, his long strides overtaking hers.

"Aw, don't be mad, Joy."

She looked up at him from underneath her eyelashes. "Wanna make it up to me?"

Ethan narrowed his eyes and hummed.

"Can I drive?" she asked sweetly, holding her hands out for the keys.

"As cute as you are, that's not gonna happen." He laughed, poking her forehead as it creased in indignation.

Joy started to defend her driving. She had only driven down a one-way twice since she moved to Austin, and really, who could blame her? She grew up driving on dirt roads and empty highways. The signs in the city could be confusing as hell. Especially those damn traffic circles. She paused her train of thought as she processed what he said, her cheeks quickly flushing red.

"You think I'm cute?" she blurted, then coughed, choking on her own spit at her blunt question.

"You're beautiful, Joy. You know that."

He said it as if he were describing the weather, an indisputable fact spoken with a kind smile and unwavering stare. She felt a flash of emotion, which she quickly stomped down. They were friends. Just friends. And friends can tell each other they're attractive. Compliments were normal. If it even was a genuine compliment. He could be just teasing her. Joy knew this and begged her heart to stop pounding so rapidly in her chest.

Ethan took a big gulp of the water he had smuggled from the theater, and Joy decided to play into his teasing with the cheesiest line she could think of.

She winked at him and said, "You're not too bad yourself, handsome."

Ethan sputtered, surprise causing him to almost drop his drink, and Joy laughed. They walked to his car in silence, both lost in thought. If Joy felt his hand brush against hers a few times, she didn't pull away, but also didn't move closer.

CHAPTER 23

Joy, Age 14

Although she now lived beyond her grandmother's reach, Joy still felt Sarah's roots in her everyday actions. She threw up at night, thinking no one heard her.

She had spent the last hour picking herself apart in the mirror, cursing the acne that never healed as she layered on foundation, the weight she never seemed to be able to lose from her thighs. She pinched at the fat, her eyes falling to the small strawberry patch on her left leg. It was a birthmark, a strip of red, raised skin that closely resembled a burn.

Joanne loved it, as she seemed to love all of Joy's flaws.

Not in a kind way, the way a mother should love their daughter. No, Joanne loved anything that made Joy imperfect, anything that proved that Joy wasn't as pretty or as smart as she was. Joanne loved being the most interesting person in the room more than she could ever love another person.

Sometimes Joy wondered about her mom. She wondered why her mother's love was conditional. She wondered if her mother even still thought of her after she moved in with Trini and Connor.

Secrets about Joy's life, about her family, were never revealed when they should have been. The things that put her at the most risk were hidden until it was far too late, and the things that would hurt her the most were told to her far too young. As with so many things that Joy wouldn't find out until she was older, her mother did think of her. Too much, actually. So much so that she threatened Trini, threatening to take Clara and Joy away from the life they were slowly getting accustomed to. So much so that Charlie, their uncle, had to drive around their small town to make sure no one had seen Joanne lately and had to patrol the roads to their house when the girls got home from school.

And now, Joy stood in front of the mirror, her head cocking to the side as she continued to look at herself, examining her reflection to see how much of her mother she had in her. She wondered how much she looked like the father she had never met. She wondered when the taste in her mouth, the bitter result of the vomit that still remained in the toilet, would fade. She was grateful it would fade, unlike the eyes she shared with her grandmother and the nose she shared with her mother. Those were constant, a permanent reminder of the past.

"Joy?" Connor tapped lightly on the bathroom door. "Are you alright?"

Joy flushed quickly, patting her cheeks and forcing a smile onto her lips as she cracked the door open.

"Yup!" she said.

"Were you throwing up?"

How incredibly blunt, and yet typical of Connor. He had no filter between his mouth and his words, often regretting the things he said mere seconds later.

She swallowed, opening the door slightly wider.

"Yeah. I think it might be the Takis. They're pretty spicy. They burn both going down and coming back up." She let out a strangled laugh.

She stared at Connor, daring him to question her. A part of her wished he would push it further. He didn't. He chuckled, stepping aside and letting her pass as she darted to her room.

"Maybe lay off the Takis next time!" he called after her.

She nodded, waving him goodnight, her lips twitching into an amused smile that fell as soon as her door shut.

As she lay in her bed that night, she couldn't help but wonder if the reaction would have been different if it were Caden or Oliver in that bathroom. If he might have been more assertive, worried instead of playful. When you're young, you notice even the smallest differences in how you're treated. You notice how your grandparents yell and cheer for your cousins at sports events but sit quietly for your games. You notice how your dad never attended your tennis matches, even those on the weekend, but took off work to see your younger sister's games. You notice how much money is being spent on your siblings, how there always seems to be a new vehicle in the driveway, parts for dirt bikes, new clothes in closets, while you're too scared to even ask for the things you need.

And maybe that was on Joy. Maybe she could have been more assertive. But the responsibility for her needs, even as a child, for reaching out and trying to connect with her family, always seemed to fall on her shoulders. That's possibly why Joy had never learned to call Trini and Connor "Mom" and "Dad." They never pressured her to do so, but she saw the joy in their eyes when she first referred to them as such and the disappointment when she stopped. She tried it out for a few weeks, but it never seemed to fit the relationship she had with them. Joy's image of motherhood was so tainted by Joanne and Sarah that she wasn't sure she could ever comfortably call someone her mom.

While Connor seemed to be ignorant of the effects of her past, Joy could tell that Trini knew, had maybe even experienced it herself. Joy's eyes might have been the color of Sarah's, but they held the depth of Trini's, the glint of being forced to grow up too young. Trini understood her, genuinely tried to be there for her, and Joy quickly found herself more comfortable with Trini than with Connor. Trini drove to all her games, took her and her friends prom dress shopping, would come home from working fifty-hour work weeks and beg for her and Clara to open up, to let her in.

She sat for hours at the foot of their beds, pleading with them to talk to her, only to be met with blank faces. Joy's empathy had been weaponized against her in the past, the love she gave twisted in manipulation as the situation called for it. Actions given by Joy in exchange for affection were taken as normative, used as a means of emotional blackmail when the need arose, and every time it was Joy who was left hurt when the debts of her love were never repaid. And so although she knew what Trini was feeling and could even see the vast distance Trini was trying to cross, she refused to meet her halfway. Sarah had taught them that silence was better than words unheard, or even worse, thrown back in their faces, that love was not free of consequence, not to her.

Trini was still young, too young to have teenage daughters who never learned to communicate, and found herself discouraged by the lack of effort. She slipped back into the habits she had learned in her marriage with Connor, avoiding conflict, serving as the peacemaker when Connor and Joy butted heads. Joy didn't have the maturity to see it that way. Instead, she saw her grandfather in Trini, always there for her physically but always siding with her spouse, even when they were clearly in the wrong. In that way, Trini became Joy's second heartbreak.

Joy was never shown affection without a motive, and so she was suspicious of Trini and her pleas. She was always waiting for the other shoe to drop, for the motive to come creeping out of Trini, to strangle her desire for connection into a reality of submission, like an addict willing to do anything for another hit. She couldn't let herself get too comfortable, too reliant on her new family. If she slipped up, which she always did, they would leave too. She had to be ready when that moment came.

CHAPTER 24

"We can still turn around. Just because we're technically here doesn't mean we have to stay," Joy sighed as Ethan pulled into the gravel driveway of a large barndominium.

Trini's new home, which Joy hadn't seen since it was first being built, loomed over her, sending a shiver down her spine. Instead of ghosts, it was haunted by the screeches of children and the wisps of dirt that tended to blow straight from the cotton fields and into her lungs—an introvert with health problems worst nightmare.

Ethan raised his eyebrows.

"Do you not want me here?"

"I obviously do, but it's gonna be a lot." Joy placed her head in her hands. "They're a lot."

Ethan laughed. He stepped out of the car, jumping to the side to avoid a blond blur rushing by on a hoverboard, a large shaggy dog nipping at the child's heels.

"Hi, Joy, hi, Ethan!" the kid called over his shoulder, rolling down the concrete driveway and along the dirt road.

"Hi, Oliver," Joy yelled after her eleven-year-old brother, but he was already long gone. She shuddered at the dirt he kicked up, mentally reminding herself to take some Benadryl as soon as possible.

"You act like this is my first time meeting your family," Ethan said, watching Oliver for a few seconds before turning back to Joy. "I love being around them. It's interesting how different they are from my family."

"By different, you mean chaotic, don't you?"

Ethan shrugged. Trini stood in the doorway, a wide grin on her face. Her fiancé, Jonas, shouted at a child from somewhere inside. Joy's younger sister, Caden, appeared behind Trini. She was taller than Joy remembered, already taller than Trini at only fifteen years old, wearing ripped jeans, slightly too short for her long legs, and thick black eyeliner that matched her black band t-shirt. She sprinted from the house, practically shoving Trini to the side as she raced toward Ethan's car. Joy stretched her arms open, and Caden threw herself into them.

"Joy!" Caden exclaimed, pulling away. "Please save me from the boys. They're driving me fucking nuts."

"Language!" Trini scolded, rolling her eyes as she gave Joy and Ethan each a side hug.

Joy grinned and grabbed her bag from the back of the car.

"How's the wedding prep going? Anything I can do to help?"

"Nope," Trini said. She bounced in her spot, eyes lighting up as she thought of the wedding tomorrow. "The caterers will be here in the morning, and all the decorating has been done since yesterday. I couldn't sleep, so I stayed up last night doing it."

Pursing her lips, Joy stared down at Trini. She looked young, freckles standing out against smooth skin and blond hair pulled back underneath an old cap, but tired, dark circles prominent under green eyes. At thirty-five years old, Trini looked much younger than she had when Joy and Clara moved in with her at twenty-nine. She looked content, happy even.

"I know I look gross. I'll wash my hair and probably crash by like eight tonight. It'll be fine," Trini said, waving off Joy's worried expression.

She ushered Joy and Ethan into the house, pointing at a room for the pair to share. Joy would have been incredibly uncomfortable with the idea of sharing a room with anyone but Ethan. She liked her space and hated not having somewhere to go at the end of the night to decompress alone. Shockingly, she had been fine when they had to share a room at Trini's old house a few months back, had found some odd peace in the soothing rhythm of Ethan's breath as he slept.

They dropped their bags and wandered through the house, Joy admiring all of the work Trini had put into it. It was the perfect balance of comfort and country elegance: large glass windows, soft blankets and fluffy pillows strewn across the living room, frames with pictures of smiling faces scattered throughout. Ethan plopped down at the dining room table, hands dipping into a bowl of Cheese-Its. Caden sat across from them, passing Ethan an energy drink and Joy a bottle of sweet tea before filling them in on the drama at her high school.

"I hate it. I literally hate all of them. They're so fake and bland," Caden complained, rubbing at her eyes and wincing as her eyeliner smeared.

Ethan reached across the table, patting Caden on the head. She swatted his hand away, and he leaned back with a grin, stretching his legs out in front of him. His knee bumped into the table as he stretched, and he winced.

"The good news is, once you graduate, you never have to see them again," Joy reasoned, reaching for the bowl of snacks.

Glass shattered upstairs, and Caden rolled her eyes.

"Mom told you not to toss the football in the house!" she yelled, not bothering to stand.

"It was Max's fault!"

"It was Henry's fault!"

Two voices shouted at the same time. Footsteps raced down the stairs, the boys bickering as they rounded the corner to the kitchen. They stopped arguing for a second to greet Ethan and Joy before starting again.

"What happened to my grandmother's vase?" Trini bellowed from yet another part of the house.

The two boys paled, their eyes widening in terror. They sprinted through the back door while Trini walked into the kitchen.

"Your grandmother's vase?" Joy questioned. She knew Trini had inherited some china and artwork from her grandmother but had never heard of a vase.

Trini snorted. "I actually got it at Ross for like $5, but I was sick of listening to their fighting. They'll be too scared to come in for at least an hour."

She plopped down in the seat in front of Joy and stole the bowl of snacks.

"So, how's it going?" she asked Joy, tossing a Cheese-It in her mouth and raising her eyebrows expectantly.

Joy grinned. As much as she had resented Trini in her teenage years, as she grew older, she began to understand how Trini's life had shaped her parenting style, her relationships, her personality. Trini was born to a paramedic mother, Sarah, whose face darkened with barely concealed apathy, and an old-school cowboy father, who was rarely found without a cigarette between his lips. She was only five when Sarah was caught robbing their small town's pharmacy and court-ordered to attend rehab. Not long after that, her parents divorced, and Sarah left to live in a different part of the state. From then on, it was just her and her dad.

At eleven, her dad was arrested for a DWI, and his license was revoked. They lost the ranch she grew up on. After being diagnosed with a lung condition called COPD, her father lost his ability to work. Trini started working, often holding two to three jobs, to support herself and her father. Other kids her age were sweating from sports games and bodies pressed against each other at parties. She was sweating from the mascot suit at Chuck E. Cheese. Other kids her age spent their evenings doing homework and eating the dinners prepared for them by their mothers. She spent her evening waitressing and sneaking food from the plates she cleared into the trash. When her father lost their home and his job, she lost her childhood and her freedom but never her spirit. She loved her father deeply, but within days of her eighteenth birthday, she signed a lease for an apartment and refused to look back.

At nineteen and within a year of meeting, Trini and Connor found themselves dating, pregnant, engaged, and married. Caden was born five months after they were married, and Oliver was born a little over two years later. A few years after adopting Joy and Clara, Trini and Connor's marriage began to fall apart. Passiveness ran through Trini's veins, while defensiveness ran through Connor. Petty arguments became a toxic cocktail, and days of silence became their chaser. Emotional distance shifted to physical distance. Fights became longer. Nights together became shorter. Conflicts became more desperate, louder, as both felt that anything was better than the silence, better than acknowledging the simple truth that the relationship wasn't working.

There is a violent silence in the aftermath of two hearts colliding at too young an age. Trini was tired of being alone, tired of the cold, tired of pretending to be okay, and perhaps that is what led her to find comfort in the warmth of another.

She cheated. Plain and simple. Except, it wasn't simple, not to her splintering family and the judgmental stares of their small town, not to Joy. It hurt Joy when she found out, not that she would ever admit it. A part of Joy hated Trini for cheating on Connor, even with their complicated relationship, especially after seeing how much cheating had hurt her grandfather. But she pasted on a smile and moved on because, as much as it had been bitter for her to accept, it wasn't about her. Trini cheated on Connor with their neighbor, his best friend, and her high school sweetheart, Jonas. The same Jonas she was marrying the next day. The same Jonas who she built a house with, across the road from the house she once shared with Connor. It seemed cruel, and Joy felt bad for Connor. But Trini was happy, possibly the happiest Joy had ever seen her, and Joy wasn't going to mention it. She had moved on, but a part of Joy wondered if Connor ever would. She wouldn't blame him if he didn't.

"Ethan!"

Joy's head snapped up, eyes unglazing as Oliver ran into

the house, hoverboard long since abandoned. He flung himself across the living room, grabbing Ethan's hand and tugging him to his feet.

Ethan laughed as he allowed himself to be yanked away from the kitchen. "Where are we going?"

"I got a new part for my PC, and I want you to look at it. I was thinking about replacing the graphic card and didn't know if it would work with my RAM. I really want a more—"

The two walked up the stairs, their heavy footsteps echoing throughout the house. Joy stole Ethan's remaining energy drink, downing it in one gulp.

"Hold on, let me just grab my drink," Ethan called, treading back down the steps.

Joy placed the drink back at his seat and turned to Trini. Ethan rounded the table, grabbed the can, and paused.

He turned to Joy, betrayal on his face, and whispered, "Revenge will come for you, Ms. Joy. Mark my words," before turning on his heel and leaving.

Joy rolled her eyes.

"Weirdo," Caden said under her breath, tapping her fingers in feigned annoyance even as a smile spread across her face.

Joy gently grabbed Caden's hand, examining the shiny, black nails under the kitchen light. She knew that Caden was taken to get her nails done at least once a month, sometimes twice, by one parent or the other. The thought made Joy feel slightly bitter, especially as she stared at her own nails, chewed off during fits of anxiety and skin flaking where she had picked at it.

On the one hand, she was happy for Caden. On the other hand, she was incredibly jealous. Caden had wanted for very little in her short lifetime. Both parents doted on her, spoiled her really, taking her shopping on a whim. Joy had been too afraid to ask for things, terrified her new family would abandon her.

For her sixteenth birthday, she had been given a beat-up black truck, a single cab, two-door vehicle that groaned as it started up and clanked violently on highways. She cried when she received it, so excited and touched by the gesture. And she loved that truck. At least, until her younger sister had turned sixteen and received an adorable Jeep, a lot nicer vehicle than she had gotten. She laughed bitterly when the car pulled up next to her own, a shiny gray Jeep and her old black farm truck with over 100,000 miles on it. She didn't say a single word to her family, instead hopping into her truck and driving away. She blamed Clara in the moment, unfairly, something that weighed on her. But she blamed her parents that night as she lay in her bed.

It was easier to villainize her adoptive parents for things like this, perceived injustices, than it was to understand they were complex people with reasons for why they acted as they did. Trini and Connor had saved money for a while to afford her truck; Clara's Jeep had been given to the family by a friend whom Trini had fundraised for after a cancer diagnosis.

Joy saw these things as two-dimensional, her sister simply getting a nicer car, instead of looking at the picture as a whole. As a teenager, it's easy to see the world in black and white, right and wrong, privileged and poor. As an adult, Joy felt guilty about this. She blew up and let herself get hurt by the smaller things.

And that's not to say her parents did her no harm. They did. In many ways, they had failed her, but not in all of the ways she had accused them of in her youth.

"Don't you think?" Caden asked.

Joy's attention shot back to the table in front of her. There was something about this house that made her feel nostalgic, stuck in the memories of the past. Stuck was a great word to describe Joy. Stuck in the hurt of the past. Stuck with a degree she only got to make her family proud and a job she hated. Stuck with powers that made her feel shitty. Stuck in a friend zone of her own making.

"Absolutely, yes," she answered automatically.

"You have no clue what we're talking about, do you?"

Joy grinned, and Caden groaned. "Nope. No clue whatsoever."

"I was saying we should run to Sonic, grab some ice cream."

The tension that had quietly built in her shoulders fled at the mention of ice cream. Her fingers twitched to check her bank account through the app on her phone, but she fought back the urge. Growing up poor doesn't leave you, not really. The habits learned as a child were ingrained in her, mannerisms she was forcing herself to unlearn, like checking to make sure there was enough money for even the smallest of purchases and feeling guilty every time she bought something not on sale. She was trying to teach herself that she deserved to splurge every now and then, to eat out occasionally without the crippling anxiety of not knowing how she was going to afford her next meal.

We get it. You grew up poor and traumatized, but you still haven't answered Caden.

"Oh, then my previous statement stands. Absolutely, yes," Joy blurted, realizing Buttercup was right and Caden was staring at her expectantly. Her eyes narrowed as a grin spread on Caden's face. "No, you can't drive."

Joy laughed as Caden pouted. She grabbed her keys, shouted up the stairs for Ethan and Oliver to join her, jotted down a couple of orders for Trini and the other two boys, and headed out the door.

"Are you sure I can't drive?" Caden asked as Joy slid into the passenger seat.

Ethan opened the driver's door. "Can you even reach the pedals, small fry?"

Caden swatted at him from the backseat and groaned as Ethan connected his phone to the radio.

Joy turned and raised a single eyebrow. "Is there a problem?"

"I don't want to listen to heavy metal," Caden scoffed, throwing herself back into her seat and pulling her Airpods out of the pocket of her jeans.

"Ethan doesn't listen to heavy metal."

Joy retorted, rolling her eyes at Caden's music blaring through her headphones and turning to Ethan for confirmation. He grinned sheepishly.

"I might have made her listen to Power Wolf the last time we went to get ice cream."

Joy's mouth opened and closed, a gaping trout breathing air for the first time, and her eyebrows knit together. "You went and got ice cream without me?"

Oliver flung open the opposite passenger side door.

"Can we help you?" Caden asked, crossing her arms over her chest and staring her youngest brother down.

He slid into the seat. "I'm coming, too."

"Why?"

Oliver shrugged. He leaned forward, his fingers dancing along the center console as he disconnected Ethan's phone from the Bluetooth.

"I don't want to listen to the crazy dog power band again," he murmured.

Joy's jaw dropped. "You took Oliver but not me?"

Ethan smiled, turned the radio up, and pulled out of the driveway.

* * *

"Can I get ice cream and a burger?" Oliver asked, unbuckling and leaning to the front of the car.

Joy rolled her eyes. "Didn't you just eat lunch?"

"Yeah, but it was a frozen pizza and Max ate like half of it."

"Fine. Figure out what ice cream you want and you can have a kid's burger to go with it."

Oliver grinned, sticking his face into Joy's as he looked out her window at the menu. Ethan laughed as Joy wrinkled her nose in disgust and shoved her brother's face away.

"Gross kid. Your breath smells like butt."

He leaned forward, blowing out a burst of warm air straight in her face.

"Alright, everyone out." Ethan pulled the keys from the ignition, opening his door and walking to the counter.

"What if I see someone I know?" Joy groaned.

Ethan shrugged. "We throw ice cream at them until they leave."

Joy grumbled but followed, slamming the car door behind her. Oliver sprinted by her, already chattering to Ethan about a new game he had bought. Ethan grinned as he looked down at the kid, occasionally throwing in a comment or asking a question to show he was listening. It made Joy feel warm, seeing the two interact so easily. It was cute really, how well they got along. She had even overheard Ethan calling Oliver 'Bubba' once or twice, the same nickname Joy used. She let herself watch for a few moments, taking in Ethan's broad shoulders, his easy smile, the way his hair curled at the ends.

"You're drooling," Caden smirked at Joy as they stepped toward the neon lighting of the menu.

Joy frowned. "Am not."

"You totally are. How long have you had a crush on Ethan?"

Joy's eyes went wide and she shoved her. "Shut up! I don't have a crush on Ethan."

Caden laughed. The corners of her mouth twitched as a car parked a few feet away caught her attention. A Ford truck, vibrating from the loud music inside and in desperate need of a wash, flashed its headlights. Caden paled and gritted her teeth. Joy had never seen her youngest sister, so bold in her fashion choices and confident in herself, so anxious. The air around her seemed to vibrate, anger pouring off her in waves, even as she kept her eyes trained on the ground and picked at her nails.

"Hey," Joy placed her hand on Caden's shoulder. "You okay?"

Caden winced as a piece of skin peeled away from her finger. "Yeah, just some assholes from school. It's fine. Let's just order and go."

Joy nodded, wrapping her arm around the kid's shoulder and tugging her forward to Ethan and Oliver.

We could get rid of the children.

Joy sighed.

We can't just get rid of people, Buttercup.

And why not. We doubt anyone would even miss them.

Snorting, Joy shook her head. The group ordered, Oliver getting his ice cream and burger and everyone else getting an ice cream. Joy's phone buzzed in her pocket, and she stepped away to answer it, not bothering to check who was calling.

"Hello?"

"Hey," Carmen's voice responded grimly.

A tense silence followed, and Joy frowned. It simply wasn't like Carmen to be silent. Usually, she'd be launching into a rant on whatever mess her children had gotten into that day or explaining to Joy that it was "absolutely essential" she come over to try a recipe she had been working on.

Something was wrong. Joy's breath caught in her throat.

"Everything okay?" she forced herself to ask, not certain she wanted to hear the response.

"I know you're back home for your mom's wedding, but there was a meeting today at work and—" Carmen sighed. "The company is going to have layoffs. They're going to announce it next week in a group setting, which is not surprising for those assholes. Mark was practically vibrating in his seat in excitement. It's disgusting how—"

Joy's heart fell from her chest, landing somewhere on the sticky concrete by her feet.

"I'm getting fired, aren't I?" she interrupted.

"I'm so sorry, Joy. I argued as hard as I could, but it came down to either you or Keith, and Mark made the final decision. God, it doesn't even make sense. You're obviously the better employee. I thought about quitting on the spot—"

"You can't. Carmen, please promise me you won't. You've got the kids to look after, and you worked your ass off for that position. I'll be fine. I have some money saved up and honestly,

I've been thinking of leaving for a while. This will be good for me."

A lie, but one Joy knew Carmen needed to hear. Carmen was quiet on the other line.

"It's not fair. You don't deserve—"

"It's fine." Joy chuckled bitterly. "Listen, I have to go, but thank you for letting me know. I'll see you when I get back."

The two exchanged goodbyes, and Joy slipped her phone back into her pocket. She clenched her fists by her side, hands shaking as she blinked away the tears quickly forming in her eyes. She swiped at a tear that broke free, smearing mascara down her cheek in the process. Catching her reflection in the window of the Sonic, she fabricated a smile. It slipped into a frown. She took a deep breath. And built back her smile. This one stuck, and she walked back around the restaurant.

A boy stood eye to eye with Caden, grinning cockily as he ran a hand through his curls. He wore a pair of jeans, a flat cap, and a beer-branded t-shirt. A walking, talking country cliche.

"What, bug eyes? Gonna cry now? Be careful, might ruin that ugly makeup of yours."

"Go jump off a cliff, Ed," Caden bit back, shaking in anger.

Ethan looked up from his conversation with Oliver, his eyebrows pinching as Joy rushed over. He stood, towering a good foot over the kid and glared down at the teenager. He crossed his arms, sleeves pulling tight along his forearms as his muscles flexed. The teenager flinched, backing away from Caden, fear flashing over his features before he replaced it with a tighter version of his earlier smirk.

"What, can't even defend yourself now?"

Caden stepped around Ethan, her confidence swelling. "Don't you have parents to go home and disappoint, Ed? Funny how you have so much time to talk shit, but not enough to actually pass your classes, you participant-trophy-winning, hotdog-water-smelling dick."

"Whatever," Ed mumbled, his ears turning pink.

He jogged away, his movement jerky as he walked back

toward the laughing teenagers still in the truck. This taunting didn't seem to be a new thing, judging by Caden's earlier reaction. Anger washed over Joy, followed by sadness and concern for her younger sister. She had no idea Caden was going through this at school. How bad a sister was she that Caden hadn't told her about it?

"What a little bitch," Oliver said, taking a big bite of his ice cream.

Joy glared at Ed's retreating form. She imagined him tripping, the ice cream in his hand splattering all over him in front of his equally horrible friends. She hated people like that, those who felt the need to bring down others to feel better, to mask their own insecurities. She hated how karma never seemed to come quick enough for those people.

She had been a bit of a dick herself in high school, had focused on herself a bit too much, but she would have never intentionally hurt someone, not like that. It made Joy feel a little better to picture the group of teenagers as adults, drinking every night in the same town they grew up in with the same people they grew up with, pretending that they didn't peak in high school. Still, that didn't dull the part of her that ached for something quicker, an instant reprisal for their actions.

As she thought that, Ed fumbled his ice cream to the ground. He fell forward, his legs flying out from underneath him as if something had yanked his ankles backward, his arms failing to reach out to catch himself. He smacked the concrete, nose hitting first with a crunch. Silence fell over the patio, the patrons holding their breath as they waited for him to get up. He lay still.

"Oh shit," Oliver whispered. Then he took another bite of ice cream.

Ed groaned, rolling onto his back. His chin quivered, eyes squeezed shut as tears dripped down his face. His nose looked bent, not quite in the same position as before, and a steady flow of blood trickled onto his shirt and down the sides of his cheeks. The blood mixed with the quickly melting ice cream, red swirling with white flecks of Oreos floating down the crimson stream.

Joy frowned, stepping closer to Ed as he writhed on the ground. Not because she cared about his obviously broken nose. She didn't. But because she could have sworn, for the briefest of seconds, she had seen black smoke surrounding his wrists, holding his arms to his side.

CHAPTER 25

Joy, Age 16

"I don't think I believe in love."

For myself.

The last part was only thought by Joy, not said aloud to her waiting parents. Her family sat at the dinner table, half-eaten plates of Hamburger Helper sitting in front of them. Joy would grow to hate Hamburger Helper in her adult life. It was a staple in their household, the go-to dinner for school nights. They had been discussing dating, with Joy having finally reached the age Trini and Connor had told her she would be allowed to date. Clara was annoyed at still being too young.

Connor narrowed his eyes at Joy as the words left her mouth. When she said she didn't believe in love, she wasn't necessarily talking about love in general. She had seen love in the way her grandfather had taken care of her grandmother, even after her infidelity and the abuse she had inflicted on Joy and Clara. Love had made him foolish. She had seen it in the way Trini and Connor bickered behind closed doors, Connor growing passive-aggressive as Trini grew silent. Love had made them confrontational. She had seen it in the way her mother wrapped men around her finger, warping them, angering them, manipulating them into the worst versions of themselves. Love had made them toxic. Joy's examples of love growing up had given her the impression that perhaps love was not something she wanted, not something she would go looking for.

And even if Joy had seen the most glittering, purest versions of love as a child, she probably would've been convinced that she was incapable of it. Even worse, perhaps she was undeserving of love. The holes left by those who had abandoned her, who had shown her that she wasn't worthy of staying, had riddled her, left her less than a whole person. And who would possibly want to love someone so fragmented and incomplete?

And yet, a part of her still longed for love, still wanted someone to tell her that someone would come along someday to prove her wrong. To show her that she could love. To show her that she could be loved, even with her scars and the ugly bits she kept hidden. That was part of the reason she said what she did. It was childish really, but she wanted her new parents to reassure her, tell her that she was loved. Instead, ice ran through her veins as Connor scowled at her.

"You can't say things like that, Joy."

Joy frowned. "It's what I believe."

"But that's not what it says in the Bible." Connor put his fork down. "The Bible talks all about love. Saying it doesn't exist is an insult to His word."

Joy stopped herself from rolling her eyes, even as her shoulders slumped. She settled into her seat, tuning Connor out in preparation for the lecture she was sure to come. She regretted saying anything. Knowing Connor, she shouldn't have been surprised that he took her words as an insult.

It was moments like this that slowly turned her away from Christianity. She still believed in God and even Jesus, but she wasn't comfortable with the Bible she had been taught. She was a sixteen-year-old who wanted to be told her new family loved her and that she would be loved by a future partner. God's love was great or whatever, but she wanted more. Yes, she knew how that sounded. Connor would tell her she was being sacrilegious, that God's love and His word should have been all she needed. But it wasn't. She needed more. She wanted the comfort only those around her could provide, but instead, she was being accosted.

Joy tuned back into Connor's rant. "It's also an insult to the love shared by Trini and me and by my parents."

Joy nodded her head and forced a smile on her lips.

"You're right. Sorry, I don't know what I was thinking."

The rest of the dinner was quiet. After the table was cleared, Joy and Clara had bickered about whose turn it was to do dishes while the kids were tucked into bed. Joy trudged to her room and flopped onto her bed. She stared up at the single glow-in-the-dark star stuck to her roof, slowly closing one eye, then the other, and squinting at its blurry form. It had been left over from when the room had been Caden's, but Joy had left it, finding comfort in the small object when night fell, and her room was dark. Her phone dinged beside her. She lifted it to reveal a text in the group chat between her, Clara, Connor, and Trini.

"Night. Love y'all," the message from Trini read.

Clara and Connor quickly responded, echoing her words. Joy thought about not responding, about turning her phone off and forcing Trini to tell her in person. This was their nightly routine, good night texts sent from rooms only a few feet away from each other. Had Joy been a braver person, she would have pointed this out, told Trini and Connor how lonely it made her feel and ask to hear the words she so desperately needed in person. Instead, she typed her response and turned off her bedroom light.

CHAPTER 26

The car ride home from Sonic was lively, Caden blaring music and Oliver complaining about not getting Ed's fall on camera. Joy sipped her drink absent-mindedly, processing Ed's fall and her phone call with Carmen.

We did not cause the boy to fall, Buttercup assured Joy.

She wasn't sure what to think about what had happened. She could've sworn she had seen the black mist, but she hadn't felt the chill of the power, leaving her with no choice but believing Buttercup. And as for her job...she didn't know what to do about that. She didn't even want to think about it, deciding she would deal with it when she returned home and was officially fired.

"So, theoretically, if someone were to... I don't know... get a pickle stuck to the roof of the car, and it leaves a mustard stain..."

Joy whipped around to see Oliver dabbing at the ceiling with a napkin, a sheepish expression on his face.

"How?!" she asked, reaching back to smack him as he shrugged.

"Whose car is that?" Caden interrupted, flinging off her seatbelt and leaning forward to get a better view of Trini's driveway.

Joy's hairs lifted off the back of her neck, her scalp prickling at an unknown danger. She didn't recognize the car either, but something about it made her fidget. Trini stepped out of the house as they pulled up, her eyes flicking to Joy and her fingers twisting her engagement ring.

Joy frowned as she exited the car. Buttercup flitted out of her fingertips, hurtling toward the house to find the threat.

"I thought she was coming tomorrow." Trini spoke in a hushed tone, shoulders bunched up around her neck.

Joy's jaw clenched. "She?"

Sarah, Buttercup confirmed, returning from its search.

"Everything okay?" Ethan asked.

"Just peachy," Joy ground out, narrowing her eyes at Trini's house.

She trudged forward, Ethan following closely behind. She ignored the whispering questions he shot Caden about her reaction.

"You might wanna sit this one out," Caden murmured back, nodding at Oliver to take Ethan upstairs.

Joy appreciated that. She never knew what to expect with her grandmother, when things would get ugly, and she didn't want Ethan seeing the version of her that only Sarah seemed to bring out.

Sarah leaned against the kitchen counter and smiled as Joy stormed into the room. Joy hadn't seen her in a few years, and age had not been kind to Sarah. Her typically crimson hair was a dull brown, her green eyes still sharp in intelligence but the intensity dulled by the dark bags drooping below. She was thinner than Joy had ever seen her, cheeks gaunt and limbs angular, and was much shorter than Joy remembered, standing at a mere 5 '2.

It was funny how distance had changed Joy's perception of her grandmother. Sarah had seemed so big when Joy was a child, not in appearance necessarily, but in her attitude, her words a wave that knocked Joy to her ass, her judgmental glances insurmountable. Now she just looked like another old woman desperately trying to clutch onto her youth—heavy foundation that pooled in her pores, ripped jeans and a tight t-shirt under a thick housecoat.

"Joy-Joy!" Sarah's shrill voice sliced through the quiet. "It's been so long since I last saw you. You know, I was worried about you when you stopped answering my texts, especially after my surgeries. But look at you! You've gained a bit of weight, huh? It's such a shame you didn't inherit my super-fast metabolism. God, I can barely keep the weight on these days. It looks good, though, don't worry."

Sarah smirked as her eyes paused at Joy's midsection. Joy wrapped her cardigan around her body.

Trini inviting Sarah to the wedding hurt. Joy hated how bitter it made her feel that she wasn't happy that Trini got to have her mother around.

If it was Caden or Oliver who had been treated so poorly, she would have never forgiven her.

Joy shook her head, but she knew that Buttercup could hear the small part of her that agreed. But Joy understood. Sarah's approval should have been meaningless. A washed-up, wannabe rock star stuck in a small town wasn't exactly the type of person Joy wished to appeal to. Nonetheless, Joy had spent the first eighteen years of her life craving it. It wasn't until she accepted that she would never have it that her life truly began.

"So, Caden, I heard you have a tennis game tomorrow," Sarah began.

Caden raised her eyebrows, hesitated, then nodded.

"Yeah. It's in Midland. Starts at noon. I was going to ask Joy and Ethan to drive me, but I guess everyone is welcome to come."

Sarah grinned.

"You know, I used to play tennis in high school. I was really good too. Maybe I could show you a few pointers."

She looks as though she could break a hip walking down the bleachers.

Joy snorted. Sarah narrowed her eyes, leaning against the kitchen table.

"Something funny?"

Joy's mind went blank, even as she searched desperately for an excuse. The tension in the room was almost unbearable. Shouts could be heard from the playroom upstairs, Ethan's complaints of being beaten in the video game they were playing overwhelming the cheers of the team that had won. Caden laughed.

"Ethan's a sore loser."

Joy broke eye contact with her grandmother. She looked at Caden, a grin stretching on her face. Joy hadn't played many video games as a child, never really liked them that much. That changed after meeting Ethan. She loved the way he talked about video games, how his eyes lit up when telling her about a new level he beat or a game that would be released soon.

She wanted a reason to keep talking to him, something they could bond over so that they could keep talking after the project was over. So she started playing, digging out the old Switch sitting practically untouched in the bottom of her closet and rushing through games Ethan suggested. She spent hours researching and practicing, learning all the mechanics and lore of the games he liked so she could play with him.

"You should see him when we play Fall Guys. I've never seen a grown man complain so much."

Caden bounced in her seat, spinning the stool toward Joy.

"Do y'all play it on the Xbox? I saw a Let's Play from this YouTuber I like, and it looked like a lot of fun."

"Yeah!" Joy exclaimed, nodding her head enthusiastically. "We play it with a couple of friends as a team. It's super frustrating because you have to navigate these obstacles with other people running into you and getting in your way. There was this one time—"

Sarah cleared her throat.

"What is Call Guys?"

"Oh, uh, Fall Guys." Caden glanced back at her. "It's a video game."

Sarah crossed her arms, her thin lips pressing together.

"I haven't seen y'all in months, years for Joy. And y'all want to talk about some stupid video game? Honestly, I don't understand how it could be fun, or even good for you, staring at a screen for that long. I came down a night early so we could catch up, not talk about all of that." Sarah wrinkled her nose in disgust.

She tapped her housecoat. Joy knew that gesture. It meant Sarah was annoyed, not that her mood wasn't obvious by her narrowed eyes, rigid posture, and sharp tone. There were cigarettes in one of her pockets, and as soon as Sarah got tired of the conversation, tired of her, she would escape to the backyard to take a drag.

It would be a real shame if the lighter in her pocket were to leak its fluid on her fingertips before she lit it.

Joy rolled her eyes. Although the thought had crossed her mind as well, she would never go through with it.

She would not die. Her fingertips would merely be singed.

Sarah gasped, hand flying to her chest dramatically.

"Did you just roll your eyes at me?"

Joy frowned. "No?"

"Don't lie to me. I saw it! You know, I drove all this way —" *It was only a two-hour drive.* "So I could see you—" *She told Trini she came early to help to see something else.* "And catch up because you stopped answering my text messages, and I was worried—" The last text message she had sent her was when Joy had just gotten out of surgery. It was a picture of Sarah's face, post-surgery to have a cancerous spot removed, and a message that read 'At least you don't look like this. I hope your surgery went well. I'm doing fine, wish you would've asked.' "And you roll your eyes when I'm simply trying to catch up on everything we've missed? You've always been like this, so defensive and rude. Even after everything I did for you and your sister. "

Sarah huffed, standing from her stool and pulling out a green pack of cigarettes from her pocket.

"I'm going to go take a drag."

She snatched her cup of water from the counter with her other hand. Water splashed over the side, leaving a small puddle on the marble. Joy and Caden exchanged a look.

"I think I'm going to head up to my bedroom before she gets back. I'm gonna be reading if you want to join me in a bit," Caden said.

Joy nodded. Caden grabbed her phone, stopped by the pantry to grab a bag of Takis, then turned the corner. As Caden disappeared up the stairs, Joy glared at the door her grandmother had left through. She smirked, an idea suddenly coming to her.

Buttercup drifted through the air, its black mist seeping through the cracks in the door. A stool was placed on the edge of the living room, facing out the window and toward the back patio. Joy walked over to it, settling into the seat to watch.

The patio was small, a concrete slab overlooking a raised flower bed. Row upon row of cotton plants were behind it, the white invisible in the dark. She searched through the night, eyes squinting and adjusting, before spotting a small figure sitting in the dark.

Sarah held the package of cigarettes in her hands, pulling one out as she perched on a rocking chair. She fumbled in her pockets for the lighter. Buttercup snuck toward her, practically invisible, even to Joy. Setting her water on the wicker table beside her, Sarah lit her cigarette and tossed the pack onto the table. Joy flicked her wrist to the side, and Buttercup followed, knocking the glass over. The water seeped into the plastic of the carton and soaked the cigarettes inside while Sarah scrolled through her Facebook. Joy waited.

"Fuck!" Sarah exclaimed, finally noticing the water dripping through the table and pooling at her feet.

She lurched forward, hands reaching out for the carton. Joy flicked her wrist again. Buttercup sent the package flying, tumbling through the air and landing in the flower bed. Smirking, Joy snapped her hand to the side and watched as Buttercup spread the wet cigarettes through the freshly spread manure. Sarah cursed, pointing her phone flashlight at the ground and picking through the poop for the damp objects. Trini always said the benefit of having a farm meant fresh products: eggs from the chickens, flowers from the garden, manure from the horse stalls. Joy couldn't agree more.

***

The next morning, Joy made her way up the bleachers, sitting a few rows above Sarah, who had yet to look up from her phone. Ethan plopped down beside her. The air smelled overwhelmingly like sunscreen, sweat, and what she assumed was a bit of whisky mixed into the sweet tea of the mom sitting in front of them. Joy snorted as the woman lifted her Yeti cup to her lips.

Caden walked over to her bench, giving a quick hug to her partner, her cousin Dalton. Dalton was tall, huge for a kid his age, standing probably an inch or two taller than even Ethan. He had the family's signature blond hair and blue eyes but was incredibly lanky. Dalton was the youngest son of Trini's half-brother Dee. Dee was not related to Joy's mother, and technically only related to Joy through her adoption. Trini and Joanne shared a mother, while Dee and Trini shared a father. Very little was simple in Joy's family tree.

Dalton waved at Joy, who smiled and nodded back. Joy slathered on some sunscreen, knowing she was likely to burn in the Texas heat. Ethan leaned in close, his breath ghosting along Joy's ear.

"I know nothing about tennis. You're gonna have to tell me when to cheer, so I don't come off looking like a dick."

Joy laughed. Connor walked through the gate, and the smile fell from her lips. Sometimes, Joy's past made her feel strong, as though getting through it had made her tougher than most. Sometimes, the past made her feel small. Connor attending

Caden's tennis match was one of those times. Joy had played varsity tennis all four years of high school and had been the girls' singles champion for her district three years in a row. Although she had never advanced beyond the district, she still loved the sport.

Connor had never once attended one of her matches, even those on the weekend. And yet here he was, on a random Thursday morning, taking off work to watch Caden play a practice game. It made her feel petty, but Joy shifted her eyes away from her father's gaze as he searched the bleachers for her.

"You okay?" Ethan whispered, bumping his shoulder into Joy's.

Joy sighed but nodded. "Yeah. Just a bit uncomfortable. It'll be fine."

"Give me the word, and I'll fake a dragon invasion. The people here will either believe me and run screaming or think I'm crazy and evacuate their children. Either way, we'll be able to make a run for it."

Joy giggled, one dimple flashing as she leaned further into him. His hand inched closer, his pinky finger brushing against hers. She stilled, her breath catching in her throat. She stared forward, refusing to look at their hands.

Caden walked to the edge of the court, twirling the racquet in her hand and adjusting the wrapping on its base.

Ethan took Joy's fingers in his hand, flipping her palm over.

Caden tossed the tennis ball in the air a few times. She stepped up to the baseline, placing her feet parallel to the line.

Ethan paused, waiting for Joy to pull her hand back.

Caden threw the ball high in the air, serving it in the box opposite of her.

Joy didn't pull her hand back.

Caden grinned at Dalton, chattering excitedly as they continued warming up.

Ethan threaded his fingers with Joy's, his cheeks tinting pink. Joy turned to look at him, a slow smile creeping on her face.

"Edgar!" Charlie exclaimed, clapping Ethan on the back and dropping onto the bleacher beside him.

Joy jerked her hand back. She wiped it on the side of her shorts before clearing her throat.

"You know his name is Ethan," Joy scolded, rolling her eyes.

Charlie adjusted his hat, a faded cap from a pool cleaning business he had sold a few years back, pushing back tufts of ginger hair as he wiped the sweat from his brow.

"How ya doing, Charlie?" Ethan asked, grinning in amusement.

"It's hot as balls." Charlie whipped out his phone, sent a text, then turned back to Ethan. "You ever had Turkish delight?"

Ethan's raised his eyebrows. "Um, not that I know of?"

"Don't. I ate some weird version of it yesterday and have flatulated more since then than I have in my entire life. Half surprised I'm not shitting carbonated foam."

Ethan balked. Joy sighed, shaking her head.

"Absolutely no one needed to know this."

Charlie smacked her cap.

"Just felt like good information to start a Thursday morning off with."

"How was your trip up North?" Joy asked.

Charlie scowled.

"Sold a lot. But it was 97 and humid as hell, like sitting in an obese man's asscrack."

Ethan burst into laughter. Charlie worked as a traveling salesman, selling hot tubs throughout the northeastern states. He was good at it, but he really only did it so he could travel. He took his time each trip, driving from Texas up through the states, stopping wherever something looked cool.

The job seemed to be doing him good. After selling his previous business, he had seemed a bit lost, unsure of what to do with his life. He had lost a lot of weight while cleaning pools, mainly from working in the Texas heat but also from not eating as much as he should. Joy had chastised him about his diet on multiple occasions. And maybe that made her a hypocrite, given her complicated history with food, but she also knew firsthand how difficult eating could sometimes be and how important nutrition was to your mental health. He had gained the weight back in the last few months, and the semi-permanent sunburn he had been previously sporting had faded to a decent tan, leaving him looking healthier than he had in a long time.

"What are you doing here? Didn't really peg you as the kind of guy who would want to watch a high school tennis match. Especially a practice one in the heat," Joy questioned.

Charlie shrugged.

"Got nothing better to do. I'm off for the next five days. And I heard the niece most likely to buy me a sailboat was in town."

"Most likely to buy you a sailboat?" Ethan asked.

"Way I see it, Joy's my best shot. Clara's probably gonna end up some famous artist, disown the family, and move to her own island where she'll be the leader of a cult. Caden's gonna marry some rich old fella, wait until he dies, and inherit his fortune. I don't want my boat bought with some old dead dude's money; he could haunt whatever I bought with it. Oliver will probably end up military, and they don't pay well enough for the type of boat I want. That leaves me with Joy."

Ethan laughed. "Fair enough."

"Um, no. Not fair enough. Even if I had the money, why would I buy you a sailboat?" Joy questioned, looking at her uncle dubiously.

"Because I'm your favorite family member outside of maybe Clara or Caden, and they're not as fun as me," he responded nonchalantly, not even bothering to look away from the court.

That wasn't a lie. Charlie was, and would probably always be, one of her favorite people. He was wild, a bit too unfiltered, and constantly unpredictable. Underneath that, though, he was kind, always there for those who needed him and never expecting the same in return.

Trini and Connor had a thriving social life and spent

most of their Friday and Saturday nights alternating between friends' houses. Caden and Oliver often went with them, but Joy preferred staying home. She had tried tagging along a few times, but Trini and Connor's friends were as young as they were. They had kids Caden and Oliver's ages, but not old enough for Joy to hang out with. Plus, kids freaked Joy out. Instead, Joy and Clara had spent a lot of time with Charlie in high school. He had served as an escape when their house was too quiet or their minds were too loud. Joy still hung out with her friends a good amount, but she found it exhausting, constantly having to be someone she wasn't, forcing laughs and going along with what others wanted. Charlie was one of the few people she felt comfortable enough to be herself around, but Joy wasn't sure she was of similar help to him.

Charlie never had kids or gotten married. Sometimes that scared Joy. Not because she thought he needed it—he was perfectly complete on his own—but because behind his often inappropriate humor and loud personality, Charlie seemed lonely. The bags under Charlie's eyes screamed of nights kept awake by unspoken anxieties. The way he carried himself also hinted at this. He would hesitate before joining a group conversation, even as he spoke loudly and seemingly confidently, as though he wasn't quite sure where he fit.

"Got it!" Caden called from the court.

Joy turned toward the match, surprised to see the game had started while she had been lost in thought. She elbowed Ethan.

"What's the score?" she whispered, eyes trained on the ball.

Ethan leaned closer to her. "I have no clue what's going on."

Joy snorted. Caden sprinted after the ball as it was returned. It landed closer than she anticipated, and she struggled to adjust. Her arm bent awkwardly, unable to fully extend to swing. The ball connected with the shaft of the racket, which sent it flying into the bottom of the net. It skidded underneath the net and rolled to the opposite side.

It had been a great volley, lasting almost two minutes of back and forth, but the frustration at having made a mistake was evident on Caden's face. Her eyebrows furrowed deeply, and she tapped the racket harshly against her knee. She wiped sweat from her face with the collar of her shirt as Sarah, finally looking up from her phone, let out a cheer.

"Great job, Caden!" she called, having only seen the ball on the other side of the court and assuming the point had been in Caden's favor.

Anger flashed over Caden's features. She took a deep breath, refusing to look up at the stands and hopping up and down as she waited for the next point. Although Joy couldn't see Sarah's features, she could picture the scowl she now wore at being publicly ignored.

The girl on the other team served, and Caden returned it easily. Sarah whipped around, searching the bleachers. Her eyes landed on Joy, who was able to confirm the scowl on her grandmother's face had appeared.

"She must get her rudeness from you," Sarah hissed. She paused, glancing around to make sure no one else was listening. "I'm sure Trini and Connor don't appreciate your influence on that girl's attitude. Makes me wonder if they regret adopting you in the first place."

Ethan stood, hands fisted as he glared down at the older woman. Joy placed her hand on his forearm and shook her head. He huffed, plopping back onto the metal seat and turning his attention back to the game. Cold flashed through Joy's body, but she couldn't tell if it was the fear of Sarah's words being true or something else. Joy smiled sweetly at her grandmother, her eyes flashing dangerously. Sarah flinched.

A flash of green rocketed through the air, a black shadow trailing it.

"Head's up!" A voice called out.

The ball smacked into the back of Sarah's head. She lost her grip on her phone on impact, and it shattered against the metal bleacher before slipping through the stands and landing on the concrete underneath. Sarah didn't react at first. The ball had landed on the seat below hers, and she stared at it. Her breath caught, her eyes widening in what looked like fear, and she shot up from the stands. She smoothed her ruffled red hair and sprinted down the steps to find her phone. Ethan snorted. Joy's own smile fell from her lips as she saw a wisp of black fog dart away from the tennis ball and disappear between the gaps in the seats.

This time, Joy knew it had not been her imagination. She had clearly seen Buttercup's smoke leaving the ball. She had thought about a stray ball hitting Sarah but hadn't asked Buttercup to do anything, nor had she felt it leave her. Or had she? She had felt a bit of a chill earlier, but it had seemed more like a flash of anxiety than the power she had grown accustomed to.

It was not us, Buttercup's voice echoed in her mind.

She wasn't sure how to respond. Although her thoughts had been invaded, she had no way of knowing if it was lying to her. Not that it had any reason to lie to her; she had been thinking of making something similar happen anyway. But she also hadn't decided yet. The ball was one of many thoughts she had been debating. Had Buttercup chosen for her?

We did not make the tennis ball hit her.

Buttercup's words did little to quell her doubt. She felt uneasy; a knot settled in her stomach as she continued watching the game.

"You okay?" Ethan whispered, catching her attention.

She nodded sharply. Ethan raised a single eyebrow, his brown eyes staring at her in disbelief. She forced a smile, excusing herself to grab a water from the country club's concession stand. As she passed underneath the bleachers, a bony hand grabbed her wrist.

Sarah tugged her arm, pulling her into the shadow.

"I saw what you did." Sarah's nostrils flared, her hand trembling as she gripped her shattered phone.

Joy jerked her hand away from the woman's grasp.

"What are you talking about?" Joy spit back.

"I saw it, Joy! Don't you try and lie to me." Sarah's eyes were crazed, her words slurring. "You have the devil in you. You use his power. I saw his darkness on the ball."

Joy didn't know how to respond; her tongue heavy in her mouth and her chest squeezing. Her instincts were torn between spouting denials and running away.

"Uh. No, you didn't," Joy blurted before sprinting in the opposite direction, leaving her grandmother under the bleachers.

She now stood in line for the concession stand, sighing internally and debating fleeing the country entirely.

Well, that was stupid.

"That's not helpful!" Joy exclaimed aloud.

The woman standing in front of her turned around. Joy flushed red, overcome with embarrassment. She gestured toward the phone in her hand.

"Sorry. Finishing up a phone call," she mumbled, averting her eyes.

The woman nodded. It was her turn to order, but she cast a concerned glance at Joy before stepping up to the window.

Yelling at strangers is not helpful either.

You're a dick, she thought.

We are you.

Joy threw her hands up in the air in frustration. The woman in front of her, now with a hotdog and large cup of soda in her hands, stepped away from Joy. She walked away quickly, tossing a few nervous glances at Joy over her shoulder.

She definitely thinks I'm crazy, Joy thought to Buttercup.

Perhaps we are.

Joy sighed and stepped forward. She ordered herself a water and Ethan a snack. He tended to get cranky when he was hungry. Then she rushed back to catch the last few games of the tennis set. The match flew by quickly, Caden and Dalton eventually finding their groove and winning the first and second sets. Joy avoided her fuming grandmother, choosing to walk up the far side of the bleachers when she returned. She didn't miss the way Sarah would occasionally turn and stare at her, as if daring Joy to meet her eyes.

"That last one was so good! Caden was like whack—" Ethan swung his arms, replicating the final point of the match in which Caden had returned the ball into her opponent's left corner, targeting their weaker backstroke and leaving them unable to return the ball in time. "And they ran so hard to get to it. I thought the mom in front of us would have an aneurysm with how loudly she was screaming at her son to get it."

The woman with the Yeti cup in front of Joy drank a bit more of her spiked tea than she should have. She stood the entire second set, swaying gently on her feet and screaming at every point her child, who Joy had figured out was the boy of the other pair, made a mistake. By the end, her words had slurred, becoming almost incoherent. Joy was fairly sure at one point, the woman had shouted, "Smash that shit, honey! Absolutely demolish that ball."

"So what's next on today's schedule?" Ethan asked, peering over Joy's shoulder as she read through her family's group chat.

"Can we go shopping?" Caden popped up out of nowhere, startling Joy.

Her face was red from the match, and her blonde hair was drenched in sweat, but the big grin on her face showed that she was in a much better mood after winning. Joy wrinkled her nose as she got a big whiff of sweat.

"Maybe if you shower first," Joy teased.

She shoved the girl away from her playfully. Caden glared back. She wiped the sweat from her neck with a towel, then threw it. Anticipating her sister's actions, Joy laughed and darted to the side. Ethan, hearing Joy's laughter, turned in time for the towel to smack him directly in the face. Joy laughed harder.

"What were you even aiming at?" she gasped, tears forming in her eyes. "He's like a foot taller than me."

Ethan picked the towel up off the ground, face blank. He stared at it. Plucking the half-empty water bottle from Joy's hand, he turned to Caden.

"You know, Caden...." Ethan took a quick step forward, and Caden gulped. "It must be hot, playing tennis in the middle of the day. I got just the thing to cool you off."

He squeezed the bottom of the bottle, and water arched through the air. Caden squealed, leaping behind Joy, who ducked in response. Charlie, walking up to the group after a quick trip to the concession stand, was met with the water hitting him directly in the chest. He didn't hesitate, acting purely on instinct as he grabbed the top of the snowcone with his free hand and threw it back at Ethan. The colored ice scattered in the air, blue specks of ice staining Joy and Caden's cheeks and Ethan's t-shirt.

"Oops." Charlie shrugged.

"Oops?" Joy questioned, plucking a piece of ice from her hair.

Charlie dug a spoon into the remainder of the snowcone. Joy's eye twitched.

* * *

They were kicked out. A member of the country club complained after Caden smacked her child in the face with a piece of watermelon from the cooler. It wasn't a permanent ban, at least Joy didn't think so, but the manager did ask that they leave for the day. Charlie had bid them farewell shortly after, promising to meet up for dinner. Caden, Joy, and Ethan walked to Ethan's car.

"So, was that a yes or a no to shopping?" Caden asked.

Joy frowned. She didn't dislike shopping, even found retail therapy to be soothing at times, but the idea of shopping in the town she grew up in and having even the slightest chance of running into someone she knew sounded terrible.

"Why?" she questioned. "What do you want?"

"I need a necklace to go with the dress I got for mom's wedding. Nothing I have matches." Caden pulled out a wallet from her gym bag. "I can even pay for it, but I need a ride."

Ethan shrugged and looked to Joy for confirmation.

"I guess, but only because I forgot the shoes I was going to wear tomorrow in Austin, and we're only going to one store," Joy said reluctantly.

Caden grinned.

They did not only go to one store. Joy followed Caden around five different stores at two shopping centers before Trini texted them asking to meet at a Mexican restaurant for a night-before-the-wedding dinner but was not been able to find any shoes. Ethan had been a trooper the entire time, smiling at Caden's jokes, teasing Joy for her lack of stamina as she draped herself dramatically on waiting room couches, and letting Joy steal sips of the raspberry ICEE he had somehow acquired along the way.

Arriving at the restaurant, Joy remembered her earlier conversation with her grandmother and flinched. She cracked her neck, hopped in place to hype herself up, and walked toward the front door. She held the door open for Caden as she sailed through, black combat boots treading on the bright red carpet. She scanned the room for a second before beelining for a table in the back. Joy puffed out a breath of air as her eyes caught a flash of dull brown hair at the table Caden was walking to. A hand landed on the small of her back, and she flinched.

"Just say the word," Ethan leaned down and whispered. "And I'll fake a heart attack. Or a family emergency. Or a sudden traumatic brain injury where I forget everyone's name and refer to them as Bitch #1, Bitch #2, Cowboy Bitch, Ginger Bitch, you get the idea."

Joy snorted. With Ethan on her side, she felt a lot more confident and a lot less likely to flee the dinner and start a new life in a different country. She was jealous of those who actually looked forward to family reunions. Hers typically ended in an odd combination of too much alcohol in her system, violence, and/or tears. Forget the awkward questions about one's career or love life; when her family got together, they tended to get morbid, joking about Joy's cancer, Charlie's singleness, their dead relatives, childhood trauma.

Her family knew no boundaries, a bad habit that had rubbed off on Joy and made her a chronic oversharer. Tonight would be different, though. The source of much of Joy and Clara's trauma sat next to Trini, tattoos peeking out of the edge of her short-sleeved shirt and glasses pushed up on her forehead.

"Nice of y'all to finally join us," Sarah quipped, a fake smile on her lips.

If Joy learned her fake smile from anyone, it was her grandmother. Although she had begun reflecting the expressions of her mother at a young age, it wasn't until she moved in with Sarah that she perfected it. A master of manipulation, Sarah wielded her smile as a weapon, a demonstration of feminine innocence that stretched her eyes unnaturally tight at the corners. Joy learned from Sarah how to thicken her accent at the right times, push out her chest, and flash a smile so pure that people couldn't help but fall for her Southern charm.

It was bullshit, how easy it was for Sarah to convince the people of her tiny town that she was a hard-working, grieving widow instead of a cunning, shrewd old woman with a habit of getting what she wanted. If there was anything that Sarah was excellent at, it wasn't singing or cooking or sewing clothes like other grandmothers. It was painting herself as a victim and making those who dared to stand against her feel guilty, villainous almost.

"Yeah, well. Traffic," Joy mumbled, her eyes trained on the ground.

Joy sat next to Charlie, Ethan settling in on her other side and Clara, Caden, and Oliver were in front of her at the long, rectangular table. Oliver was absorbed in a game on his phone, only looking up to say a brief "hey." Caden was trying to convince Trini to let her get a margarita, a request that caused Trini to sigh deeply. Clara smiled at Joy.

"Hey," Clara said simply, nodding.

Joy grinned back.

Clara was only fourteen months younger, but Joy had always felt so much older. She blamed it on their childhood and having to take care of Clara at a young age.

In some ways, looking after Clara growing up had shaped how Joy viewed her. When Joy saw Clara now, she couldn't help but notice all the ways Clara had changed from their youth. Joy had only been taller than Clara for a few years, Clara quickly catching her and shooting up to 5'10. Her once brown hair was now dyed a harsh black. Her skin, once tan, was now pale, striking against her black hair. Her brown eyes were hidden beneath thick makeup, her figure hidden beneath a pair of ripped jeans and t-shirt. Her phone case had a picture of Michael Cera on it. Her phone lit up as she received a text message. Joy almost laughed at Clara's background, a bright pink image with bats scattered among characters from Animal Crossing. It seemed to contradict itself, bats and the animated animals, the bright pink background and Clara's much darker aesthetic, yet it made perfect sense.

"Did you work today?" Joy asked Clara, tuning out the argument Ethan and Caden were having about an anime they had both watched.

"Yeah," Clara confirmed. "Ten to six. Wasn't terrible, but it was busy. My feet are killing me."

Clara worked at the only restaurant in their tiny town, if it could even be called a town. Lenorah, Texas, was less a town and more a scattering of houses connected by fields of cotton and highways packed with oil-field truckers driving a few miles over the speed limit. The Grill, half gas station and half restaurant, was, outside of the school, the only landmark for miles. It was an oddity. One would expect a restaurant literally in between two cotton fields not to be the best, to say it nicely, but the food at the Grill was delicious. Their breakfast burritos were the finest in West Texas, with giant tortillas, the good, thick bacon, fluffy eggs, all held together with gooey cheese. And the suckers were huge, big enough that Joy used to buy one for breakfast before school, eat half, and save the other half for her lunch. Joy still made it a point to buy one when in town, having not yet found a suitable replacement in Austin.

"That's not bad. You have tomorrow off?"

Clara nodded.

"Yup. Gonna stay the night at Trini's if you want to hang out later."

Clara's eyes flicked from Joy to Ethan and back. A sly smile crept onto her lips. Joy narrowed her eyes and she attempted to shake her head subtly.

"So, Ethan..." Clara began, ignoring Joy's hiss of disapproval. "How long have you had a crush on my sister?"

Ethan choked on his drink, coughing up water onto Caden in front of him. Caden wrinkled her nose in disgust, stealing a napkin from Oliver and wiping the spit off of her face. She didn't say anything, listening eagerly for his response. Conversation around the table died as everyone waited. Joy knew she should have said something, interrupted and scolded Clara, but the words stuck in her throat. Her heart pounded wildly in her chest, and she could feel heat rising to her cheeks. Ethan turned to her. His brown eyes searched hers as if his response could be found there. He cleared his throat.

"I—"

"Who ordered the carne guisada?" The smiling waitress asked, plates of food balanced in a tray on her hand.

Joy's hand shot up, excited both at the thought of the food and the idea of changing the subject. She thanked the waitress as the dish was put down and eyed it eagerly. Three hours of shopping with Caden had left her drained, and her stomach rumbled as the smell of the stewed meat and homemade tortillas drifted through the air.

While the conversation around the table resumed in waves

of quiet murmurs, Clara's question remained on Joy's mind, especially as she watched the pink in Ethan's cheeks slowly fade. Could Ethan actually like her that way? Sure they spent a lot of time together, went out to eat at least three times a week, and saw a movie together every weekend... That sounds a lot like...

He only views you as a friend. A best friend, but a friend nonetheless.

Joy shook her head, Buttercup's words slicing through the thoughts jumbling in her mind. She grabbed a tortilla and scooped a bit of the meat up. Her mouth watered as she topped it with beans and rice.

"That's an awfully big plate you have there, Joy. Are you really planning on eating the whole thing?" Sarah's voice was like a bullet.

Her stomach turned. The food that had made Joy's mouth water seconds before now made her want to vomit. She thought back to years spent forcing herself to throw up in high school, to an entire decade where she was unable to look in the mirror without seeing all the flaws Sarah so casually reminded her of when they spoke.

Joy sat back, eyebrows furrowing. It seemed any fear Sarah might have felt earlier was gone, replaced by disdain and a cruel smile. Joy placed her hands in her lap. Ethan placed a large hand over hers, and she looked up at him in surprise. He smiled, nodding at her calmly. Joy felt a sudden surge of confidence, and she turned her narrowed eyes at her grandmother.

"I am. Is there something wrong with that?" she challenged.

Sarah glared back. Sensing tension, Trini turned from her conversation with Jonas. Sarah's features instantly slackened, her smile returning and eyebrows raising in mock concern.

"I was just teasing you. There's no need to get so worked up."

Clara scoffed, rolling her eyes as she took a bite of her own food. Sarah glanced around the table. She realized many family members were still staring at her, suspicious looks on their faces.

Sarah forced a laugh. "I was hoping to steal a bit. It smells so good and I only ordered a taco."

Joy sat quietly in response, not wanting to ruin Trini's dinner. Still, her face burned with embarrassment at her grandmother's dig. Something was building inside her, a resentment that pressed into every corner of her being. Her hands trembled. She shivered at the sensation of Buttercup leaving her. The black mist spread beneath the table and throughout the restaurant, leaving a thin film of black on the floor of the building.

Joy let out a shaky breath. She wanted Sarah to hurt. She shouldn't; she should let it go and save a confrontation for another day. Tonight and tomorrow weren't about her. It was Trini's special week. She could suck it up. She could handle this.

"So, Clara…" Sarah started. "Whatever happened to that art career of yours? I heard you're working in a convenience store now."

Joy clenched her fist. The water in her cup rippled. Joy's vision blurred, and her arms shook violently as if she was lifting something heavy. Ethan looked at her in concern. The ground below them began to shake, plates and forks clattering along the table and shattering as they fell to the floor.

"Earthquake, get down!" A server shouted, but Joy didn't move.

She couldn't control the anger that had built in her, try as she might. The room began to spin, the brightly colored lights twirling around Joy. A glass fell from the table, breaking a few inches away from where Clara had ducked beneath the table. A sliver hopped from the ground, and Clara hissed as it left a pink streak on her pale cheek.

Ethan grabbed her shoulder. A painting fell from the wall behind them, the corner of the frame clipping his shoulder. He groaned as it knocked him forward. The noise shook Joy from her stupor, and she unclenched her fist. The room stilled.

CHAPTER 27

Joy, Age 17

Joy and Clara giggled as they pushed through the door, a few friends with gift bags walking in behind them. They paused in the entrance, eyebrows furrowing as Trini waited for the group with red-rimmed eyes.

Joy couldn't explain why, but she had felt something was wrong all day. Trini had excused herself from Clara's birthday dinner, telling the group that she would meet them back at the house after the movie they were planning on seeing. After she left, there was a tension in Connor's shoulders, his eyes downcast even as his temperament remained unchanged. He had served as their chauffeur, driving them place to place, but had ducked out a few times, speaking in whispered conversations and avoiding Joy's inquiring looks.

"Hi girls, we had a family emergency come up. We've already talked to your parents. Taylor and SB, your parents are on their way to pick you up. Gemma, your mom said you could drive home, just avoid the highways and drive safe," Trini said with a wobbly smile.

Joy and Clara exchanged worried glances but remained silent. A car pulled into the driveway, and Taylor murmured a quick "Happy Birthday" to Clara before walking down the stairs and into the vehicle. Gemma gave Joy and Clara a hug and followed, getting into her car and driving away. The group waited a few tense minutes for SB's father to arrive. With a final hug, SB left, and Trini ushered Joy and Clara into the living room.

"There's no easy way to say this," Kenny started. "Your grandfather killed himself. They found his body this morning."

The world stilled. Joy's head throbbed as she stared back at Kenny. Her parents watched the girls, eyes searching for their reactions.

"How did he do it?" Joy asked, surprising herself with the calmness of her voice.

Kenny shook his head, confusion blatant on his face.

"I want to know how he did it. They're going to be talking about it. I want to know before I find out some other way."

Kenny hesitated. He looked to Trini, who reluctantly nodded. "He shot himself in his car."

Joy nodded. Clara began to cry, but Joy didn't think she was crying. She reached her hand up and swiped it along her cheeks, confirming they were dry.

"Are you okay?" Trini asked, reaching out to Joy and Clara. Joy leaned up, avoiding her mother's touch. She caught the flash of hurt on Trini's face but kept her own expression blank. "We're here if you want to talk."

Joy nodded.

"I think I'm going to go to bed now. I'd like to be alone." Her voice sounded cold, uncaring, even to herself.

Trini and Connor started to protest, but Joy ignored them, walking to her room and quietly shutting her door.

She lay down on her bed and pulled out her phone. She wanted someone to confide in, someone to rant to, to cry to. As she stared at the lit screen, she realized there was no one she trusted, no one who would understand. She placed her phone on her nightstand, took a deep breath, and then imploded.

Outside of the anger she was still trying to unlearn, Joy was usually reserved with her emotions, quiet by nature and even more so in the confines of her room. Grief, however, does not remain within the molds of one's personality. That night Joy's grief, as much as she tried to muffle it, was loud.

She sobbed, swore at her ceiling fan, screamed at the hidden sky. She cursed a world in which someone so bright and full of life had died while she, dull and unimportant as she thought herself, lived.

Joy called for her grandfather, mouth pressed against her pillow, again and again and again until her voice could no longer be heard. She mourned until her eyes were too swollen to see and her throat was too raw to speak.

And then a thought.

A thought so cruel, so life-changing, that she shot up in her bed.

She wrapped her trembling arms around herself.

She thought back to her life in Miles, the life she had so carelessly abandoned. She thought of leaving Tom in that house with Sarah, of his sad eyes and the dejected tone of his voice in their phone calls.

The thought bounced through her head, rattling her, chilling her to the core.

Joy wondered if it was possible to love someone away from the edge. Perhaps not, but as her mother and father had abandoned her, she had abandoned him. Worse, she left him with her, the woman who still haunted her dreams, who had a way of making people feel small, worthless. Could Joy have shown him that he was worth so incredibly much? Had she not been selfish, had she stayed, would he still be alive?

The thought echoed.

This was your fault.

The nightmares started that night.

CHAPTER 28

"If you don't put down my damn burrito, I swear to you I will burn this bitch to the ground," Caden shouted from next to Joy's door.

After returning from the restaurant, everyone went their separate ways. No one had been seriously hurt; her family had left sporting only nicks and bruises. The news called it a freak accident, an earthquake that only targeted the tiny area of the restaurant, a result of too much fracking in the oil capital of Texas. Joy knew better.

She had spent the night in the guest room she had dropped her bags off in, which was unfortunately located right down the hall from the kitchen. Jonas had dropped off breakfast burritos for all of the children but had grabbed too many sausage burritos. The bacon ones had quickly been claimed, leaving only one for Caden and Oliver, the last to wake up other than Joy, to fight over. Not that Joy had actually been there when it happened. No, she had been fast asleep, woken only by the sound of Caden throwing things at their youngest brother.

"I'm going to murder both of them," Joy grumbled, ripping open her door and stalking into the kitchen.

Ethan sat atop a stool, still dressed in his pajamas, hair mussed from sleeping on the couch in Oliver's room. Joy had expected them to share a room and had even been secretly looking forward to it, but Oliver insisted on Ethan staying with him so that the two could play some new game he had downloaded. If the bags under Ethan's eyes were any indication, they hadn't gotten much sleep.

"Are they always like this?" Ethan whispered to Joy, passing her a sausage burrito as she plopped down beside him but not bothering to take his eyes off of the fighting siblings.

Joy watched in amazement as Oliver sprinted around the dining room table and leapt over the back of the couch, feet sliding only slightly upon landing on the wooden floor in his bright yellow basketball socks.

She laughed, leaning over Ethan to grab a packet of hot sauce. "No, they're usually much worse."

There was a knock on the front door, followed by a pause only long enough for Joy to swallow a bite of burrito.

It swung open, Charlie strolling into the house with a cheery, "Sup, nerds."

Joy nodded in greeting and turned back toward Oliver, slowly lifting the burrito to his mouth. Oliver licked the burrito, and Caden let out a screech, a combination of a dog whistle and silverware scraping along the bottom of a porcelain plate, a demonic wail that seemed to summon Trini from the depths of the house. Using Trini stepping into the room as a distraction, Oliver darted toward Joy and Ethan, Caden sprinting after him in a blur of black, fluffy pajama pants.

"He's not coming," Trini sighed, resignation slipping onto her face before she masked it with an optimistic half-smile.

Joy raised her eyebrows, assuming Trini meant some distant relative that Joy wouldn't have been able to recognize anyway. Oliver skidded to a stop, Caden smacking him on the back of the head as she passed and grabbing one of the sausage burritos before leaning against the counter.

"Who?" she asked.

"The pastor," Trini deadpanned.

Joy's lips parted in shock. A silence fell over the room as the siblings processed their mother's words.

"I'm sorry, what was that?" Joy asked, setting her burrito to the side and standing.

We kill him.

No, Joy thought back.

You're right. Too kind. We kill his family?

Still a no.

His dog?

"That dickwad!" Caden fumed, pacing the kitchen in her pajamas and picking up her phone. "I knew something like this was going to happen. He and Dad hang out a lot. What did he say?"

Ha. She called a preacher a dickwad.

Trini ran her hand through her hair. "Just that he wasn't comfortable officiating. He said he usually meets with the couple a few times before doing a wedding, for counsel. We've been texting him all week trying to set up times. He finally responded this morning, saying he wasn't coming."

Biting back her anger, Joy asked, "Do you have a backup?"

Trini hesitated.

"We do..."

Her eyes flicked up to Charlie.

He grinned. "Hell, yeah."

* * *

The heels that Caden had loaned her sat mockingly on the dresser. It was stupid how a pair of shoes had the ability to make Joy feel so insecure. They were adorable, black and strappy, and would undoubtedly look great with the outfit Joy had planned for the wedding. Joy stared down at her bare feet, wiggling her toes on the wooden floor. The problem with the shoes was that they were open at the top. The same toes pressed against the cold floor would be on display for anyone to see. Wrinkling her nose in disgust, she tossed the shoes into the back of the guest room closet.

Her favorite shoes in seventh grade, before she moved in with Trini and Connor, were a pair of basketball shoes. She lived in those shoes, wearing them, working out and practicing in them, for hours a day. That was not to say she was a gifted basketball player, far from it. But basketball practices and games kept her at the school longer, meaning she didn't have to go back as early when things began to fall apart. A part of her felt guilty. While she stayed on the court, Clara walked home alone, faced Sarah alone, became quieter, more reclusive. But Joy had made friends with some of the older girls while playing, and it was addicting, not being lonely anymore. It also gave Joy something to do at home. Tom loved basketball and had played in high school. On the rare occasions he was home, he was in the driveway with Joy, playing Chicken or teaching her a new post move.

The shoes themselves weren't bought by her grandparents. A coach had felt bad for the small girl trying to play in beat-up sneakers and bought her a pair. Joy had been too excited to tell her they were a size and a half too small. Her toes bled from rubbing against the top of the shoes. Before every practice, she would hide in the locker room toilet stall, wrapping her feet in layers of toilet paper so the blood wouldn't rub off onto the fabric of the shoe.

She continued to wear the shoes a year after she moved in with Trini and Connor. It wasn't that they wouldn't buy her shoes. They probably would have if she hadn't been too scared to ask. She didn't want to be a burden, didn't want them changing their mind about taking her and Clara in. So she wore the shoes all through the school year. In high school, the school athletic program bought all the basketball girls new shoes, and Joy tossed the old ones. She assumed the blisters on her feet would fade with time. They didn't. Instead, the skin had hardened into calluses, a big lump of flesh on top of each of her toes.

She hated sandals, wearing sneakers even in the hottest of

weather.

Although she loved the look of the shoes Caden had loaned her, she pulled out a pair of flats from her suitcase and slipped them on.

* * *

As Ethan accepted yet another invite to dance, this time with Jonas's mother, Joy sat and watched the couples sway to an old country song. The ice in her Coke and rum had slowly melted, the condensation of the glass leaving her hand uncomfortably damp. She wiped it against the white tablecloth. The decor of the wedding was rustic, pearl cloth on antique wooden tables and sparkling lights strung in the trees overhead. Atop each table sat a white candle and a bouquet of blushing peonies, white roses, and snapdragons placed in thin wooden vases.

The wedding itself was small and short, Charlie doing surprisingly well as the makeshift preacher. Joy thought there must be a better term for this. Speaker? Officiant? Likening Charlie to a preacher seemed sacrilegious in a way, especially as he managed to slip in two dirty jokes, three usages of the word fuck (oddly enough, completely separate from the dirty jokes), and likened marriage to an anchor that forever weighed a person down.

Still, he pulled it together with a sweet comment about how glad he was his little sister had finally found her happiness and only grimaced slightly as he told Jonas he may kiss the bride.

Jonas swung Trini around the makeshift dance floor—a mahogany platform perched atop grass—her blonde hair bouncing around her shoulders in carefully crafted curls, head tipped back in a burst of laughter.

"She looks happy," Clara noted, plopping herself into the chair next to Joy.

Joy raised her eyebrows at the bottle of vodka clutched in

Clara's hands.

"You good?"

Clara shrugged.

"Figured it would help with dealing with Sarah."

Joy stared at her, then reached for the bottle. She took a large swig, the alcohol burning on the way down. Someone cleared their throat behind her, and she turned, eyebrows raised and one hand still holding the bottle of alcohol.

"Dance with me."

Ethan stuck out his hand, nodding toward the patio. Joy narrowed her eyes but bit back a grin. Grabbing his hand, Joy led him to the edge of the patio and wrapped her arms around his neck. He placed his hands on her waist, tugging her close enough that the two stood chest to chest. She glanced up at him, neck straining to meet his eyes, and smiled when she noticed his red-tinted cheeks. The music, a soft country song sung by a man with a deep voice, drifted over the porch and through the night, and the two swayed to the beat. Joy relaxed in his arms, resting her head against his chest.

Joy was a terrible dancer. Born with two left feet and no sense of rhythm, she had spent many a prom, quinceanera, and spring fling with her arms stiffly around her poor partners, eyes fixed on the ground to avoid stepping on feet. With Ethan, dancing felt different, calmer, gentler. He was her goofy best friend, the one person who would never mock her for the awkwardness of her step.

"You look beautiful in that dress," Ethan said, his voice rumbling through his chest.

She had been told she was pretty many times as a teenager, usually by adults who tutted about enjoying her youth. She had only been told she was beautiful a few times by family members, but never in the way Ethan said it. It wasn't his first time telling her she was beautiful, and hopefully it wouldn't be the last, but there was something about the way the stars twinkled in the country sky, the velvety voice of the man crooning about first love, and the giggles of kids running through the backyard that made Joy want the moment to never end.

Not for the first time, her breath caught in her chest at his words. She pulled back from him, her eyes shining with unshed tears, and looked up.

As she looked into Ethan's eyes, she saw herself. She could tell he really saw her. Not the anger. Not the anxiety. Not the bitterness of her youth. He saw her as she was. Broken, desperately trying to hold it together, to be the perfect sister, daughter, friend. Worse yet, he could see the loneliness. The pure, all-consuming loneliness. And he didn't flinch. He was unyielding in his friendship. Joy realized Ethan was, and might always be, her favorite person.

"You know, you two remind me so much of Tom and me back when we first got married. Before everything went to shit," Sarah's voice rang out from over Ethan's shoulder.

NO.

Joy flinched. She pulled back from Ethan, who looked at her in question. Forcing a smile, she let go of Ethan's hand.

"Sorry, I think I'm going to get something to drink. Do you want anything?"

She turned from him as heat flooded through her, body tensed as it waited to flee. Ethan reached out, placing his hand on her shoulder and forcing her to look back at him.

"Um, no. Not really. Do you want me to come with you?"

We're not her.

"That's okay, I'll be back in a minute."

Joy jogged away, practically sprinting as she slipped inside and locked herself in the restroom.

"Get it together, Joy. You're fine. It's fine."

We are not fine.

I am fine. I will be fine.

Joy slapped her cheeks, glaring at her reflection.

We will never be her. We're nothing like her. We should make her suffer for even thinking we would ever be anything like her.

Not here. Not today. Not at Trini's wedding. I'm fine.

Everything is fine, damn it.

Joy puffed out a breath before pasting a smile back on her face. She grabbed a drink from a cooler in the kitchen without bothering to look at what it was and trudged her way through those gathered around the snack table to glance out the back door.

In the short time Joy had been inside, her grandmother had managed to corner Jonas, who laughed awkwardly at whatever she was telling him. Trini was chatting to a distant cousin a few feet away, her eyes flitting nervously to the pair every few seconds. Joy opened the door and nudged her way by a group chatting by the stereo, inching her way closer to hear what Sarah was saying.

"I'm surprised she chose to wear a dress that short. She always had such shapely legs." Jonas's eyebrows furrowed as Sarah spoke. She laughed, placing her hand on his arm. "Oh, I'm not saying that as a bad thing, obviously. I'm sure you're into that kind of thing. Bigger girls are seen as so attractive these days. Course, I don't know where she got that from. Her dad was always so skinny, and I mean it obviously didn't come from my side."

Jonas looked away, searching the crowd to make sure Trini wasn't close enough to hear her mother. Trini simply looked hurt. Her smile had been so happy, so content, and now it turned at the edges as if she were willing her joy not to fade at the comment.

Get Sarah away from them.

Joy paced down the concrete, grabbed her grandmother by the arm, and tugged her into the garage.

CHAPTER 29

Joy, Age 17

"Will you pass me the tape?" Sarah asked.

Joy passed it to her silently, staring at the walls of the living room she had grown up in. Sarah was being kicked out; the house now legally belonged to her aunt, Tom's biological daughter. Joy, Connor, Trini, Clara, Kaelyn, and Oliver had driven down to help her pack.

Joy didn't want to be there, in the house that had caused her so much pain. She hated it but hated its emptiness even more. Gone were the traces of her childhood, the paintings on the walls, the collection of the nerdiest possible DVDs in the cabinets.

Her grandfather's art room had been stripped bare long before Sarah was forced to move, items claimed by various relatives mere hours after the funeral. Her grandfather's mother had led the charge for stripping the house, passing out objects to Tom's biological niece and nephew.

Joy didn't think to stop and grab something for herself, even as Trini, bless her heart, tried to break her out of her stupor.

"Is there anything you want?" Trini had asked.

Tom to be alive, she nearly responded.

The entire day had been overwhelming, and the last thing she wanted was to pick through her dead grandfather's things the same day as his funeral. It felt morbid. She wished she had snapped out of it and thought to claim more, any reminder of him she could, but she only watched as his things were divided among his family, the toys she grew up playing with and the comics she grew up reading shoved into the hands of others.

Tom's biological family ignored Clara and Joy as they grabbed the things they wanted, which only enforced Joy's hatred for herself and the idea that she was to blame. It was as if she wasn't worthy of his things now that he was gone, as if she had only been tolerated while he was still alive to defend her.

And maybe she wasn't worthy of being defended, not when she knew how far he was slipping and did nothing to prevent it.

"Oh, you like Star Wars, right?" Tom's mother asked as she handed yet another of the movies Joy had grown up watching to her cousin.

Joy said nothing as he took it eagerly.

The case for *The Princess Bride* was lifted from Tom's drawer, wordlessly passed from cousin to cousin before being tossed in a donation pile. Joy plucked it from among the other rejects, clutching it tightly to her chest. When she got home after the funeral, she hid it under her bed, afraid some unknown force would steal it from her.

Although months had since passed since his funeral, the emptiness didn't subside, wouldn't subside. Night after night she thought of joining him, convincing herself that no one would miss her anyway. She was an extra piece, a child unwanted, a burden.

And now here she was, pretending it was just another Sunday, as if her grandmother had simply bought a new house. Joy wasn't sure how she felt about that. She didn't like Sarah being in the same room as her, making her heart thump harshly in her chest, even as she put on her most polite smile and spoke only the most civil of words. This was the way it worked in her family. She was expected at all times to put up a good image, to act like everything was fine and that she wasn't helping the woman who had abused her for almost a decade, something that was never talked about within her family, move into a tiny house on the other side of town.

She was tired, physically from helping move boxes, but more so mentally. She was sick of her family pretending everything was okay, of them enforcing their expectations of obedience. Even worse, she was expected to be in a good mood, a cheerful mood, so as not to scare her younger siblings.

No one spoke about Tom.

Instead, they trashed his daughter, calling her names and tutting about how immoral Sarah's eviction had been. They made it sound like Sarah was a victim, this poor grieving widow who suddenly became homeless, instead of the woman who had mooched off Tom for years, living in his house long after the ink on their divorce had settled and sleeping with his best friend on the vacations Tom paid for.

Joy felt gross as she watched them toast with beers and pass out pizza, an anger building in her like she had never known. She was still in mourning, and her family was acting like they had something to celebrate. Sarah had actually said she was excited for a "fresh start." She didn't understand how she could say that so happily. Where was her grandfather's fresh start? How could she be so flippant about the situation, so uncaring?

On the final trip from the old house to Sarah's new house, Joy had been startled by a thumping in the next room, the gasp that she recognized as Clara's making her leap into action. Trini and Connor had taken the younger kids to the new house to finish eating, leaving Joy, Clara, and Sarah. When she came into the room, now empty except for a small box lying on the carpet and the trash Sarah had purposely left lying about the house, she paused. Clara stared down at the box, its lid slightly ajar, her hands shaking and eyes wide with fear while Sarah leaned against the doorway casually.

"What is it?" Joy asked.

She didn't really want to know.

Clara only shook her head.

Sarah shifted, pulling a pack of cigarettes from her sweatpants and lighting one.

"That's the one," she sighed.

Only Joy knew it wasn't a real sigh. Joy had grown to understand her grandmother's masks, the way she lilted her words and cast her eyes downward in an attempt to seem sad. It wasn't real sadness. Sarah was not one to grieve without an audience.

Clara rushed out of the room, her head shaking rapidly and tears swarming down her cheeks.

"What. Is. It," Joy demanded, iciness seeping into her tone as she stared down her grandmother.

Sarah took a drag. "The one he killed himself with."

"What the fuck."

"Language," Sarah chided, pushing off the wall and scooping the box up.

Joy didn't look, couldn't force herself to even if she had wanted to. Sarah strode by her, cigarette lit in one hand, the box with the gun her grandfather had used to kill himself in the other. But Clara. Clara had seen it. Clara would never be able to unsee it, as she would tell Joy years later after a few too many gulps of wine stolen from Trini's fridge.

Joy would also find out where the gun had come from—Sarah's dresser—and how it had been returned to her, a box on the porch left by Tom's biological daughter. Joy didn't know how much of the story she was told was true—Sarah had a way of framing a situation such that she was always the victim—but apparently, Tom's daughter had invited Sarah out to lunch. The conversation had been civil, pleasant even according to Sarah, but had ended with Sarah being served an eviction notice. A few minutes after parting ways, with Sarah too stunned to speak (although Joy very much doubted that), Tom's daughter had texted Sarah to check her porch. The box had been sitting on the concrete, waiting for Sarah, Tom's daughter simply telling her that she was returning it.

Gruesome. And so very fitting for Joy's family.

After Clara found the gun, they returned to Sarah's new house, where music was playing and chips of bags were being opened, forming an impromptu housewarming party. The casualness dug deep into Joy, Sarah's grin burning under the surface of Joy's skin. A rock song pounded through the air while Clara slouched in a corner, staring at hands that had held the object that killed Tom.

Joy snapped, her composed mask finally shattering. Her exact words had been washed away by the years, but her family looked at her with such disdain, such disgust at her outburst, that she simply left. She packed herself back in her truck, Clara climbing into her passenger seat, and sped away from that tiny town, praying she never had to return.

"Joy, slow down."

Clara gripped the sides of the seats. Joy accelerated well past the speed limit. Tears slipped down her face. Her vision blurred, and Clara yelled in her ear.

"Joy! STOP THE CAR."

Joy slammed on the brakes and pulled to the side of the road. She sobbed then, shoulders quaking.

At seventeen, Joy had never been taught how to communicate beyond superficial remarks and passive-aggressive comments. And so she found herself alone. She didn't know how to talk about the sorrow and bitterness she was feeling, or even who to speak to.

For the last few months, she felt she had been screaming. Not literally, but everything in her felt wrong, angry.

She didn't feel like eating and couldn't get out of bed.

Although she didn't say a word, she was begging for someone, anyone, to notice that she wasn't okay. Her family, her friends had to have known. How do you live with someone, ask them about their day, tell them you care about them, and not see the way they beg for help? How can you look someone in the eyes over a dinner table and not see the emptiness in them? And yet they did nothing. It could be because they didn't know what to do, or that they were afraid they would make it worse, but it felt like they didn't care.

What Joy didn't understand was that a silent scream might be seen but was never heard, even by those closest to you.

CHAPTER 30

"Slow down, Joy. Where's the emergency?" Sarah chuckled, yanking her arm out of Joy's grip.

"You don't get to act like everything is fine," Joy gritted out, her arms quivering from the intensity with which she clenched her fists at her side. "You don't get to make your little comments. Not today. Not on Trini's wedding day."

Sarah's smile tightened.

"What do you mean? I don't appreciate the way you're speaking to me. I know we had our differences in the past, but we're still family."

Joy laughed darkly.

"If that's your idea of family, I don't want it. I'm not going to ignore years of abuse and neglect."

Sarah glanced around the empty garage, searching for any witnesses as she let her carefully crafted mask slip, and then scoffed.

"I would hardly say we abused you. You had food to eat and a roof over your head."

"You gave me an eating disorder! And I wasn't the only one! You continually belittled us until I felt like I wasn't worthy of love." Joy unclenched her fists and forced a shaky breath. "I couldn't look in a mirror for years. I've just started getting over that. And you were physical. Just because you used a belt and would call it punishment doesn't make it not abuse. I was seven the first time you used a belt on me, for saying a cuss word I didn't even understand. It wasn't only us, either. You were horrible to Tom too. You used him, divorced him, and then continued to use him."

Let us out.

"Tom and I loved each other," Sarah ground out.

A trickle of sweat ran down Joy's neck. The garage was suddenly too hot and small, the walls creeping closer as her vision blurred.

"He loved you. You treated him like a servant and then cheated on him. With his best friend, one of the few he had, multiple times."

Make her pay.

"He sent me, alone, on that trip and then never asked if anything happened. He was practically begging me to cheat."

The lightbulb flickered and dimmed, casting shadows crawling through the room. Cold shot through Joy's body, and she fought back a shiver, even as sweat trailed down her spine.

Joy snarled. "You're wrong. He sent you on that trip because he knew you were using again and thought getting away would help you get clean. He didn't want you around us because you were unstable, but he had nowhere he could take the two of us. We had nowhere to go, so he sent you away instead."

"He didn't do shit for y'all. I was the one who begged him to take you two in." Sarah rolled her eyes.

"Even if that's true, he showed up for us. While you were shit-faced, he was working multiple jobs. You couldn't even keep one."

"I worked my ass off." Sarah shoved her finger into Joy's chest. "And don't forget I sent you to Trini's. I gave you a second chance at a new life."

"It was Trini who fought for us to live with them. She knew what was happening. You going to rehab was her last straw."

Sarah flinched, her eyes widening as she took a few steps back. Joy smiled cruelly at her grandmother's surprise. Sarah, who collected secrets, who traded in insecurities shared in confidence, should know better than to think Joy wouldn't have learned a trick or two from her.

She needs to learn that those who are bold in their hatred and cruelty should hold no exploitable weaknesses.

"Yeah, that's right. I know all about your stints in rehab. I know how you got run out of your last town for breaking into the pharmacy. Just because you've convinced everyone else in that stupid little town that you're some sorry widow doesn't mean you actually are one. I see who you really are. I know all of your little secrets. And I'm going to make sure everyone else does too, you manipulative old—"

Sarah's hand shot out, cracking across Joy's face.

"Learn your place, you little bitch. You would've been nothing without me. I took you in when even your own parents didn't want you. I did you a favor, sending you to Trini. You think I'm a bad guy, but I knew. I saved you because I knew he was going to kill himself. I got you out before he could," Sarah hissed.

Her attention was no longer on Joy. Instead, she was watching the door as voices floated by.

She knew.

"You knew..." Joy whispered, cradling her cheek.

Sarah bucked up, squaring her shoulder and lengthening her spine. Joy stood, unflinching, waiting.

Make her pay. Make her hurt.

She took a step back, and Sarah's eyes flashed in triumph at the way Joy seemed to bow down to her. Joy didn't move because she was afraid of Sarah or being hit. It was the opposite. She stepped back because she realized she wanted Sarah to hit her again, wanted a reason to let Buttercup go, to fight back.

Looking at her grandmother's frail body, Joy knew it wouldn't be hard to hurt her, to make her pay for all the pain she had inflicted on her. But that wasn't the kind of person Joy wanted to be. She didn't want to stoop to her level. She wasn't

Sarah. She wasn't her mother. She didn't want to feed into the anger that she had inherited.

Sarah rolled her eyes again, her lip curling upward in disgust.

"Of course I knew. I was surprised he didn't do it sooner. I was waiting for the day—"

Buttercup shot out, its solid mist connecting with Sarah's nose with a gruesome crunch. Joy stood unmoving, numb, as the older woman fell to the ground. She sighed, then cracked her neck from side to side. A few moments passed in silence, Sarah stunned as red began to drip from her nose. When Joy finally spoke, her voice was calm and even, no hint of emotion in her tone.

"I always thought it was unfair how you got to live happily. How you have your little food truck and get to walk around like nothing ever happened. I used to fear you, but now? Now I pity you. You're a failed rockstar wannabe who piggybacked off of everyone around you. Don't show yourself around me again. Don't text me. Don't even look in my direction. Or I will tear down the life you've managed to build. I will not stop until each and every person you know hates you as much as I do."

"That's a gift from the devil," Sarah whispered. "You go against God every time you use that power."

Joy squatted, placing herself at eye level with her grandmother. "So now you're interested in God? I distinctly remember you telling Clara she looked 'too poor' to go to church and that God would hate her if she showed up in jeans. Think we might have different ideas of what God would be against."

The garage door opened then, Caden typing on her phone as she stepped into the room. She glanced up, saw Sarah on the floor, then slowly backed out of the garage, slamming the door shut behind her.

So what now?

CHAPTER 31

Joy, Age 18

Joy stared at Connor, her eyebrows furrowing in confusion. He paused, dart in hand, and turned to look at the girl.

"I think it would be good for you. Community college is a great first step, and you could always transfer out. It'll give you time to save money and adjust to living on your own," he repeated.

Joy wasn't sure what to say. It felt like the breath had been sucked out of her. She had done everything she thought she was supposed to in high school. She was president of the student council and the Fellowship of Christian Athletes, helped lead the science team, played varsity tennis and basketball, even joined the One Act Play in an odd bid to make herself more likable.

She did well in academics, incredibly well, with teachers often praising her intelligence and peers coming to her for homework help. She was set to graduate Valedictorian in the spring from her admittedly incredibly small school. She scored well on her ACT, well enough to get her into any school in-state she wanted and the majority of those outside her state.

"I don't want to go to community college," Joy muttered from her position on the bar stool.

There was nothing wrong with community college, but Joy had bigger plans for her life. She was the smart child, the successful one. She wasn't the kid who had been left behind anymore. She wasn't the poor kid anymore. She wouldn't let herself be looked at with pity, as she imagined she would be if her friends found out. She wanted, NEEDED, to be the child that her parents could brag about to their friends. If she wasn't impressive, wasn't attending the best school possible, would they even talk about her anymore? If there was nothing to be proud of, would she simply fade from the conversation, forgotten as another child who wasted their potential? She wouldn't let herself be abandoned, not this time.

"I understand that, Joy, but will you be able to afford to go to a different college? Even UT is almost $20,000 a year."

Her stomach dropped. There it was, the real reason he was suggesting community college. Something flared in her then, an anger so deep and so red that it scared her. When she and Clara moved, she had expected things to be different. She was hesitant, but more than willing to give up control. If anything, she was excited to finally get the opportunity to be a kid.

As she went through high school, Trini and Connor's house never felt like home to Joy, simply the lesser of two evils. There was no nurturing on Connor's part, no building of a relationship. There was a clear boundary between her and her new family, one she didn't know how to cross. There was Joy, and there was her family, but there seemed to be no space for the two to exist simultaneously. Joy ran parallel to her family, always in the same proximity, but never crossing. He continued while her anger built.

"We'll try to pitch in, but you know we won't be able to help much. There're always loans, but you don't want to get a whole bunch of debt for a degree that's just as good as one you could get around here. I'm just saying it's a good option."

Joy wanted to laugh. She wanted to scream. She knew he would be paying if it were one of his actual kids who was going to college. If little Caden batted her eyes and told him she wanted to go to college out of state, he would gladly pony up the money.

Joy had become someone she hated in order to be accepted by this man, and it was at this moment that she realized she would never truly fit into his life. She had been so desperate for affection and acceptance that she shaped herself to please those around her. She had mirrored the actions and mannerisms of the popular students at her school, molding her personality into one she thought her peers and her new family would accept. At school, she craved attention and fought to keep it. She felt so empty being this person, hollow inside. Her voice was shrill and noisy to her ears, her laugh fake and harsh.

"I never asked you to pay for college. I'm going to go to UT. I'm going to get scholarships and take out loans and do everything right. I'm not going to end up stuck in this stupid little town for the rest of my life. I'm not going to end up knocked up and miserable, going to the same stupid bar with the same stupid people I knew in high school. I'm not going to end up like you," she practically spit.

She felt guilty as soon as she said it, her neck hot and chest tight, but she refused to take it back as she sprinted from the barn, ignoring Connor as he called after her. She didn't slow down until she was safe in her bedroom. All her bravada and indignation crashed the moment she stepped inside. In her room, she was quiet. She lay in bed, covering herself in blankets and curling her body in on itself as she hid from the fatigue, from existing, from the uncertainty of never knowing what it was she wanted. She felt like screaming, but not a whisper escaped her lips. All of her hard work, all of her desperate trying to be well-liked, had been for nothing.

Did Connor hate her now?

She hated herself, but she had tried so hard to be liked by him. What if all of it was not enough?

Desperate for any source of comfort, she draped herself over her bed and allowed her fingers to drag against the floor.

They bumped against hard plastic, and she yanked out the *Princess Bride* DVD case she had rescued after Tom's funeral. She didn't have a tv in her room but maybe she could wait until everyone was asleep and then use the subtitles so she didn't have to—

The case was empty.

CHAPTER 32

Joy gasped, shocked at the words that had slipped from her lips. She towered over Sarah, even in her flats. She took a step back. Then another. Then sprinted away from her speechless grandmother and back into the house.

She gasped out, "Not today. Jesus, Joy, not today."

Why not today?

It's Trini's wedding, Joy thought back.

And she invited the woman who abused Clara and us.

Joy nodded at Caden as she passed her in the hallway, forcing herself to slow down to a casual walk. She stopped at the kitchen window, looking out at the happy couple. The wedding was winding down in the backyard, guests slipping away in the night, goodbye hugs and final congratulations being given to a beaming Trini and Jonas.

That's not an excuse to lose my temper like that. I know better. I am better.

Why should you be? Why did you, even as only a child, have to be the bigger person? You don't have to forgive, don't have to force yourself to move on. Trini chose to invite Sarah to hurt you.

But Sarah's her mother. Of course, she'd want her mother here.

And Trini's your mother.

And?

And why should she need her mother here while ignoring her duties as ours? It's funny how often you call us selfish while forcing our feelings down at every chance. Trini has it all. A new house. A new husband. New children. She had plenty, but it wasn't enough. No, she also had to invite Sarah, to force us to act civilly like she hadn't placed us in a position to interact with the woman who ruined our childhood. We have every right to be upset.

"I can't..." Joy mumbled, shaking her head. "It's too much. I can't deal with this right now."

In the span of two days, Joy had caused a minor earthquake, lost her job, and confronted her grandmother. Trini was going to be pissed off with her, she had no idea how she was going to pay her rent, and she was losing control over her powers, using Buttercup for the stupidest and pettiest of things. It was all too much, problems overwhelming her from every angle. She needed to step back, get a good night's rest so she could wake up in the morning and start planning.

She spun on her heels, intent on telling Trini and Jonas goodnight and sleeping off her clawing anxiety. She rubbed at her eyes, her heavy fake eyelashes suddenly itchy, and grumbled out a quiet apology as she bumped into a firm chest.

"Hey, I've been looking for you," Ethan said, wrapping his hands around her shoulders and guiding her away from the back door, through the kitchen, and back into the garage. Sarah was nowhere to be seen, but a small pink spot dotted the concrete where she had been. "Everything alright?"

"Yeah, I was about to head back to the—"

"I'm in love with you."

The world stopped. The humming of the deep freezer and muffled music from outside, the dirt bike and power tools lining the walls, the chatter of guests and the beeping of cars being unlocked, all faded to the background, leaving only a blushing Ethan.

"What?" Joy whispered.

Ethan stepped back, allowing room for Joy to process his words.

"You knew. There's no way you didn't know. And I'm sorry

that I blurted it like that. I just." Ethan took a deep breath. "I'm tired of us acting like we're just friends, like we both don't want something more."

Joy blinked. "But you're my best friend."

"Yeah."

It grew quiet, Ethan searching her eyes for a response. Joy hated it. It was intense, how incredibly vulnerable she felt under his warm gaze.

"Joy. I've loved you for years now. I know it. You know it. So what is it that you're so afraid of?"

"I can't," Joy shook her head. "I can't be with anyone, not like that."

"And why not? Because your old ass, incredibly abusive grandmother and crazy biological mother say you can't? You're still letting them ruin your life, even when they're no longer a part of it."

"You don't understand," Joy gulped.

"You're right. I don't understand. So tell me! Help me understand what it is you think is so unlovable about you! Because I know you, Joy! Probably better than any of your family members ever did. And I can tell you, you are so worthy of love. You are smart and beautiful and kind. And yeah, you're a bit of a dick sometimes. And you're awkward as hell other times. But I would not change a single thing about you, because I see it. I see all of it. The way you light up around your siblings. The tiny acts of kindness you do when you're so certain that no one is watching. Your ridiculous obsession with romance novels and secret love of all things nerdy. The sadness in your eyes. The anger. The bitterness. I see it. And I am going to accept every part, all of the darkness and all of your light, because I love you." Ethan took a deep breath. "So please. Please help me to understand."

"What if they're right about me?" Joy whispered.

Ethan threw his hands up in frustration. "You mean when they say you're like them? You're not. I promise you're not."

"Yeah, it's easy to say that, but you don't know. That anger and that bitterness that's in me? That's them. That's them in a nutshell. I've seen what love does to people, how it hurts them. Trini and Connor, my grandparents, my mom and her boyfriends, all examples of how toxic relationships can be.

"I've seen families ripped apart, people who loved so hard that when it was ripped away from them, it broke them, people who became monsters because of their partners. I watched Trini grow silent and passive and Connor grow dismissive. I saw my mom bring out the worst in every single man in her life. And Sarah was so angry all of the time, so manipulative and cruel while my grandfather just watched."

Ethan grabbed her hands, pulling her closer to him.

"You're not them, Joy. We're not them."

"But what if that's what's waiting for me?"

Ethan shook his head.

"It's not."

"What if I bring out the worst in you?"

His shoulders slumped.

"You've never been anything but supportive."

"What if I can't control my temper?"

Joy's chin dropped to her chest.

"Then you'll go to therapy. I can't help you with it, but I can be by your side as you learn."

"What if I can't make you happy?"

"You already make me so happy!" he shouted, shaking her hands gently.

"And if I don't and you leave and I lose you as a friend too?"

"I'm not going to leave, Joy. Jesus, you've written us off before we've even tried. Not everyone in your life is going to hurt you."

Perhaps not on purpose.

"Not everyone is going to leave you."

And yet they have so far.

"People love you and want to be more in your life. Your parents, your siblings, me."

"How—" Joy began, but choked a sob.

Ethan waited.

"How am I supposed to make you happy when I don't know how to make myself happy?"

Ethan opened his mouth to respond. He closed it as Joy continued.

"I can't even imagine what it would feel like to be happy. Like truly happy. Fuck, I don't even know if I have a right to be happy. I've always been a bit selfish, even as a kid. I didn't stand up for Clara enough when we were kids. I didn't stay in Miles with Tom, even though I knew he wasn't okay, and I didn't reach out enough when I left. I was mean and fake in high school. Maybe all of this shit I've been through has been some form of karma for being selfish, for not being enough, for not trying harder. So maybe instead of wanting to be happy, I want to feel okay. Not sick. Not anxious. Not waiting for the other shoe to drop, just okay."

"Joy—" Ethan stood, reaching out for her.

She jerked backward, away from his reach. "And I don't want that for you. I don't want 'just okay' for you. You are so kind and happy all of the time, and I don't want you to have to settle for my 'just okay.' I don't want to bring you, or anyone else, down with me."

Ethan's brown eyes met her blue ones, searching for any way into the wall she had built around herself so long ago.

"So that's it then. No chance for us."

Joy swallowed, then shook her head no.

"You deserve better than that, Joy."

She flinched at the anger in his voice.

"You say I don't deserve to settle for just okay, but neither do you. You were a kid, Joy. Just a kid. None of what happened has been your fault in any way, but I'm not going to push you on this, not tonight. When you're ready to accept that you deserve happiness and all the best things this world can offer, I'll be waiting. For now, I think we should get some rest. We have a long drive tomorrow."

* * *

Ethan hadn't returned to their bedroom that night. Joy had been worried, insistently texting her siblings until Oliver confessed he was sleeping on the floor in his room. Joy climbed out of bed when she read the message, fingers resting on the doorknob.

Sarah hadn't said anything to Trini about what had happened and had spent the next half hour after their confrontation avoiding Joy's eyes until Joy decided enough time had passed to slip into her room without her family questioning it. Her phone vibrated in her hand, and she opened the message to a picture of Ethan fast asleep in a sleeping bag on the carpet.

She retreated from the door and trod quietly back to her bed. After a few seconds of deliberation, she tugged the comforter off the mattress, settling onto the wooden floor, phone clutched in her hand in case Ethan woke up and wanted to text her. He did that sometimes, sent her random videos on nights when he couldn't sleep.

Joy didn't sleep.

The next morning, she dabbed on as much concealer as she could, painting on a happy grin as she bid farewell to her family. She climbed into the car with promises of coming to visit soon while Ethan hugged her siblings and mother goodbye with a smile that didn't quite reach his eyes. Trini looked questioningly at Joy, eyebrows creased, but Joy only shook her head, silently begging her not to say anything.

A few hours passed as the brown fields shifted to green pastures, and the country roads slipped into two-lane highways. Music played over the speaker, but neither Joy nor Ethan spoke, Joy too afraid of what he was going to say, and Ethan seemingly deep in thought.

Ethan broke the silence of the car, his gaze straight ahead.

"What if I move on?"

We'd kill her.

Joy gulped. She turned to Ethan, forcing a smile on her lips.

"Then I'll be happy for you," she choked out.

He nodded sharply but said nothing as his fingers flexed on the steering wheel. Joy tightened her fists, her fingernails digging into her palm. Was this it for the pair? Could they still be friends after this? What if in trying to protect their friendship, she had actually destroyed it?

"Ethan—"

"I don't want to talk about it right now," he interrupted.

Joy folded into herself.

The honking of multiple cars interrupted the tense silence, and Joy whipped around in time to see a red car sideswiping a truck in the next lane. The car zipped through the traffic, crossing lanes and cutting Ethan off.

"Fuck," Ethan swore, pounding his foot against the brake.

The minivan behind him honked and swerved to avoid rear-ending the two.

The red car continued accelerating down the highway. It rolled down its window, a burly hand sticking out a middle finger as it bounced from lane to lane.

"God, I wish people like that would get off the road," Joy said.

An image flashed through her mind of the vehicle crashing, of the driver slamming his brakes, swerving, and hitting a median. She pictured the wreckage, the angry driver stomping out of his vehicle, hurt, but not seriously so, as he complained about his car being totaled. She was torn between smiling at the image and frowning at the pettiness that had created it.

Ethan muttered a quick agreement as he resumed driving.

We can help with that.

Joy felt Buttercup leave, the cold drifting from her fingertips before the words even registered in her head. She watched the fog dart from the car and through traffic before slowing down beside the vehicle. The red car swerved from the exit lane, where it had been passing other cars, back onto the main highway.

"I didn't mean it," Joy pleaded, dread filling her.

She flicked her hand away, waiting for Buttercup to return, to move, but the black mass continued.

"Mean what?" Ethan asked, glancing at her from the corner of his eyes.

Buttercup stilled beside the vehicle's back right tire.

"No!" she shouted.

Ethan startled, jerking the wheel to the side. The car swerved for a second before he was able to regain control. Joy shot her hands out, bracing herself against the dashboard.

Tears filled Joy's eyes, a quiet whimper falling from her lips. "Please."

Buttercup slammed into the tire of the car, and it went careening, the tail end crashing against the metal railing, sending it spinning a few hundred feet in front of Ethan and Joy. Joy closed her eyes as the crunching of metal filled the air, cars plowing into each other.

Ethan pulled to the side of the highway, hopped out of the car and headed toward the pile of wrecked vehicles. Joy remained in the car, eyes squeezed shut and fists balled together, too afraid to see what she had done.

Is that not what you wanted?

Buttercup's words were monotone, as they always were, and yet Joy felt they were mocking her somehow. She didn't bother with a response. She glanced up slowly, taking in the consequences of her intrusive thought.

Ten or so cars piled up in front of her, bumpers dragging along the ground and doors dented from impact. Glass and pieces of metal littered the pavement, sparkling in the setting sun. People stood on the side of the highway, examining their cars and checking others for injuries. A few held phones up to their ears, faces grim as they spoke. Joy reached out a trembling hand, opened her door and stepped onto the shoulder. She trod carefully, stepping around the fragments of the vehicles and searching for Ethan.

"Damn it. I just bought this car," a woman groaned from beside a badly damaged black sedan. She held a fast food napkin to her arm, red seeping through the white paper.

Two children sat beside a silver SUV, a teenager and a young boy who sobbed into her shirt.

"Yeah, we're okay." The girl talked into her phone as she rubbed the child's back. "Just a couple of cuts and bruises, but nothing serious. The car is pretty messed up, though. Is Dad on his way?"

Joy dragged herself forward.

"Has anyone seen my dog?" An elderly man called out, frantically searching around an old blue truck. Blood dripped down the side of his face, spotting the road as he bent down to look under his vehicle. The tailgate had been smashed in, and Joy noticed a large hole in the windshield as she passed the front of the truck.

Joy shook her head, stomach burning. She caught a glimpse of long, brown hair atop a tall figure, and she walked faster, quickly approaching the red car that started the pileup.

She crossed the lane, stopping and staring at Ethan's back as he tapped on the window.

"Sir? Can you hear me?" Ethan tugged on the driver's door. He grunted as it refused to budge.

Joy's attention flicked to the inside of the car, saw a man slumped back in his seat, and looked away.

"Open the door," she whispered.

"I'm trying," Ethan responded. "The doors are still locked."

Buttercup passed through the cracks of the vehicle and pressed on the button to unlock the car. Joy stepped around Ethan and grabbed the door handle.

"I just said it was—" Ethan paused as Joy pulled the door open.

The driver woke slowly and blinked up at Joy. He was a middle-aged man, slightly balding, wearing a tight t-shirt and a pair of jeans. He shifted in his seat and lifted his arm to his face. Fast food wrappers lined his floorboards, and a six-pack of beer, with one missing, was sitting in his passenger side door.

"Are you okay?" Joy asked.

The man unbuckled himself and rubbed at his chest. He moved both arms, then both legs. He twisted his head from side to side. Looking back at Joy, he nodded. Sirens sounded somewhere in the background, and the man glanced at the six-pack in his passenger side. Without a word, he grabbed it and tossed it into his backseat. Ethan yanked Joy back, eyes narrowed, and stepped toward the man.

"You've been drinking, haven't you, asshole?" he asked.

The man scoffed. "And if I have?"

"Are you kidding me? Look at the mess you made. Dude, there're kids in some of those cars!" Ethan yanked the guy by the shirt, tossing him easily onto the highway as a police car and ambulance raced to the front of the wreck.

The man landed on his hands and knees, scrambled to his feet, then stood, his frame reaching a good head shorter than Ethan.

"Hadn't had a sip yet. Can check if ya want. All them bottles still got their lids fully sealed. Don't know what caused my car to fuck up like that, but it wasn't me."

A policewoman jogged over to the pair, scanning them for obvious signs of injury.

"Sir, I'm going to need you to step back." She gestured at Ethan, then turned to the other man. "Is this your vehicle?"

"Yup." He looked the officer up and down, gaze lingering on her chest.

She crossed her arms.

"Great, we're going to have some questions for you. Please stay by the vehicle as we assess the situation."

Ethan stepped away, standing beside Joy.

"Are you two injured?" the officer asked.

"No, ma'am," Ethan responded, pointing toward his car. "We weren't in the wreck. We saw him hit the guard and stopped when the cars started piling up."

"Please return to your vehicle. We can handle it from here," she instructed, dismissing the pair.

Ethan nodded, his hand slipping into Joy's as they picked their way through the wreckage and back to the car. The old man sobbed on his knees at his truck, a bundle of red fur clutched in his arms. Ice ran through Joy, and she rubbed her arms, averting her eyes. Ever the gentleman, Ethan shrugged his jacket off and placed it on her shoulders.

"I'm sorry," Joy whispered, tightening her hold on Ethan's hand.

"For what? Our argument? Joy, we've needed to have that conversation for a long time. And it's not over yet. We're going to sit down and talk through this, but not today. Today we're going to go home and rest." Ethan stopped, placing his hand on her chin so she would look at him.

"Not for that. The wreck. It was my fault."

Her vision spun as she looked at the scene around her. The sun bathed the destroyed vehicles in an orange haze; the wind carried the sound of sirens and sobs through the air.

"Joy, we weren't anywhere near the car. Asshole probably got an ad for Pornhub and wrecked trying to unlock his phone. Everyone's fine. The kids seemed a bit shaken up, and there're probably a few people who need a couple of stitches, but they're otherwise okay. And that creep will have to be off the road for a while, so that's definitely a bonus. With the way he was driving, it was only a matter of time before he crashed. We're lucky it was today, where no one was seriously hurt."

See, it was deserved. We probably saved someone's life by taking him off the road.

There is no we. Not anymore. This was a mistake, Joy thought. I'm never speaking to you again and I'm sure as hell never using you again.

We'll see.

Joy laughed as she stumbled toward the edge of the road. She sat, hands tightly wound in her hair. Ethan kneeled beside her, a hand hesitantly raised as his eyebrows furrowed. Joy's laugh morphed, her voice growing hysterical as tears spilled down her cheeks and darkened the pavement.

"I can't—" Joy choked out, her chest tightening painfully.

Ethan blinked. In the short time it had taken them to walk back to the car, Joy had gone from apologizing to laughing to sobbing. His mouth opened, then closed a few times. He nodded, sitting beside her with his hand on her shoulder.

"Is she alright?" a man in a suit and a cellphone pressed to his ear asked, looking down at Joy before turning to scrutinize Ethan.

Joy laughed harder. She tucked her knees into her chest, her body caving in on itself and her shoulders shaking.

"Just a rough day. She'll be fine, thank you for asking," Ethan responded.

The suited man nodded sharply, turning around as he mumbled into his phone about insurance claims and rental car choices.

The drive home was short, though Joy barely noticed. The scene played in her head over and over again, the children crying, the red bundle in the old man's arms. She had done that. She had hurt them. She wouldn't, couldn't, allow that to happen again. People like her weren't meant for powers like Buttercup and she would be damned if she didn't find a way to lock it away for good.

With a new goal in mind, Joy finally snapped to her senses, frowning as Ethan pulled into the parking lot of her apartment complex.

Ethan rubbed his neck.

"I assumed you would be more comfortable here, given..." He trailed off into silence. He sighed. "Anyway, I have work tomorrow from 10 to 6, if you want to swing by while I'm gone and pick up some of your things."

Joy felt herself nod, even though all she wanted was to jump back into his car and go back to the apartment she had quickly learned to call home. Ethan escorted her up the stairs, pausing as she unlocked her apartment door. He stared at her, studying her features as desperate to commit her face to memory.

"If you need anything, please call me. I know we're in this weird middle ground thing right now, but I'll always be there if you need me." He placed a finger underneath her chin, tipping her gaze from the concrete floor to his warm brown eyes.

"Always," he promised.

With that, he spun on his heel and walked down her stairs. And Joy watched as he left with the few pieces of herself she had learned to freely give, not her entirety, but enough to leave her feeling empty, incomplete.

CHAPTER 33

Joy, Age 18

"You're just like me."

Joy clenched her jaw as she read the message over and over again.

"You think you're special because you got a whole bunch of fancy awards in high school and you're going to a nice college now? I did that too. I won all of the awards, topped all of my classes, and look at me now. All because I got pregnant with some brat who doesn't even understand what I gave up for her. You ruined my life. It's funny, because as much as you hate me, you are exactly like me. The same anger. The same selfishness."

Comments flew from Joy's mother, one after the other.

"Fuck you, little girl. You ruined everything."

"How could you talk to me like that, and on Mother's Day?"

Joy debated not responding, thought of throwing her phone across the room and ignoring it for the rest of the day.

She didn't ignore the comments. She grew up to be petty, and she wanted this woman to hurt like she had hurt her so many times.

"You were never my mother. You were never here for me like Trini was. I hadn't spoken to you in months, and sometimes I went whole years without seeing you," Joy typed out, only pausing for a second before hitting send.

Joanne had called Tom a coward on Facebook. When Joy called her out on it, Joanne attacked her and claimed his suicide was cowardly. While Joy had been angry at Tom when he died, disappointed in herself for not being there for the man, she had never thought of him as a coward.

Tom had lost himself in his art. It served to save him, to allow him to express himself, but it also pulled him to depths where Joy couldn't reach. She wasn't artistic, never had been, and had no way to connect with him in the way he so desperately craved. Tom had been the most loyal person, the most gentle and kind, that Joy had ever known. He gave everything freely, never expecting anything in return, never accepting any gratitude for what he claimed he was happy to do. He gave and he gave until there was nothing left for him to take except his own life. That was not cowardice, not a weakness. That was him using his strength until none remained.

"Just because I didn't want to be your mother doesn't mean I'm not. Whether you like it or not, I am your mom, and all of that smart, all of that drive, that pretty little face of yours, it all came from me."

Her messages soon became manic, the comment chain extending to dozens of comments, only three or four of which came from Joy.

"@Sarah, u see? How she's treating me on Mother's Day?"

"Fuck u."

"I gave up everything to have u."

"Your only their with Trini because I let u go."

Joy typed one more response, contemplating how to finish the chain before blocking her mother for good.

"*You're, *There."

Joy smirked, showing the phone to Clara, who laughed. Clara had shown the first comment to Joy, fully expecting her older sister to rebuke their mom. And Joy, not wanting to disappoint Clara, had jumped right into it. Clara didn't want to do it herself, had only stepped in when her mother went too far, and only left a simple comment asking her mom to stop blowing up Joy's phone. She wouldn't say anything more than that because she still had a relationship with their mother. A toxic one, built on Facebook messages and ten-minute, supervised visits, but one nonetheless. Joy had never been Joanne's favorite, even before her siblings had been born, but now it was as if she didn't exist to her outside of the occasional birthday text on the wrong date.

A bitterness climbed up Joy's throat, threatening to spew resentment at her sister, so Joy left the living room, walked into her old bedroom, what was now Caden's room, and shut the door. A plastic horse bit into Joy's leg as she sank to the floor. Joy felt like a disaster, the body of a grown woman stuck with the mind of the unwanted child she had been. She clutched at her chest and let out quick, shallow exhales.

Joy's phone, dropped on Caden's carpet, buzzed as it lit up with one final message.

"You are exactly like me."

CHAPTER 34

A few days after the accident, Joy threw herself into searching for a new job. She avoided her ever-growing loneliness and guilt. She wanted to talk to Ethan about what had happened but didn't know how to start or if he would even want to talk to her.

He probably does not.

She ignored Buttercup, as had become her custom over the last few days, stared at the screen of her laptop, and sighed as she hit submit on yet another application. She was perched on the couch in her living room, feet propped up on her coffee table and computer balanced on her lap. The microwave in her kitchen chimed, and she stood, shutting her laptop and tossing it onto her armchair.

The smell of her cup noodles bit through the lavender candle. It was an odd mix of sickly sweet and artificial beef flavoring that made her gag as she passed it. The candle was a poor attempt at relaxing. She had Googled ways to alleviate stress, figuring she could think of a better way to apologize to Ethan if she didn't have her job hunt, increasing debt, and extreme fatigue weighing her down. She found it difficult to think, to eat, or even to want to get out of bed. She knew she was responsible for her own happiness and wanted to make sure she was the best version of herself before jumping into a relationship with him.

Because he had been right. She did have feelings for him. She did deserve to be happy. And they could be happy together, but not without her working on herself first. So she had turned to Google, who in turn told her to seek therapy. Fair, but out of her budget. She tried Google again, searching "how to relieve" without noticing she had clicked the autofill below her actual query.

One bout with diarrhea later helped her to realize she had instead searched "how to relieve constipation" and that extra fluids and Senna, a herbal remedy (laxative) whose instructions Joy had not bothered to examine, do not help with anxiety.

After correcting her search, she was left with exercise, sleep, and meditation. Sleep came easily to Joy, to the point where it was no longer healthy. She spent the first few days after the accident curled up under her covers, ignoring her phone and ordering delivery she couldn't afford.

Meditation, on the other hand, sucked ass. Every time she closed her eyes and took deep breaths, following along with the soothing voice in the YouTube videos, she thought of the dog in the old man's arms, the cuts and bruises littering the bodies of those who were in the accident.

That left exercise. She tried to take a walk, completely overlooking that she lived in a terrible neighborhood. After a brief incident with a man who followed her for a few blocks singing what sounded like a love song in Spanish (she wasn't quite sure; she had only barely passed her Spanish classes in college), she decided it was safer to stay home.

Her phone dinged as she walked back to the couch, instant noodles in hand, and she put her meal down to pick it up. Trini had messaged her, asking how work and Ethan were and updating her on the latest struggles with the busybodies of her small town. Trini had lost a lot of friends after separating from Connor. She had never been an incredibly outgoing person, but it had still stung when so many picked sides. She never expected them to pick her, never wanted that, but she had expected her old group to have the maturity to not create a division in the first place. They didn't. They were petty, going so far as to exclude her from work activities. Trini and Connor's marriage had been deteriorating for years, with both of them at fault to some extent, but it was Trini who took the brunt of the blame.

Joy secretly loved the little dramas that Trini told her about. Up until recently, her life had been quiet, dull even. She lived vicariously through Clara, Caden, and Trini, finding amusement in the messiness of their lives. Overall though, they both seemed happy with the lives they had carved out for themselves, Trini with her new house and husband and Clara with a job she loved and doing art on the side.

Joy typed out a quick reply, telling Trini that work was great, but her fingers twiddled over her screen as she debated including her fight with Ethan. Trini gave great advice, having been through so much at such a young age, and might have an idea on how to make things up to Ethan. She sent a message explaining that she and Ethan were in an argument and she needed advice on how to work through it. Seconds later, the phone began to ring in her hand and she nearly dropped it in surprise.

"Hello?" she answered, glancing down to see Trini's name flash across her screen.

"Have you tried apologizing?" Trini asked, forgoing a normal greeting.

Joy blinked. "Uh. To Ethan?"

"Duh." Joy could practically hear Trini rolling her eyes.

"No. Not yet at least. I don't know. I think maybe I should go big with it. I really screwed things up, even told him I would be okay if he moved on to someone else."

"And would you?"

Joy's stomach churned.

"I'd be happy for him, but I don't know. No, I guess? It would really suck."

"The morning of the wedding, Ethan woke up a couple

hours before you did. He sat on the back porch with me and drank a cup of coffee."

Joy's mind spun as she tried to connect Ethan drinking coffee with her mom to Joy's apology.

"That's nice?" Joy hesitated. "What did y'all talk about?"

"You."

Anger shot through Joy at the vague statement. Her first response would normally have been snippy, frustration seeping into her tone. Instead, she forced herself to take a deep breath, to think through Trini's words. Panda sprinted around the corner as Joy opened her mouth to respond, meowing loudly and rubbing her chubby face against Joy's legs to get attention. Joy bent down, lifted the cat, and placed her on the couch, absentmindedly stroking her soft fur.

After a moment of silence, Trini explained. "I thanked him for being such a good friend to you. Told him I had been worried about you living in a big city and that I was grateful you had him there, and you know what he said?"

"Dear God, please make that gremlin come back to West Texas so she'll stop beating me at Mario Kart and begging me to make her grilled cheese at three in the morning?"

"Nope, but that's probably what he was thinking." Trini snorted. "He thanked me for giving you someone to look up to. He said he was so grateful I had given you a safe environment to grow up in and that you had done more for him than he could ever describe. Said you made him want to be a better man."

Joy swiped at a random tear that fell on her cheek. She held the drop on her fingertip, staring down at it in confusion. She had never been much of a crier, but one nice comment from Ethan made her want to sob like a child.

"I damn near cried, it was so sweet. But that might have been hormones. Or the shot of whiskey I put in my coffee to help with the wedding nerves." Joy let out a watery chuckle as Trini continued. "Either way, that boy has it bad for you. You say the word, and he'll be there. I'd bet all the money in the world he misses you more than anything. Just apologize. Plain and simple. And finally tell the kid how you feel. Jesus, Joy, it's been like two years."

Joy thanked Trini, promised to keep her updated, then hung up. It had been almost two years since she had fallen in love with her best friend, and she wasn't going to let any more time pass without telling him how she felt. She opened her Instagram, searching for cute coupley confession videos, and cringed at the results. They were really sweet, but she would rather die than plan a big public confession. A popup for a new video from a YouTuber Ethan enjoyed, Greg Flowers, also known as Phase Matrix, caught her eye and an idea quickly formed.

"One last time," she said to Buttercup, who remained silent. "Go find him."

The black mist drifted quietly, scattering among the warm air of her apartment before shifting and squeezing through the cracks of her closed door. It tugged her attention in a hundred directions as it spread throughout the city, brief pictures of faces flashing through her mind as Buttercup searched. The farther Buttercup floated from her, the thinner it stretched, and the weaker she felt. Her knees buckled as the images kept coming, one after another, blurring together people, trees, and buildings.

Regret kicked in hard as a burning sensation traveled from her scalp and down her spine. The smell of smoke filled her nostrils and her hands stung, a dull numbness escalating into needles jammed into her palms. Squeezing her eyes shut, she placed her hands over her ears and focused on the passing faces, searching through the never-ending cycle for one in particular.

"There!" Joy shouted, willing Buttercup to converge in front of a man leaning against a hotel check-in counter. His cap was pulled down low over his eyes, but Joy was certain it was him. After all, she had spent hours watching his videos with Ethan, nights watching nerdy play-throughs and gaming commentary she didn't quite understand but had grown to enjoy.

"Stay with him," she demanded, leaping up from the floor.

* * *

A shower, change of clothes, and a quick drive later, Joy was walking a few feet behind the man, visible but unseen in her casual jeans and loose-fitting t-shirt. She wanted to fit into the streets, not stand out in a positive or negative way. The easiest way to obtain someone's trust was to come off as completely ordinary, not capable of harm nor relevant enough to attract attention. A plain ole Texas girl willing to show some southern hospitality to someone in trouble. Or someone who would soon be in trouble. She smirked, then followed the man as he entered a parking garage.

Greg Flowers was taller in real life than he seemed to be through a screen. He was about Ethan's height, maybe a bit taller, but less broad, his frame thin and features slim. His dark hair was still tucked into a dark blue hat, but sunglasses now covered most of his face. Joy watched as he stepped into the garage's elevator, sending Buttercup after him to see what floor he was headed to.

"Fuck. Shit. Damn," Joy chanted under her breath, jogging up the stairs to the fourth floor.

She stopped when she reached the door, peeking her head through the glass window and ducking below it when she saw Greg leave the elevator. Hands on her knees, she panted and wiped at the bead of sweat that had dripped down her forward with the edge of her t-shirt. After a few moments, she allowed herself to glance back through the window, watching as he strode across the concrete toward a row of cars.

Reaching into his pocket, Greg pulled out his keys and unlocked an expensive-looking car. The ridiculously clean seats and freshly vacuumed floorboard hinted that it was a rental. He tossed the keys, followed by his phone and wallet, onto the console and began lowering his body into the driver's seat. With a wiggle of her finger, Buttercup floated after him, tugging his hotel key from his back pocket and dropping it a few feet from the car. Joy winced, expecting the man to be confused by how far the object had landed, but he didn't even blink, instead groaning as he lifted himself from the seat and trudged the few steps to grab it.

Joy flicked her wrist, and Buttercup slammed the car door shut, keys and wallet still on the center console. Greg stood, mouth gaping as he looked at his possessions inside his locked vehicle. Joy fought back a smile as the man let out a string of curses.

"You alright?" Joy thickened her accent, pulling her "I" into a southern drawl and stepping closer to him.

Greg tensed at the sudden question, but relaxed as he turned to see a normal-looking woman with a smile that was carefully crafted to look friendly: not too wide but still prominent, a dimple winking in her right cheek. She knew exactly what she was doing as her eyebrows furrowed in concern, disarming him using the same moves she had watched her grandmother use in their small town. It made her feel gross, but she ignored the way her skin crawled at the similarity and reminded herself it was for Ethan.

"I locked my keys in my rental car. Is there any way I can borrow your phone?" he smiled sheepishly.

Joy nodded, passing her phone over to him. He took a few steps away, leaned against the railing, and pressed the device to his ear. Buttercup tapped his elbow, and he watched in horror as the phone tumbled out of his hand and over the edge. He turned to Joy, eyes wide.

"I am so sorry," he said. "I'll buy you a new one, I promise."

He ran his hand over his face, stopping to look at the time on his watch.

"Shit, I have a meet and greet in like twenty minutes."

Joy pursed her lips in contemplation.

"I would offer you a ride, but I was planning on Ubering home and my phone..." Joy gestured vaguely at the area where her phone would have dropped.

Yes, because people typically come into the fourth floor of a parking garage to request an Uber. He's going to see right through us.

Joy ignored Buttercup, choosing to study Greg, whose frown deepened with every passing second. She didn't miss the dark circles under his eyes, guilt eating at her as she realized how exhausted this man was.

Deciding to put him out of his misery, she leaned in close, prompting him to do the same, and whispered as if they were co-conspirators. "Okay, I'm going to do something, but you can't judge me for it."

He hesitated, then nodded.

She pulled a bobby pin from her hair, stepping up to the vehicle. She jammed it in the lock, twisting it back and forth for a few seconds before Buttercup drifted through the cracks of the car and pressed the unlock button. Greg narrowed his eyes, and Joy shrugged.

"I lock my keys in my car all the time. I was embarrassed when the locksmith started recognizing my number, so I watched a few YouTube videos and—" Joy opened the door, and the man laughed.

"How can I thank you—"

"Joy," she supplied, sticking out her hand.

He shook it, replying with his name. Joy let her eyes widen with recognition. Seeing the recognition on her face, he smiled.

"Did you not recognize me?" he teased.

She shot him an embarrassed grin, ducking her head and willing the blood to rush to her cheeks. He ate up her sudden shyness, his smile stretching further as he cocked his head to the side.

"I'm sorry, my friend is a huge fan. Actually, his birthday is coming up." Joy bit her lip, pretending to think. "Tell you what, I'll call it even for my phone if you don't mind doing me a small favor."

After contact details were exchanged, Greg drove off, and Buttercup floated the undamaged phone into Joy's hand. A DM from Greg waited, a picture of a confirmation code for VIP tickets to a future show of his inside. Joy grinned, pulled out her car keys, got in her car, and drove home.

* * *

Joy paced her kitchen, going through every possible scenario in her head. She ran through each conversation she could have with Ethan, different ways he could respond, even looked up the menu of the coffee shop across the street from his apartment so she knew exactly what to order.

"Hey. Can you..." She typed on the notes section of her phone, then immediately erased it.

"Hi. Would you—"

Maybe it would be better if she called. It would save her an awkward text message. But then she wouldn't be able to think through what she wanted to say. And what if he didn't want to talk to her? Then instead of an awkward text, there would be an awkward silence.

"Screw it," she muttered under her breath as she clicked Ethan's contact.

It would be fine. He was probably in class, and it would go to voicemail, and she could—

"Joy?" Ethan answered, confusion evident in his voice.

"Oh," Joy simply said.

Silence lapsed as Joy stared at the phone in her hand.

Ethan coughed. "Uh. Are you still there? Everything alright?"

"Yes. I... Yes?"

"Did you mean to call me?"

Joy nodded, then remembered he couldn't see her.

"Yes!" she blurted.

Ethan snorted like he was trying to hold back a laugh.

Joy took a deep breath and forced herself to continue. "I was wondering if you wanted to meet me at the coffee shop at four?"

Silence.

"Sorry, I can't."

"Oh." Joy breathed out in disappointment.

It made sense; he was probably busy. Who would want to make time for the girl who turned him down right before getting into a car accident? Still, Joy's heart fell through her chest, landing and shattering somewhere around her feet.

"Yeah, I have class until five. Wanna meet me at five-thirty? I have plans after, but I should have about twenty minutes if that's enough time?"

Her heart was a traitor, a dramatic, overreacting bitch.

"Yeah!" She forced herself to calm down, wincing at the excited pitch of her voice. "Yes, five-thirty works great."

"Okay, cool. See you then." Ethan paused. "Are you sure everything's alright?"

The promise of seeing Ethan again, and the lack of anger in his voice, made Joy feel like it would be.

* * *

"Hey," Ethan greeted, sliding into the seat in front of her.

Joy blinked, thrown off by how casual he was being after the two not speaking for almost a week. It had killed her, going from texting nonstop to nothing but silence and regret. She hadn't thought of anything but him, losing sleep, their argument in a constant loop in her mind. And here he was, perfectly calm, acting as if nothing had changed. Something twisted in her stomach.

"Hi," she forced herself to croak out.

She took a sip of her drink, a fancy iced coffee that cost her way more than her jobless self should spend, to help with the sudden dryness in her throat.

Ethan raised an eyebrow. "Everything alright?"

Joy nodded.

"Yeah."

"Okay. I'm going to go grab a coffee. Do you want anything?"

Joy shook her head and gestured vaguely at the drink in her hand.

Ethan frowned but stood and walked over to the counter. His phone dinged on the counter, and Joy cast it a quick glance. It was facing the opposite way, but Joy could still make out the words "are we still on for tonight?" from a Wendy. Whatever it was that had twisted in her stomach traveled upward, grabbing onto her heart and squeezing. It felt disgusting, how jealous she got from six words on the screen. Could it be a friend, someone from a study group?

He does not like study groups, Buttercup chimed in.

Buttercup had been mostly silent since the accident. She had grown accustomed to its random interruptions, but now, after a break, it was disconcerting, its monotone voice suddenly cutting through her jumbled thoughts.

I know. But maybe it could just be a friend, she thought back.

Perhaps. But you did tell him that you would be happy for him, should he move on.

The conversation flashed through Joy's mind, the way her chest had hurt and the disappointment in Ethan's eyes as the words left her mouth. This conversation suddenly felt like a terrible idea. She wasn't sure she could handle him moving on, not when she finally understood what she felt and was ready to try.

She had been through so much: abandonment, neglect, her grandfather's suicide, working two jobs and taking a full load of college credits while undergoing cancer treatment. She had spent so long expecting the worst and receiving it. Ethan was her exception, her only exception. Life had taught her not to want big things. Wanting Ethan's heart was no small thing, but she was willing to try. With him, she allowed herself to want again. With him, she could see herself finally being content, maybe even happy.

But what if he had already slipped from her fingers? What if she had pushed him away for good?

She let out a shaky breath and glanced over to where Ethan stood in the front of the line. The barista smiled at Ethan, looking up at him through long eyelashes. Joy couldn't hear what they were talking about, but the barista laughed at something he said and placed her hand on his arm. Joy looked away.

Ethan returned a few moments later, a drink in one hand and two brownies in his other. He passed one over to Joy, sat, then waited.

Joy let her thoughts turn over a few times, flitting from one introduction to the next. Grabbing the brownie, she took a large bite as she debated. She swallowed.

"I like you," she said, her calm voice a complete contrast to the emotions swirling inside of her.

Ethan smiled. "I know."

Joy blinked.

"Okay."

She took another bite of her brownie.

"Like more than a friend. I like you romantically," she continued.

Ethan chuckled and leaned back in his seat.

"I know."

Joy tilted her head to the side and pursed her lips. She studied him, searching his warm brown eyes for any sign of what he was feeling. The grin never left his lips.

"Oh, uh. Good?"

"Good?"

Ethan's phone dinged, reminding Joy of the previous message. She puffed out a breath of air and set down her brownie.

"I understand if you found someone else. I saw the message earlier, from Wendy." Joy looked down and picked at her nails. "I know I'm… a lot. And I understand if you want something easier. I'm not sure I'm worth—"

Ethan placed a hand over Joy's, stopping her from pulling at the skin. With his other hand, he tugged her chair and pulled her closer to him. He grabbed her chin gently and forced her to look at him.

"You are worth everything and so much more than any man or woman could give you." His thumb brushed over the back of her hand. "But I'll be damned if I don't try. I love you, Joy. I meant what I said in that car, and that's not going to change. I want you, all of you, all of the time. I'll be here, as your best friend, your boyfriend, your partner in crime, whatever you're comfortable with. I'll take any part of you that you're willing to give."

"But Wendy…" Joy's cheeks flushed.

She felt silly, asking about another woman after Ethan's sweet words. She flinched, waited for him to get upset, to change his mind. Instead, he laughed, startling her and those sitting at the neighboring tables.

"Wendy is the mom of a high school kid I'm tutoring in math. I'm meeting him after this to help him study for his final."

Her chin slumped down to her chest and she stared at the ground.

"Oh."

The knot in her stomach unraveled, spreading warmth throughout her body. She grinned, even as she tried to hide her red face in the hood of her jacket.

"So…" Joy breathed, finally flicking her eyes back to Ethan. Her breath caught in her throat as she realized how close he was. He had scooted his chair to be right beside hers, his face only a few inches away. Her eyes trailed down his face to his lips.

"So?" Ethan asked.

Joy glanced back up to see Ethan's gaze drop to her mouth. This close, she could smell his cologne, spicy and citrusy, and caramel from the ridiculously sugary drink he had downed. She wondered if he would taste like caramel.

"So," she murmured, voice airy and light, "what's next for us?"

Ethan leaned closer, and she let her eyes flutter shut. She could feel the brush of his breath, warm and sweet, against her mouth.

An alarm sounded on Ethan's phone, and they both jumped. Ethan looked at the time and groaned.

"I really have to go, or I'm going to be even later." He gathered his possessions and surprised Joy by pressing a quick peck to her cheek.

Disappointment sparked through Joy, but she swallowed it as she raised an eyebrow.

"Even later?"

Ethan laughed nervously and rubbed his neck.

"Well. If we were to be technical, Wendy was texting me earlier because I was supposed to be at her house by five-thirty."

"And the alarm?"

"Was my, 'if I don't leave by now, I'm definitely getting fired' alarm."

Joy sighed, but couldn't manage to suppress her smile. "You better get going then."

Ethan smiled back, then dropped to his knees in front of her.

"What are you doing?" Joy hissed, grabbing his arms and trying to pull him up. "People are staring. Get up!"

"Go on a date with me?"

Joy's expression went slack. "What?"

"A date? The thing people go on when they like each other?"

Joy swatted at his arm, and Ethan laughed before continuing. "Let me take you on a proper date. I'll plan it and everything. You just have to show up. Tomorrow. I'll pick you up at eight?"

"In the morning?" Joy's nose wrinkled.

"No," Ethan chuckled. "Even I'm not stupid enough to try and get you up that early on a Saturday. Eight PM. Dress comfortably. Sweats or pajamas are fine." He glanced at his phone. "I really gotta go."

He dashed out the door, throwing up his hand in a wave and jogging to his car. Joy watched him leave, a stupidly happy-looking grin on her face.

CHAPTER 35

Joy, Age 19

A ceiling fan spun in lazy circles above Joy's head.

She stared up at it.

She shivered, her stomach rolling violently. Turning to her side, she pulled the covers closer to her chin. Clothes lay scattered around the floor of the room, clean ones mixing with those disgusting from being worn in the Texas heat. The small TV perched on top of her dresser blared the opening song of the anime Joy had been half-heartedly watching. She didn't even flinch.

A phone dinged from somewhere within her blankets, and she groaned. Flailing in the covers, Joy ran her hands against her sheets, becoming increasingly angry as she failed to find the device. She rolled off of the twin bed and shook the blankets. Something fell from within, a loud CRACK sounding through the room as it connected with the metal frame of the bed. Joy frowned. She stared at the phone as it lay facedown on her shaggy brown carpet. The sun painted on the phone's case seemed to mock her as she contemplated not picking it up, not flipping it over to potentially see a crack on its surface. She glared at it. The sun, an orange circle painted on a black case by Caden, glared back.

Her stomach rumbled.

She walked around the phone, leaving it on the floor, opened her door and stepped into the kitchen she shared with her two roommates. She had decided not to live in the campus dorms for her freshman year of college, finding it cheaper to live in an apartment a few miles away. Her roommates were nice, one student a few years older than her and a woman in her late twenties who worked at a store in the center of the city. At first, she had found it weird, living with a grown woman as a student, but the woman was nice and shared cooking tips with Joy. Joy soon found it comforting living with someone older than her; she had someone to turn to for advice, especially about the common adulting things that Joy had not learned at home. She learned the benefits of fabric softener, how to shop coupons and have her groceries delivered, how long to boil an egg. Plus, the roommate had a dog, an adorable little chihuahua with anxiety problems that Joy could never pet, but still enjoyed watching run about as her owner cooked in the kitchen.

Joy flung open her refrigerator door and sifted through the expired carton of almond milk, bottle of off-brand Worcestershire sauce, vegetables in various states of wilting, and Styrofoam container of Greek food she had ordered a few nights earlier that sat on her designated shelf. Shrugging, she pulled the takeout box from the fridge and threw it in the microwave. The container spun as it heated, and Joy rubbed her eyes, still red and stinging from crying that morning. The microwave dinged. Joy grabbed the food with one hand and a plastic water bottle from the pantry with the other. Stalking back into her room, Joy kicked the door shut, scowled at her phone, and plopped down on her bed.

After the food was gone, Joy leaned over, legs remaining on the bed as she bent to grab her phone. She sent up a quick prayer to whoever was listening and flipped the device over. She grinned. Unlocking the device, she glanced through a few text messages, Facebook notifications, and Instagram comments, all wishing her a happy birthday. The smile fell from her lips. She knew those messaging her meant well, but it just felt so... lonely.

She hated her birthday, always had, and not in the bashful way those who secretly loved the attention claimed they hated their birthday. She wasn't sure when it had started. Perhaps it was when she turned five and a friend asked her what her mom and dad had given her for her birthday. She hadn't heard from her mom that day, and hadn't heard from her father in years.

Perhaps it was the year she was sick and had to stay home with Sarah, who promptly left her alone in the living room for the day, too weak to move or make herself something to eat.

Perhaps it was the two years that no one came to her birthday party. She wasn't sure why. She had always felt awkward, overcompensating with her reactions to hide that she simply did not know how to react. Maybe the other kids had secretly not liked her, and that's why no one came. Maybe the other kids had heard stories about Sarah and her mother. Either way, she had spent those two birthdays crying in her closet, only being coaxed out by Tom's promise of letting her pick out all the candy she could carry from the local grocery store.

Perhaps it was the isolation she felt, comparing herself to others her age. As the years flew by, Joy felt like she was falling behind. Others her age seemed so happy, so content with being a kid and hanging out with their friends. Joy had never felt that. Being around others made her anxious, as if she was one misspoken word away from being left alone. The pressure she placed on herself grew as she did. She wanted to be successful, and each year, she felt like she didn't make it.

This year, she hated her birthday because she was alone. It had fallen on a Wednesday, the middle of the week. Her family had come down the weekend before, taking her out to eat and exploring Austin. It had been nice, but ended with Clara warning Joy that Trini and Connor were planning on kicking her off of their phone plan, a way to "encourage her to be more responsible." She wasn't sure how she could be any more responsible, working two jobs while attending school, but she supposed it was bound to happen anyway. Joy had spent the morning of her birthday shopping for a new phone, trying to find a provider that she could afford on her tiny college budget.

She came home to an empty apartment. Her roommates probably didn't know it was her birthday, and even if they did, they weren't close enough to celebrate it together. She wasn't sure she had anyone outside of her family that she was close enough to celebrate it with.

When Joy came to college, she had been tired of smiling, tired of being loud, tired of fighting for attention. She was tired of forcing herself to be someone she wasn't. So she let her smile slip. She didn't force herself to be cheery but still smiled at those around her. She was friendly, but didn't force herself into friendships, didn't mold herself to be likable, as she had in the past.

For the first part of college, she allowed herself to just be herself.

For the first part of college, she was incredibly lonely.

She found it difficult to make friends as herself. She knew a few people enough to chat before class and to wave when running into them on campus, but not well enough to text them randomly or invite them to hang out. She spent most of her time alone in her bedroom, skipping classes, living vicariously through others via social media. Her grades were great, which sort of disappointed Joy. She thought college would be fun, challenging even. Instead, she had coasted through her first semester of classes, barely studying, only attending half of the lectures she was supposed to. She had heard college would be the best time of her life, but she hated it.

On the evening of her twentieth birthday, Joy stared at herself in the bathroom mirror, thoughts of her childhood and words spit at her by family members echoing through her head. Although she had slept most of the day, she was tired, more so than she had ever been before. Her reflection stared back at her, and all she could see were the flaws. She had gained weight in college, the extra pounds clinging to her torso. Her skin was oily, broken out from the nights she was too tired to wash the makeup off her face. Her hair hung in clumps from being thrown into ponytails and buns without brushing it.

She couldn't find the point of keeping up her appearance. She simply didn't know how to want to be alive anymore. She was tired, so incredibly, mind-numbingly tired. The things that had once brought her happiness now exhausted her. She couldn't find it in herself to be happy for her friends, to celebrate their accomplishments, to comment on their Facebook posts about engagements and children and new jobs while she was stuck in her room, in her head. She knew it was selfish, but she pushed them away, resigning herself to a life of loneliness. Food was bland. Movies were predictable. And she couldn't find the excitement that life had held when she was a child looking forward to growing up. She had been told that life would get better. It hadn't.

Her phone continued to ding beside her with messages celebrating her birthday. She swallowed the pills, trying to make it her last.

CHAPTER 36

"When are you going to tell me where we're going?" Joy rolled her eyes but chuckled under her breath as Ethan turned up the music and pretended not to hear.

Joy smirked. A popular pop song drifted through the air and she proceeded to sing along as loudly and obnoxiously as possible. Ethan winced. He reached forward, turning down the song. Joy continued to sing along, her eyebrows raised in a challenge.

"If you're taking me somewhere to murder me," Joy paused her singing, watching as the city lights faded in her side mirror, "you will not be getting a second date."

"How cliche. If I was going to murder you, I'd do it somewhere fun."

"Somewhere fun?" Joy echoed.

"Yeah, like an amusement park. Or an arcade." Ethan flicked on his brights as he turned down a narrow road lined with tall trees. The road glistened from the rain they had gotten a few hours ago, a surprise freeze leaving the roads a little more slippery than usual, and Ethan was driving almost twenty miles under the limit to compensate. "I'd kill you and stick you on some bumper cars."

"God," Joy chuckled. "Can you imagine? Some poor kid goes to bump me, and I just slump forward. Pretty sure it'd scar them for life."

"Their therapy bill would be ridiculous. But they'd have a really good truth for two truths in a lie."

"I broke my collarbone playing basketball when I was sixteen, I hate broccoli, and the first time I saw a dead body was when I was eleven at Disney World while riding the bumper cars." Joy made her voice higher, ticking off her fingers.

"Uh, the last one?" Ethan deepened his voice as he replied.

"No. I actually love broccoli."

Ethan laughed. Joy tapped her fingers against her phone, her knee bouncing and head bopping to the music. She really should be patient, wait until Ethan told her what the big surprise was.

"Sooo—" she began.

"So?

"Where are we going?"

Ethan sighed, but then smiled, giving in to her curiosity.

"A cabin. A few weeks ago, you mentioned how much you missed the stars. There's no way we can see them in the city. The cabin has a telescope and a hot tub, and I have snacks, wine, and a cake."

Joy cocked her head to the side.

"A cake?"

Ethan's smile widened.

"It's almost midnight," he explained.

She clicked the power button on her phone to check the time, completely ignoring the perfectly good clock on the car dashboard, as one does, smiling and shaking her head as she saw the date.

If her life was like one of the romance novels she read so frequently, this would be the end of Joy's story. A sweet friends-to-lovers story with slight undertones of angst, but a happy ending, her favorite. There would perhaps be an epilogue with a wedding, a couple of kids running around in their shared home, or, more realistic to her, a cat purring on her lap as she read and Ethan dove into a new video game. A simple life with the man she loved.

But life had always been cruel to Joy, and tonight was no exception. Tonight, Joy found herself shielding her eyes as two beams of blinds blinded her.

"What is that?" Joy asked, blinking away the fuzziness in her vision.

Headlights approached the pair from the other side of the road. A black truck drove toward them, swerving in and out of its lane.

"Fuck."

Ethan grabbed the wheel, yanking it sharply to the side. The car spun out, the tires sliding along the ice, leaving it sideways and half on, half off the road. Joy squeezed her eyes shut, bracing herself as the truck plowed into the side of the car.

When Joy tried to open her eyes, she found herself surrounded by a dark mist. She waved her hand, Buttercup retreating, and listened as glass fell to the carpeted floor. Turning her head to the side, she squinted against the black truck's headlights. Ethan lay slumped to the side, his head hanging on his neck at an unnatural angle. Glimmers of light sparkled along his skin, glass that had embedded itself in his face and arms.

"Ethan?"

Ethan let out a sound, a rattle of a breath, almost like he was choking on an invisible object. He twitched once.

A door slammed shut, and footsteps rapidly approached the car.

"Holy shit," a deep voice slurred.

A man stood in front of the headlights, looking into the car. He swayed slightly, then bent down and threw up. Joy could smell the alcohol on his breath from the other side of the car.

"Help him," she whimpered, turning her attention back to Ethan.

A trail of blood dripped from both of his nostrils. His breathing stopped.

"HELP HIM!" she screamed.

She tried to unbuckle herself, but the seatbelt was stuck.

She jammed her fingers into the button, over and over as she shouted at the other driver.

"HE'S NOT BREATHING, PLEASE! PLEASE HELP!"

The driver's eyes widened. He shook his head rapidly.

"No no no no no. This isn't happening," the man said.

"HE'S NOT BREATHING!" Joy could taste copper as she screamed.

She pulled at her seatbelt.

"FUCK!" the driver shouted. He looked at Ethan once more, then took off in a sprint.

Joy prayed he was going to grab a phone, a first aid kit, something to cut her seatbelt off. He didn't. The man hopped into his truck, slamming his door shut. He sped by the car, his headlights passing and leaving Ethan and Joy in the dark.

"No," Joy whispered.

She looked around for her phone but couldn't see it in the pitch black of the car.

"NO!" she shrieked, jabbing her finger into the button of her seatbelt. Her middle finger popped, the bone snapping, but she continued.

"Ethan. Ethan. Please open your eyes. Please. Just open your eyes," she begged, shoving him with her left arm. He slumped away from her. She couldn't see his features, couldn't find the rise and fall of his chest in the dark. Her other hand brushed against her phone, and she pulled it up with trembling fingers. She was surprised to find it undamaged. She clicked on her flashlight app, pausing as it illuminated the dashboard. A tear dripped down her cheek. She turned the light toward Ethan slowly. Ethan stared back at her, eyes open but unseeing.

He is dead, Joy.

"Shut up." Joy shook her head violently, dropping her phone but picking up a long, jagged piece of glass from the floorboard. She gripped it tightly, warmth flowing from her palms, and began to saw into her seatbelt.

Buttercup drifted from her nostrils, pressing itself into the button of her seatbelt. When it did not budge, the black fog pried the glass from her hand and snapped the canvas with one powerful thrust.

Now free, Joy lunged forward, grabbing Ethan by the shoulders and shaking him with both hands.

"Wake up," she demanded.

She slapped him roughly across the cheek. His head rolled around his neck, angling backward. His empty eyes stared at the ceiling.

"He needs a doctor. A doctor could fix this." She opened her car door, spilling onto the dirt road. "HELP. WE NEED HELP," she shouted, cupping her hands over her mouth.

Joy, he is gone. There is nothing we can do.

"SHUT UP," she screeched, pulling at her hair. "He's fine. He's going to be okay. I just have to get him to a doctor. He'll see a doctor and he'll have surgery or something and he'll be super sore and he'll wake up and complain about not going on our date. He wouldn't... he wouldn't leave me. He promised he wouldn't leave me."

She sprinted around to the other side of the car and yanked on his door. It refused to open.

"Buttercup. Get him out of the car."

There is no point. He is dead.

"Get him out, or so help me God, I will never speak to you again. You will live the rest of your days in silence."

As you wish.

Buttercup slipped through the cracks of the car. It lifted Ethan over the center console, his body flopping around the car as it dragged him over the passenger seat and through Joy's open door. It dropped him at Joy's feet, his body reduced to a heap of broken bones and bloodied clothes.

We will carry him no farther. He is gone, Joy; you must let him go.

Joy lifted him by the armpits, walking backward as she heaved him along the road. She panted, sweat dripping down her back and forehead as she tugged him along, his legs dragging in the dirt.

"Ethan... this.. would be so much easier... if you would just wake up," she panted.

Her arms shook with effort. Eventually, she could no longer see the car, only a narrow road with trees that seemed to loom over her. Tears fell steadily from eyes and blurred her vision, but she was unable to wipe them with her arms holding Ethan.

She stumbled.

She fell flat onto her back, Ethan's cold body landing on her lap. A flat box fell out of his coat pocket, and she picked it up with one arm, the other wrapping around Ethan's torso in a morbid embrace.

She turned it upside down, shaking it until its lid fell to the ground. A note floated down, a small silver necklace with a sunflower plopping down on top of it. Joy shoved the necklace into her pocket, then grabbed the note.

"Happy Birthday, Joy," she read aloud.

Her limbs ached, and her eyelids grew heavy. She dropped the note and looked upward. Through the tree limbs, she could see the stars.

CHAPTER 37

Joy, Age 20

"They found a tumor during your operation. They had it shipped out to a lab and tested. I'm sorry, Ms. Hayes, but it was malignant."

Joy clenched her trembling hands together. The room suddenly seemed too small, the lights too bright. The doctor's face blurred.

"Malignant.... That's..." Joy choked out.

"Cancer. It was a neuroendocrine tumor, a hormone cancer." The doctor smiled patiently. "It was a good thing they found it. These types of tumors aren't usually detected unless they are seen in a scan or found by accident. The appendectomy allowed the surgeons to successfully remove the tumor. I'm setting you up with an appointment to meet with an oncologist to discuss next steps. You'll want to—"

Joy tuned out the doctor's words, instead staring at the sheet of paper she had been given. Two weeks after an emergency surgery, which she was told was a routine appendectomy, the last thing Joy thought she would hear was that a tumor had grown through the tip of her appendix, causing it to fail and confirming that she had cancer. The irony of the situation was not lost on Joy. She had spent years wanting to die, but now that she was faced with that possibility, she suddenly wanted nothing more than to live. She didn't know whether she wanted to laugh or cry. She was angry, at the world, at herself, at God. She flipped through her emotions like a magazine, leaving her an unstable mess with unshed tears.

Cancer was one of those things that lingered in the back of everyone's mind. A four-letter word stretched to six, a topic for a dark joke, a side character irrelevant to the plotline, the monster under a child's bed. Looking at the doctor sitting in front of her, that same patient smile on her face, it felt real, too real, too much at one time, and Joy didn't flinch, didn't move, just smiled. She nodded and thanked the woman, her smile never slipping at the receptionist and the man who held the door for her.

Even as she got into her car, set the paper with the address for her first oncology appointment to the side, sent a few text messages, swiped at the tears on her face, slammed her fists against her steering wheel, tugged at the roots of her hair, cursed rapidly at the roof of her car. She. Just. Smiled.

Because what else could she do? If her grief showed, if she mourned the life she had become adjusted to, the one she finally began to enjoy, who would like her? It was pathetic, really, how her first thought was how people would treat her if they found out. How people would not want to be around her anymore if they knew how scared she was, how angry, how sad. So she continued to smile, waved off any concerns her family had, and told her friends how someday it would be a good story. She declined invites for family to visit her as she returned to the city.

She spent her days trapped in bright white walls, her phone occasionally pinging with messages of support from her friends and family. She spent her nights in her dark room, hiding away from the rest of the world. She forced herself into solitude lest her family find out she wasn't handling it quite as well as she claimed to be. The worst part was the fatigue. She was too tired to go out, too tired to take care of herself, but she kept forcing.

She took a full load of classes, continued working part-time —anything to distract herself from the needles, the nausea, the pain. Her hair matted against her scalp; she didn't have the energy to wash and brush. Knots formed in her blonde hair, prominent against her paling skin. She wore long sleeves to cover the brushes left from the needles, even in the middle of a Texas summer. She lay in bed, sweating every night, fevers a constant side effect, a bucket beside her for nights she couldn't get herself to the bathroom to throw up.

Her family asked if they should visit during her second surgery. It was hard to determine intention through a text. Did they actually want to come down? Were they annoyed by the inconvenience caused by having a daughter with cancer? Joy had declined, but it shouldn't have even been a question. She didn't want to let them down, to show how weak she had become, how desperate she was for an escape from her loneliness. She told them she was fine. That she could only have one guest at a time anyway.

Although she betrayed herself when she didn't tell them how badly she wanted them to come, they betrayed her when they didn't overrule her. When they sent her texts after surgery instead of calling. When they went about their lives as usual, posting on Facebook about their everyday accomplishments and enjoying their lives while she sat in her hospital bed, fingers fumbling as she attempted to do homework with pain medication still in her system.

The next few months were some of the darkest in Joy's life. She was terrified of needles, and had been since she saw her mother using them as a child. She was tired of surgeries, of staying overnight in hospitals. Hell, she couldn't even swallow pills at first; the little capsules always seemed to get stuck in her throat. But she learned.

She also learned that treatment was expensive, her medical bills piling up after every appointment. She found herself buried in debt, and why? Because she wanted to feel okay again? Because she didn't want to die?

The only thing that got her through was Ethan.

Ethan, who visited her every day after her second surgery, her only visitor during her hospital stay. Half of her colon had been removed, and he bought a stuffed version of the organ, to replace the part she lost, he said.

Ethan, who held her hair back as she threw up, brushed the knots out with incredible patience when she was too weak to do so herself.

Ethan, who drove her to every appointment, even though he wasn't allowed inside with her.

Ethan, who got her a cat, so she wasn't alone in her apartment while he left for class.

Ethan, who emailed professors for her when she was too sick to attend class.

Ethan, who slept in his car when she was rushed to the emergency room.

Ethan, who helped her with chores.

Ethan, who brought her groceries.

Ethan, who loved her.

Ethan, who was gone.

CHAPTER 38

Ethan's friends and family sobbed around Joy, his mother clutching his sister, and silent tears trailing down his father's face. People Ethan knew in high school, those who he had not seen or even thought of in years, sniffed in their seats.

A black casket had the place of honor in the front of the church, two rows and three seats away from Joy. It would take her five steps, perhaps seven, to walk to it. Her best friend, partner, favorite person in this entire world lay seven steps away, but she could not reach him. She would never reach him, but she didn't cry. She sat in her seat, eyes fixed on the wall.

"My brother was..." Ethan's older brother began his eulogy.

He stood tall, his voice wavering only once. He was dressed sharply, crisp black pants with an ironed button-down shirt and black dress shoes, his hair combed and styled. Had it not been for the red rimming his eyes, he could have been on his way to the office. Joy glanced down at herself. Her own black pants were wrinkled, creases deeply ingrained in their fabric from being shoved into a backpack.

"...Never again with a stranger." The crowd around Joy let out a watery chuckle as Ethan's brother finished a story from Ethan's youth.

Joy tugged at the collar of her sweater, heat coursing throughout her body. Ethan's brother stepped away from the podium, red socks flashing as the bottoms of his pants swayed.

The color reminded her that Christmas was in a few weeks. She couldn't find it in herself to care. So many holidays had been spent with Ethan and his family. They had welcomed her with open arms, buying her Christmas presents and Easter baskets, inviting her on vacations and asking her about how school was going, if she liked her job, how she was feeling.

She couldn't help but wonder if this was the last time she would see them. Three years of friendship, two years of being in love with her best friend, and one car accident to lose it all.

The preacher took Ethan's brother's spot, standing beside the altar, Bible in hand. He opened his mouth to speak, but Joy could not hear it. Instead she heard

Buzzing.

Buzzing so loud and intense that she closed her eyes and focused on her breathing.

Buzzing that muffled the preacher's words.

Buzzing that lessened the sniffling around her.

Buzzing that only allowed her to hear her own heart beat, thudding painfully against her ribs. It was cruel, only hearing the pounding in her chest while knowing that Ethan's remained still.

And then she could hear everything, all at once. The preacher shouted from the front of the church. Every sniffle was a sob. Every sob was a wail. The blowing of noses were bombs exploding in her ears, shattering her eardrums. She willed herself to calm down, willed her breath to return to her lungs, and yet every gasp of air only sought to choke her more.

She stood. The room fell silent. People who loved Ethan, some of whom had known him far longer than she had, stared as she panted.

There was one whisper, then another. Soon, the entire church was whispering. Joy wondered what they were thinking. Did they blame her? Did they know she could have saved him? They must hate her so much. Yet again, she stood in a room with a dead man she loved, a man who deserved to live far more than she thought she did. Her eyes fell on the exit, and she sprinted, leaving behind her belongings and ignoring the mutterings of those around her.

Throwing herself through the wooden doors, she continued running down the road until she couldn't physically run any longer. She hunched over, throwing up in a grassy area. Vomit dripped through her nose, the acidity making her eyes sting. Standing, she wiped the back of her mouth with her hand and looked at her surroundings.

Anger burst through Joy, so quick and powerful that she couldn't keep it contained. She screamed, dropping to her knees as Buttercup hurled out of her in a violent wave of black. It connected with the stop sign across the street, snapping the metal pole and sending it flying. She panted as she listened to it clatter along the road.

We have to go back. We cannot abandon him in his last moments.

Knowing Buttercup was right, she forced herself to walk back to the church, pausing outside its doors. She could hear the sermon continuing, the opening notes of "Amazing Grace" drifting through the wood. Her hand hovered over the door handle, but she couldn't will it to reach down to open the door and chose to instead slide down the brick wall and sit with her arms wrapped around her knees. The service soon ended, people filing through the doors and into their cars. No one stopped to check on Joy, and if they noticed her, they said nothing. Someone sat beside her, sighing as their knees cracked.

"I don't think there's anything I could say to make you feel better," Connor said. "I've never been very good with words. I'm actually pretty terrible with them, as I'm sure you know. But I don't think it's me you would want to talk to anyway. Ethan's mom said they're about to load him up to take him to the cemetery. She said she can give you a few minutes, though, if you want to say goodbye."

Joy nodded, pulling herself to her feet. Connor offered her a sad smile as she helped him up.

"Caden, Oliver, and I are going to head to the reception. Do you want us to wait for you? You can ride with us if you want?"

Joy shook her head no, not trusting her voice. Connor patted her shoulder. She turned, staring at the church, her hand trembling as she opened the doors. Stepping into the room, she shivered as a blast of air conditioning raced through her clothes. She walked slowly toward the altar, stopping beside the closed casket. The chapel was empty now, save for the piano player shuffling her music sheets into a folder. She smiled at Joy, grabbing her papers and leaving out the back door.

"I'm sorry," Joy whispered.

She stood silently, mouth opening and closing as she tried to think of what to say. How does one apologize for something so grim as choosing oneself over the life of another? How could mere words express all of the sorrow and guilt she carried? She knew nothing she said would ever be able to encompass everything she felt toward Ethan in that moment, in the years she had known him, in the way she had cared for him.

So instead, she said something she had known for a while. Something she had never told him. Something she should have said, at least once, while he was still alive.

"I love you."

She didn't attend the reception, nor did she go to watch Ethan's casket be lowered into the ground. Instead, she got into her car and drove. It took her five hours to get home, only stopping once to get gas.

Her only thought on the road had been to go home, that he would be waiting there for her, that this was all a mistake somehow, a bad dream. He would be sitting on the couch, Xbox controller in hand. He'd toss the controller to the side, stand up, hug her, ask her how her day was. They would go on dates. She would watch him graduate from college, cheer with his family as he walked the stage. They'd move in together permanently, argue about whose turn it was to do laundry, cry during sad anime scenes.

She pulled into the parking lot, yanking her keys from the ignition and locking the car behind her. She trod up the stairs and unlocked the apartment, only to be met with darkness.

It didn't matter, Joy decided, he was running late, caught up in homework at the library or running a DND campaign at the shop down the road. She took off her shoes, setting them off to the side.

She lay down in front of the door, the cool of the wood keeping her alert, her phone clutched in her hand in case Ethan wanted to text her. He did that sometimes, sent her random videos on nights when he couldn't sleep.

CHAPTER 39

A single candle lit up her childhood bedroom in a scene Joy knew too well. For the first time, she was somewhat aware that she was dreaming, an inkling of recognition wiggling around in the back of her brain. She knew of the glass on the floor, of the scraps of air freshener and seatbelt that lay somewhere within the mess, of the mirror that hung on the door she would never be able to go through.

She sat on her bed, legs crossed, and stared into the dark. A voice muttered from the figure still trapped in the mirror.

"Who's there?" Joy heard herself whisper, as she had dozens of times before, but she remained on the bed.

"You let me die," the reflection screeched.

Joy thought she knew this scene, had lived through it countless times, and yet her head cocked to the side. Her fear was still there, tucked inside of her and showing in her trembling figure, but confusion overwhelmed her.

"YOU COULD HAVE SAVED ME!" The figures in the mirror bellowed, voices causing the mirror to shake against the door.

Wait.

Something was wrong, different.

A flicker of a second shadow moved in the mirror.

"My Joy..." it said, its voice familiar and sad. "Why didn't you save me?"

The mirror fell from the door, and the glass shattered. Two

figures crawled out from underneath the mirror's frame, one scrambling toward Joy on its hands and knees while the other stood and walked silently behind it. The door opened behind them, revealing nothing but darkness. Joy didn't move, didn't cry. She accepted her fate, ignoring her grandfather as he inched closer. He was a demon she was used to, a ghost she had come to accept. Instead, she focused on Ethan, unflinching as he stopped in front of the bed frame and lowered his head to hers.

Ethan's eyes were black, his head hung unnaturally from his neck, and his face sparkled in the candlelight, glass reflecting from where it stuck to his skin. He reached a hand out to Joy, and she nuzzled her cheek against his cold palm.

A burst of cold air ran down Joy's spine and she shivered, reaching for Ethan to pull him closer. He stepped back, his face obscured by the shadows of the room. Black mist floated from the corners of the room, swarming around her body. Cold tendrils wrapped around her waist and her legs. She opened her mouth to scream, but the fog shot down her throat, choking her into silence.

"Oh, Joy," Ethan sighed from somewhere in the room. She could no longer see him, could no longer see anything through the dark cloud.

"You do not belong in the dark," Joy jumped as his voice whispered directly into her ear. "You are the dark."

The rope at her waist pulled, yanking her off the bed and onto the glass-covered floor. She didn't react to the pain of the shards pushing into her skin. She didn't feel it. Just like she didn't the night Ethan died. Instead, her mouth opened, throat straining against the mist in a silent, desperate plea as it dragged her through the door and away from Ethan.

* * *

Joy shot up from her position sprawled on the floor, her eyes blinking rapidly as they adjusted. A dull throbbing in her left hand drew her attention, and she looked down to see her phone still clenched within her fist. Footsteps echoed outside. Joy glanced up at the white door. Ethan's front door stood untouched in front of her.

She held her breath and stared at it, willing it to open, hope growing as the footsteps drew closer.

"Please. Come home, Ethan," she whispered through the night.

The neighboring door opened, warm voices escaping through the chill of the morning. Ethan's door remained closed.

Joy's phone vibrated in the pocket of her black dress. She pulled it out to see Clara calling her. She declined. She picked her way through the living room, intent on grabbing herself a glass of water to soothe her dry throat and chapped lips.

A shower would do us good.

She didn't know when she started talking to Buttercup again, but she now found the voice comforting. It had been there for her, coaxing her into taking care of herself, never leaving her mind, never abandoning her.

Joy found herself walking into her bathroom and turning the shower on to heat up. Steam drifted through the bathroom as she undressed.

Joy sucked in a deep breath before releasing it slowly.

"Why didn't I save him?" she asked, finally gasping into the world the question that had plagued her since the accident.

Because we didn't think to do so.

"What?"

When the truck hit, we wanted to save ourself. At that moment, we did not think of Ethan.

Buttercup's words hit her harder than the truck had. She rushed to the toilet, the small bites of food she had managed to choke down that morning forcing themselves back up.

Her family had called it a miracle that she was unharmed.

They had been sad, of course they had. They had liked Ethan well enough, even considered him an honorary part of the family. But he hadn't belonged to them, not like he had belonged to his family and Joy. They understood her grief, as much as they could, but they were able to see the positive in the accident. Joy didn't think Ethan's family saw it that way.

And now. Now that she was to blame. Now that she knew she could have but didn't save him. How would she ever look at them again? How could she even look at her own family, knowing they were grateful she was okay while not understanding she was to blame? How could there be a positive when their daughter was a murderer?

The drunk driver is the murderer. Our reaction was only natural.

Joy heard Buttercup but didn't care. Regardless of what it said, she knew she was to blame. She pulled a piece of her hair from her mouth, sticky from her vomit, and pushed the rest off from where it clung to her sweaty face.

She sat in the shower, her back to the stream of water, suddenly too tired to move. Pressing her palms to her eyes, she inhaled sharply. There was a tightness in her chest that unraveled far quicker than she could suppress it, and she sought to force it out, banging her hands against her body, her shower walls, anywhere she could reach. She pulled at her hair, tugging harshly at the roots, gasping for breath. Heat coursed through her body even as she trembled, and she bit down on her fist to prevent the silent scream clogging her throat from escaping.

Ethan's eyes had replaced her grandfather's in her nightmares, their faces blurring together every time she closed her own. The two most important men in her life, gone. Both deaths had been her fault. If only she hadn't thought of only herself. If only she could have been less fucking selfish. She was worthless. She_

"Breathe," Joy choked out.

It's a panic attack. We've been through this before. This is only temporary. We're going to be fine.

She closed her eyes.

Joy sat up straight, the warm water of the shower dripping down her back. She took a deep breath, filling her stomach and chest with air and relaxing her shoulders as she exhaled. Breathing in again, this time, she imagined a feather rising as she inhaled. The feather floated down with her exhale. She repeated this cycle for a few minutes, letting her body relax further with every breath.

When she felt more stable, she stood, pushing her wet hair off of her face, and rubbed at her temples to alleviate the throbbing.

I'm fine. I'm fine. I'm fine.

Long after her fingers pruned, Joy turned off the faucet and stepped out of the shower. She headed across the hallway, feet automatically leading her to the guest bedroom. A picture of Ethan and his family sat framed on the bedside table. She stared at it before turning and tucking herself into her bed.

CHAPTER 40

Scrolling through Facebook, as it turns out, does nothing to help one hide from grief.

It isn't fair.

It wasn't. Her attempt at a distraction, scrolling through social media on her living room floor, had failed. Those around Joy carried on with their lives, oblivious to her loss, ignorant of her pain. Even worse, those who had hurt her in the past, who had traumatized her childhood and left her questioning her worth, were thriving.

Her mother was married, living in a small house and creating art on the side. Trini was still posting pictures of the wedding, Ethan peeking into the frame every now and then. Joy forced herself to swipe away at every glance of his long hair and tall frame. Connor shared an update from the road trip he had taken with Oliver. Even her grandmother seemed to be doing well, her food truck succeeding in her small town. It burned to know that everyone else was fine, that the world had moved on while Joy was still stuck in her abandonment.

A glutton for punishment, she clicked on the Facebook account for Sarah's food truck. The food looked mediocre, but the page itself already had hundreds of likes, including a like by Trini. Had Joy been a better daughter, a better person even, perhaps she would have tried to see it from Trini's point of view. Sarah was her mother, as shitty as she was, and maybe people don't really grow out of seeking that affection. But Joy was tired of being a good person, exhausted from forcing herself to understand the feelings of those who consistently invalidated hers. She stared at the most recent post, attention catching on those who shared it.

Her anger stilled, rivers of cold hurt freezing the hot banks of her rage. One of the shares came from the mother of one of her closest childhood friends. Her friend was one of the few she confided in about her abuse, the one who showed up with trash bags of clothes when she couldn't afford new ones, the very same clothes Sarah had stolen from her and yet mocked her for wanting. Her mom had helped with school supplies, given her coats in the winter. Her father had been friends with her grandfather, making small talk in the local grocery store and sharing beers when they bumped into each other at barbecues. They had watched him wither firsthand and saw how Sarah's infidelity and manipulation diminished him until he was nothing but a shell of the man he once was.

And yet there was the share. Joy glared at it, hunching obsessively over her bright screen from her seat on the floor of her dark room.

Maybe she hadn't shared it for Sarah. She could have shared it for Sarah's business partner, a woman Joy had never met or heard of before. She could've shared it thinking she was supporting a small business. She could've not known it was Sarah running the food truck. Joy didn't care what the reason was; it still hurt.

Had she not been alone, maybe she wouldn't have cared as much. She could've turned to Ethan, ranted for a few minutes about the lack of cosmic justice.

Maybe he would've kissed her, coaxing her to relax in the sweetest way possible.

Maybe he would've held her hand and pulled her into a hug, reminding her how lucky she was to have him in her life.

But he didn't. Because he was dead. Gone. Not coming back.

So she sat alone, scrolling through her social media,

desperately searching for a distraction. Her neighbors thumped at her bedroom wall. Once. Twice. A squeak. A moan.

Disgusting.

"It's like two in the afternoon."

And a Tuesday.

"Assholes," Joy murmured.

A red truck flashed through her mind.

Ethan's killer, the driver of that truck, was out there somewhere, living his life, posting pictures on Facebook, dating, fucking, working. And pretending nothing had happened.

Joy hated it.

The phone burned her hand, and she threw it across the room. It landed safely on her couch cushions. She slapped her hands against the hardwood floor, palms stinging on impact, in response to the lack of a satisfying crack.

I could find him.

"It wouldn't be hard."

I could make him pay.

"I could scare him," Joy justified. "No one would even have to get hurt. I could set up a camera, make him admit what he's done, then turn it into the police. He doesn't deserve to live normally."

I remember what he looks like. It wouldn't take long.

"He has to be from around here. He had a Texas license plate and a sticker on his truck for one of those sleazy college bars on sixth."

I could get justice for Ethan's death.

For the first time since her birthday, Joy smiled.

***

A few hours later, Joy found herself standing at the edge of a tree line, a smattering of trees behind her and black bars in front of her. The driver lived in a nice neighborhood on the outskirts of Austin, his house backing up to a small stretch of woods. The house itself was mostly glass, large transparent walls with black framing, and the backyard was surrounded by a wrought iron fence.

Not only was the driver a dick, judging by the size of the house, he was also a rich dick.

I don't think anyone is home.

"There were no cars that I could see. And only cameras in the front."

A poor choice, really.

Buttercup drifted outward, condensing into dark steps. Joy strode forward, climbing the stairs over the fence and hopping onto the grass of the backyard. Something squished beneath her right shoe.

A five-million-dollar house...

"And they still can't pick up their dog's shit." Joy sighed, dragging her shoes against the grass.

She let herself in through the back door, using Buttercup to flip open the deadlock. Slipping into the house, she was surprised at how normal it was. There were no sex dungeons, no secret murder rooms, no hint of anything in the living room other than white modern furniture, an electric fireplace, a large tv, and framed pictures. She stopped in front of one of the pictures, her head cocking to the side as she studied the man she had seen the night of Ethan's death.

He looked underwhelmingly ordinary, average height, brown hair cut short and a white strip of perfectly straight teeth. He was attractive enough to get a second glance at a bar but not memorably handsome. One of his arms was around an equally attractive, obviously pregnant woman, the other holding up a toddler with blonde curls and a wide grin. If there was ever a picture of a typical upper-class white family, this was it.

Joy walked down the hallway before opening the door to what appeared to be a home office. Framed awards lined the walls, and a diploma hung proudly above an antique desk.

"A doctor. That's ironic," Joy mumbled.

She traced her gloved fingers along the certificates, reading the man's various accolades, relishing how Buttercup sent them scattering to the ground at her touch. They were mostly for charity work, a few from medical publications the man had contributed to, one for volunteering with Doctors Without Borders. She knocked the next hanging item off the wall without bothering to look at it but stopped it mid-air when a flash of bright color caught her attention. Buttercup drifted the frame to her waiting hands.

It was a picture of a family drawn in crayon, a mother and father, a small girl with a blue dress and yellow curls, and what was either a swaddled baby or large carrot hung among the displays of accomplishment. "Happy Father's Day!!!!" was written in bright orange beneath the drawing. For the first time since entering the house, Joy thought about leaving, forgetting the grudge, moving on with her life.

Ethan was still alive when the accident happened, and the driver was a doctor.

"He probably couldn't have saved him anyway. He didn't..." Joy let out a shaky breath. "He didn't last long."

Yes, but the doctor did not know that. The doctor saw him breathing and heard me scream for help.

Rage filled Joy, sudden and blazing, as she thought of the doctor leaving, the darkness that he left behind as his truck pulled away. Joy tossed the drawing to the side and watched the glass splinter on the carpet. The shards crunched, and the paper crumpled under her foot as she walked out of the room, slamming the door shut behind her.

She paced through the house, Buttercup tearing apart any item that caught her attention. When she finally stopped in the living room, chaos surrounded her, and she felt a chill run through her in the silence of the house. Flipping on the electric fireplace, Joy settled onto the couch and waited.

* * *

A half-hour later, keys jingled in the front door. Joy turned her attention to the turn of the door knob.

Thank God, I was starting to get bored.

"Hi," Joy said, uncrossing her legs on the couch.

The man startled as he walked through the front door, dropping his phone but managing to catch the small package he held. She pointed at the phone and Buttercup snatched it from the ground. Pocketing the device, she studied the man. He looked exactly like the pictures, objectively handsome, body toned from obvious hours at the gym.

"Who are you? What are you doing in my house?" he fumed. His eyes flicked to the door. "I'm going to call the police if you don't get out right now."

Joy blinked. She cocked her head to the side, silently observing. She thought when she saw him again she would be filled with hatred, overcome with righteous anger and the need for vengeance. Instead, she felt discontent, the image of the man standing before her and the one who had fled that night not quite connecting.

"With what phone?" she asked, her voice calm.

"What is it that you want? Why are you in my house?" he repeated.

What do I want?

"A confession."

"A confession?" he parroted, still standing in the entrance.

The man grew angry then, as if a switch had flipped, his eyebrows furrowing as he decided that Joy was not a threat. He stomped over to her, nostrils flaring, and reached a hand out to wrap around her bicep. Joy smirked at the muscle jumping in his jaw. Buttercup rammed into his chest, sending him sprawling. He landed on his back, coughing and gasping for breath as he stared at the ceiling fan for a few seconds.

"I have a couple of questions for you," Joy said, peeling herself from the admittedly comfortable couch and walking to stand over the man.

The man rolled over with a groan and began to stand. "You crazy bitch. What did you hit me with?"

"Sorry," Joy flicked her wrist, and Buttercup followed, striking the back of the knees and returning him to the ground. "I think you might not have heard me. I said I have a couple of questions for you, not the other way around."

The man glanced at the open front door. Joy pointed at it, and it slammed shut, the lock sliding into place. A bead of sweat formed on his forehead.

"Where were you the morning of November 8th? About midnight?"

The man's expression fell blank. Joy had spent a lifetime with women who knew how to manipulate their emotions at will, and this man's confusion was genuine. Joy gritted her teeth. He didn't even remember the date he took a life.

"Should I refresh your memory then?"

Buttercup yanked the man to his knees, pinning him against the wall.

"You were driving a black truck down a country road. Had a couple of drinks, maybe more. You swerved into the other lane, hitting another car. A girl sat in the passenger side, begging you to help her. A boy sat in the driver's seat, badly injured. You looked at them, got back in your truck, and then drove away. Does it ring a bell now?"

Joy pulled down her mask. His eyes widened in recognition.

"Hello again."

"I'm sorry," he whimpered, tears rushing to his eyes.

"I'm afraid sorry isn't enough."

"What. What do you want from me?"

"I want you to pay for what you did. I want you to remember his face every single time you close your eyes. I want you to suffer the same way he did. I want you dead, like he is." The man flinched at this.

"You feel this power?" Joy lifted him higher along the wall. "It can find you. No matter where you go, how far you run, how fast you run, it will find you. And that's if I'm feeling nice. If I'm not, I won't start with you. I'll start with the woman in those pictures, then the kid. Hell, I'll even find your parents, your siblings, their kids. I won't stop until every single person you care about is dead. Or. Or—" Joy patted him on the cheek.

"—You can turn yourself in. Admit what you did, serve your time, let your family look at you like the monster you are. Your choice. I'll give you until tomorrow morning. Say your goodbyes. Arrange whatever you have to arrange. Then head to the police station. Or. I kill every person you know. Simple as that."

Joy dropped him then, letting him fall to the ground. She stared at him, contemplating. Then shoved his head into the wall, watching as he crumpled.

"Oops," she shrugged.

And then, Joy did something careless. She turned her back to the man, assuming him incapacitated for a few moments, and walked to his front door. She didn't hear the man get up, but she did hear the glass shatter as he broke the mug from the counter over her head. Buttercup left her in a second, restraining him against the wall as Joy stood.

Warm liquid slid from her forehead down onto her white shirt, dotting the fabric with red. She looked back at where the man stood, his face paling in fear. She brought a hand up to her face and flinched as her fingers brushed against the cold glass protruding from beside her temple.

She gripped the piece gingerly between two fingers and pulled, her eyes never leaving his. She felt the glass drag through the cut before it tugged free, a few beads of blood smearing her fingertips. She dropped the shard into her pocket, careful not to let any of the blood drip elsewhere.

"Do you know what happens when you break your neck?"

Buttercup wrapped one tendril around the man's throat, another shooting down it.

"It starts with losing feeling in your limbs. Your arms and legs go completely numb."

The man's breath slowed, his eyes bulging as Buttercup circled in his chest.

"You lose oxygen as your body loses the ability to breathe. Your heart slows down, then stops beating completely. You can feel it, feel yourself start to die as you suffocate. It's not an instant death, not always. Ethan, that was his name by the way, didn't die instantly. Instead, I watched him try to breathe. A minute doesn't seem like a long time. Only sixty seconds. But I felt each one. Each second tick by. Sixty seconds stretched into a lifetime as I heard his final breath."

"I didn't mean to," the man gasped out. "Let me go, and I promise I'll turn myself in. It was an accident, I promise."

"An accident?" Joy leaned in close. "So you weren't drinking? You didn't swerve into my lane?"

The man kicked his legs out.

"Let me go, you crazy bitch!"

There was a pounding in Joy's ears, drowning out the shouts of the man.

She sighed. "That's the problem with men like you. You never know when to stop talking."

Joy flicked her wrist. The man's head snapped to the side. Buttercup receded, and the man dropped to the floor in a heap.

Joy blinked. The man lay still. All at once, her thoughts raced.

Who would find his body? The cherub-cheeked girl in his pictures? The angelic woman grinning next to her? Bile rose from Joy's stomach, through her throat, and out of her mouth, Buttercup stopping it from hitting the wood floor. Her vomit hovered over the ground, floating amid the black mist, the smell making her dry heave once more.

Joy popped her hoodie over her head and sprinted out the door. Halfway down the driveway, she paused. Buttercup shattered the camera on the doorbell before Joy turned back to look at the man's SUV. The driver-side door was open, the keys still in the ignition, the AC blasting and a song playing over the radio.

Keep going.

Joy shook her head, cocking it to the side as a small sound escaped through the crack of the car door. She stepped toward it.

Don't do that. I have to leave now.

The music drifting through the air was wrong. It didn't fit with the image of the man. The lyrics were too simple, the melody too cheery. Joy took another step.

I just killed a man. I have to leave before the police show up.

A sticker on the back of the vehicle caught her attention. A yellow diamond with three words. Joy's vision swam.

I don't want to know. If I leave now, there's no proof. I can go, pretend this never happened.

A gurgle. Then a soft coo.

Joy held her breath as she opened the back door. A small face stared back at her, eyes wide with innocence. A small hand reached for her, the small form straining against the buckles of the car seat. It babbled, opening its mouth into a toothless smile.

Shutting the door, Joy walked back inside the house. She squatted next to the man, avoiding looking at his face, and pulled his phone from his pocket. She dialed 911 and waited until an operator picked up.

"There's a baby in a parked car in front of a house. It's been there for a few hours. The front door of the house is open too."

"What is your location?"

Joy rattled off the address, and the operator assured her that a police officer would be there soon. Leaving the door open as she left, she turned the phone off and pocketed it.

"Buttercup, stay here and watch over it. Make sure nothing other than a police officer gets into the vehicle."

Okay.

Joy walked a few blocks before tossing the phone into the dumpster of a convenience store. A police car whizzed by her, sirens blaring. Joy ducked inside the store, buying herself a bottle of water and a candy bar. Sitting on the pavement outside, she chugged the bottle of water and waited for Buttercup to return. She felt the cold mist before she heard its words.

The child is safe.

Joy stood, candy bar forgotten on the concrete, and walked home.

CHAPTER 41

The next morning, Joy stood in her kitchen and watched as her coffee machine brewed. The smell of coffee soon filled the room, and she picked up the warm cup as it finished, taking a small sip and grimacing as the taste mixed with the leftover toothpaste from her freshly brushed teeth. She had come home the evening before and crawled into bed, not moving until well after the sun had come up. The toothpaste erased the taste of the murder she had committed, but not the sight of the man's neck snapping, the cries of his baby as she ran just like he had.

Heat flashed through Joy's body, and her vision blurred.

The mug slipped from her fingers, shattering and spilling the light brown drink on the tile floor. She staggered to pick it up, nearly losing her balance completely. She leaned against the counter, head tilted downward as the world around her spun. Her head pounded, and sweat dripped from her temple onto the floor.

Pulling her phone from her pocket, she opened the camera app and flipped the screen toward herself. She reached up, her fingers trembling as they hovered over her face. A thick black liquid oozed from the cut on her temple and streamed downward toward her chin.

"What the actual fu—" Joy's words were interrupted as a groan slipped from her lips.

There is a cost to power. One that has been paid before.

Her body flushed hot, and she dropped to the floor as a blinding headache overcame her. She clenched her eyes shut as her hand flew up to cradle her face. The pain faded after a few moments, leaving Joy panting on the ground.

"What's gonna happen to me?" asked Joy, wiping her sleeve along the cut and smearing the black goo along her cheek.

It isn't real.

"I know," she admitted in a whisper. She looked down at her fingertips, then rubbed the blood onto her jeans, staining the denim a dark crimson. She had picked at the scab left from the man hitting her with the glass while she waited for her coffee to brew. "A mysterious illness caused by your powers would have been a lot cooler, though. I could go off on an adventure. Look for a cure to a gift given by the ancient gods. Or something like that."

That would be cool.

"The hot flash was real, wasn't it?"

It was real, Buttercup confirmed.

"It's back."

It's back.

"Huh." She looked at the medical bills on her coffee table, stacked neatly in order of greatest to least. Placing a hand on her stomach, she ran her clean fingers over the raised scar from her second surgery. "How long do I have? Is it treatable this time?"

I have no way of knowing.

She nodded. Perhaps she should have been scared by the thought, but she was so tired. If it was what she thought it was, she wasn't sure she had the strength to keep going anyway. For now, she would focus on what she could control, push everything else away for another day.

She cleaned up the coffee, Buttercup tossing the mug pieces in the trash as she mopped up the liquid with a dish towel. She was reminded of the glass shard in her jeans and went to retrieve it, mistakenly sticking her hand into the wrong pocket. Her wallet slipped out, opening as it hit the floor. The smiling face on her driver's license looked odd to her. Her eyes were bright, and her hair was a wild mess.

"Joy Aurora Hayes," her name read below.

When she was a child, she was a firm believer that names held power, that they could shape someone's life. Her name meant happiness and light, something she clung to even when she was at her lowest. It had never really seemed fitting for someone as gloomy as herself, but now it especially seemed ill-suited. Maybe her mother had known how she would turn out. Maybe her name was the darkest joke ever told.

Still, maybe names were important. A name, after all, would last long after a person died. To take a name from someone would be like taking their life from them, to reduce them to nothing. A name—

Joy had never thought of herself as a particularly good person. She tried to be kind when she could afford to be, fair when she couldn't. Even after murdering a man, she still felt fairly gray, not great, but not the worst person to ever live. One thought changed that.

"What was his name?"

I don't know.

"I saw it. I know I saw it. It was on the diploma and the awards. It was... It was..."

I don't know.

"I killed a man. And I didn't even know his name. Holy fucking shit.

He killed Ethan.

"And I killed him!"

He deserved to die.

Joy paced through her apartment, walking from room to room in a frenzied panic.

"What gives me the right to make that decision? Some power I never asked for?" Joy's voice elevated in pitch, rising to something akin to a dog whistle. "I just...I just took a man's life. What if he was a good person who made a bad choice? Jesus, what about his family?"

A bad choice? He left me to die. He let Ethan die as he fled.

"I can't... I can't undo that, though. He's never going to blink again. Or breathe again. He won't even get the opportunity to make up for what he did."

He can do so in Hell.

"Jesus! What if..." Joy gulped, the thought making her feel guilty. "What if someone finds out it was me?"

The body was not touched, and no DNA was left behind. The house was torn apart. It will look like a failed robbery.

She grabbed the nearest object to her, a cookbook, threw it across the room and watched as it collided with an accent mirror. The mirror fell, breaking further as it landed on the hardwood floor. Immediately feeling guilty and wanting to clean the mess, she kneeled in front of the shattered object, her face staring back at her in the shards.

Joy's eyes were glued to those in her reflection. They were pitch black, and a mocking smile stretched across her mouth. She screamed, scampering backward on all fours until her back hit the wall. She squeezed her eyelids together tightly, shaking her head as tears dripped down her face.

Her phone buzzed from somewhere in her pocket, and Joy yanked it out, desperate for someone to talk to.

"This is a call from a debt collector on behalf of Southwest Medical. Our records show that Ms. JOY HAYES has an outstanding balance of..."

Joy laughed, then screamed.

Blood interchanged with spit as her throat, raw from the force of her scream, from the emotions she so carefully bottled up, closed.

The world around her imploded upon her scream. Buttercup thrummed through the room, glass shattering and wood splintering at its touch, leaving her panting for breath.

What now?

CHAPTER 42

Joy, Age 23

"What now?" Joy laughed, swiping the tears from her cheeks and gritting her teeth.

The smile dropped from her face.

She looked at the empty *Princess Bride* DVD on her shelf.

Then at Ethan's jacket.

Then at herself in the mirror.

Now I have nothing holding me back.

CHAPTER 43

Joy really needed to get a handle on her social media consumption. She sat at the restaurant table, flipping between TikTok and Instagram as she waited for Caden to return from the restroom. Joy had returned to West Texas a few days ago and was staying with Trini and Jonas for an extended Christmas vacation. Caden had begged her this morning to take her to try out a new brunch place in town, and she had reluctantly agreed.

A news alert caught her attention—red letters against a white background that made her phone vibrate.

"New updates on the robbery and abduction of Alphagraph CEO John Dongle."

Joy bit back a smile and clicked the link. An embedded video began to play on the news website. A bald, tall man stumbled into the street wearing nothing but a pair of heart print underwear. Joy turned the volume up on her phone and pressed the speaker against her ear as the man rambled about being attacked by a ghost. The clip then switched to the night before. The man, now fully dressed but still stumbling about due to his obvious intoxication, waded his way through a packed college-bar street.

Joy paused the video, screenshotted, then zoomed in on a woman in the corner of the shot, almost out of frame, who smiled at the street camera. She glared at the image. The glasses she had worn that night weren't as flattering as she would have liked. She made a mental note to buy a new pair. A news anchor could be heard speaking in the background of the article.

"Police believe he was jumped by... missing wallet...and with a broken arm." She winced at the mention. She hadn't meant to break his arm, but... "John was recently accused of sexual assault by four of his employees in a lawsuit that was dismissed for lack of evidence. While Alphagraph has yet to release an official statement about the situation, the morning of the attack, pictures and emails confirming the allegations were sent from John's phone to a mix of national and local news stations, as well as a company-wide email. The headline of the email simply read 'Suck it, John.' "

Joy snorted, sipping on her mimosa and putting away her phone.

A middle-aged woman at a neighboring table cleared her throat and a heavily pregnant waitress with her brown hair braided into pigtails turned to her.

"How can I help you?" the teenage server asked with a kind smile.

The customer, who had the roundest hairstyle Joy had ever seen, scoffed. "This isn't what I ordered."

Joy frowned, listening in as Bowl-Cut pushed her plate across the table.

I'll kill her.

Damn, Buttercup, Joy thought back. You really got to work on not trying to murder people when they cause a small inconvenience.

"Oh, um..." The younger woman responded, pulling her notebook from her apron and flipping to a previous page. "Eggs Benedict with bacon and a fruit cup on the side?"

"Great, I'm so happy you can read. Now, tell me what's wrong with it."

The barista remained silent and scanned the plate.

"Are you stupid?" The woman shoved a finger in her face.

"Does this look like an Eggs Benedict to you?" She gestured at the food.

"Um. Yes?" The waitress's eyebrows furrowed.

The woman slammed her hands on the table and stood, her pink puffer vest squelching as she rose to her mighty height of 5'3.

"Is this a joke? It's on a soggy ass piece of bread."

"Oh, but." The teenager stuttered over herself. "That's an English muffin."

The woman balked, her hands flying up to her hips in frustration and eyes narrowing. Joy knew this look, had seen this entitlement in many people when working at Olive Garden the summer after her senior year of high school. The woman held the same stance as the man who had hit her in the face with a restaurant pager after she told him it would be a ten-minute wait—on a Saturday night—in the middle of downtown.

She took a deep, calming breath, willing herself not to lose her temper at the woman.

"Are you saying I'm lying? I know what an Eggs Benedict is and it's on a biscuit. Not whatever the hell this is."

"Of course I'm not accusing you of lying." The waitress waved her hands. "I just...that's what Eggs Benedict is usually served on?"

"I want a new one. With a biscuit like this one." The woman grabbed a biscuit from the plate of a passing server and took a bite. He mumbled in protest before hanging his head and taking the plate back to the kitchen. A couple at a different table watched their order sadly as it was returned.

"People like you are why I told my kids they have to go to college and why I won't let my daughter date," the woman said, her mouth full. "So they don't end up ruining their life with an unexpected pregnancy. You don't know how to take care of yourself, much less a child at your age. Why don't you wrap up the food, and I'll take it to go. And get me a caramel latte to go too."

The waitress nodded once, blinked away her tears, and rushed back to the kitchen.

"You're the worst." Joy plopped down in the seat next to the complaining woman.

Pink jacket squared her shoulders, spinning in a circle to point her biscuit accusingly at Joy.

"Excuse me?"

Joy grabbed a piece of bacon from the discarded plate and shrugged. "This bacon is wonderful. I'd say you should try it, but it's amazing, and you're the worst. You don't deserve to get to try this bacon."

"How dare yo—"

Buttercup flung from Joy's fingertips. It tore off a piece of the biscuit from the woman's hand, shoving it into her mouth and down her throat.

"It's not wise to talk with your mouth full," Joy said calmly.

The woman gagged and set the rest of her biscuit back on the table. She wrapped her hands around her throat, her eyes bulging. She attempted to speak, to cough even, but found she was unable to. Joy watched for a few seconds as the older woman's face turned purple. She cocked her head to the side, then sighed.

Joy waved down the server from before on his way back from dropping off the couple's fixed plates. "I think she's choking."

He sprang into action, threw a chair out of the way, got behind the woman, and patted her on the back roughly. The pregnant waitress returned, setting a cup of coffee on the table and watching the scene with wide eyes. Pink vest pounded herself on the chest while the server wrapped his arms around her and squeezed. Joy grabbed the freshly made coffee. Popping the bacon into her mouth, she smirked.

That's good enough, she thought. She motioned for Buttercup to come back.

Buttercup shot from the woman's throat, pulling the biscuit piece with it as the server gave her a final thrust. The restaurant patrons cheered as the woman dropped to her knees and coughed. She reluctantly thanked the server, her face returning to its normal orange color.

Looking around the crowd that had gathered, the woman's eyes caught on Joy, who smiled in response. She shivered, grabbed her purse, and darted out of the shop. The server leaned against the hostess stand, a smile on his face as customers came up to him with praise.

Joy sipped the coffee, enjoying the warmth and flavor of the caramel, and walked back to her table.

Caden returned a few moments later and complained about the quality of the toilet paper as the two looked over their brunch menus.

"How's the job hunt coming?" Caden asked, passing her menu over to the waitress after ordering the largest stack of pancakes she could find.

Joy shrugged. She thanked the waitress, then turned back to Caden. "I'm not all that worried about it. I have a good amount of money saved up from working over the year, so I have a couple of months until I need to get serious about it."

Only part of what she said was true. She wasn't worried about money, hadn't been in the months since Ethan's death, but not because she had any money in her savings. In all honesty, Joy hadn't been able to save any money while working, her credit card bill and medical debt far exceeding her biweekly checks.

Revenge, on the other hand, turned out to be quite the lucrative business. Although absolute scumbags, the people she chose had big pockets, big enough to allow them to get away with crimes ranging from sexual assault to second-degree murder and definitely big enough to have wallets with hundreds of dollars in cash. She didn't keep all of it, only enough to cover her rent, groceries, and biweekly nail appointments. The rest she would send to a select few of the victims who had suffered because of her targets, always in a white envelope and unmarked.

"Need anything else?" the waitress asked, clearing the plates from the table.

Caden sat back and groaned, her hand on her stomach. "I'm stuffed."

"I think we're good, thank you." Joy took the check from her, not bothering to look at the total as she slipped four one-hundred-dollar bills into the black plastic.

"God, I'm never eating again." Caden walked toward the front of the door, and Joy stood to follow.

The waitress's eyes widened as Joy handed the bill back.

"Are you sure? The bill was only for $30," she whispered, obviously wanting the large tip but hesitant to accept it.

Joy smiled. "Boy or girl?"

The waitress placed a hand on her stomach.

"Girl."

"Girls are trouble," Joy laughed. "Have a nice day."

She left the restaurant, rolling her eyes and breaking into a jog as she realized Caden hadn't bothered to wait for her. Caden stood at an intersection, waiting for the light to cross and ignoring a man, no taller than Joy and probably ten years older, who leaned against the street sign.

The man shuffled a bit too close to Caden, a smile stretching on his chapped lips. "Well, aren't you a pretty one?"

"I'm a minor and you're ugly," Caden deadpanned.

The man's nostrils flared and he stood straighter, reaching his hand out to grab Caden's wrist. "You should learn to take a compli—"

Buttercup shot out of Joy, intent on stopping the man from touching her sister, but it was beaten by a tendril of smoke lobbing itself out of Caden's fingertips and striking the man in the dick.

Joy's jaw dropped as she stepped around the man now crouching on the sidewalk, his face an odd shade of green.

Caden, seeing Joy's shock, smirked. "Did you think you were the only one?"

A laugh burst out of Joy. "I mean...yeah? I don't exactly

expect other people to have superpowers and a creepy ass voice in their head."

"Voice?" Caden's head tilted to the side. "What voice?"

ACKNOWLEDGEMENT

To the people who helped make this book less of a hot mess — my editor Margaret, my book designer Kelly, and Heather, who outlined my marketing. You are all absolutely wonderful and I am grateful for your help in making a dream of mine a reality.

To the pastor who refused to do my mom's wedding the morning of, the only part of the wedding scene that is true, for breaking me out of my writer's block.

To my mom. Her joy, her healing, her renewed excitement for life, is an inspiration to me.

To my dad. His growth as a father, his willingness to listen, his openness to our differences, are all inspirations to me.

To Dusty for calming me down when the nerves got to be too much and riling me up when I needed inspiration. And for all the ice cream runs. And for all of the movies. And for all of the hundreds of things you do.

To my abundance of siblings, but especially my sisters, for being way cooler than I was at their age and inspiring me in the most chaotic of ways.

To my real life Ethan, mainly for not being dead. You're wonderful. Thank you.

To my friends and family. I had cracks in me, shatters from a childhood lived as a forced adult. I don't think there are words that can explain how grateful I am for those who came forward with cement and plaster, sometimes silly putty or duct tape, to help me fill my cracks.

ABOUT THE AUTHOR

Draven Aurora

Draven's early life was a hot mess, but during her childhood in West Texas she learned to solder, grew a deep and unwavering hatred for roosters, and participated in everything from one act play to the school's science team. She graduated Valedictorian from her high school, which is made less impressive by only having twelve in her graduating class.

She attended the University of Texas at Austin, majoring in rhetoric and writing and minoring in business. She had every intention to go to law school, which she would have hated, until she was diagnosed with cancer at 20. After beating cancer and graduating, she took a nice, quiet office job in Austin and began writing her first book.

Her debut novel, Things We Inherit, was released in June of 2023. Draven enjoys writing dark, contemporary fantasy/ paranormal novels with strong, complicated female leads. Although she loves a happy ending in the romance novels she reads (ironically her favorite genre), she makes no promises for those she writes.

She currently lives in Austin with her fiance, cat, and an overwhelming number of books and video game systems. In her free time she enjoys playing video games, drinking fancy lemonades, watching rugby, and exploring renaissance festivals.

https://www.dravenaurora.com
https://www.tiktok.com/@dravenaurora
https://www.instagram.com/dravenaurora